Despierto

By: Amina Moore

Chapters

Though it took longer than anticipated, I'd like to dedicate this book to Isis. You helped bring me out of a period of stagnancy. Isis, you helped me finally complete something that should have been finished a long time ago. Though you are no longer with us, may you live on with this book in your memory.

Isis Angela Moore-Johnson

Chapter 1
So, It Begins

"Have you seen Samantha's new boyfriend? I think he's gorgeous. She doesn't deserve him," said Emily to Amelia.

"Yeah, I've heard of him, but he's way too, I don't know. He seems kind of shallow to me."

"Well, whatever you think about him, you have to admit he is gorgeous! No matter how vain, or shallow, or self-centered he may or may not be."

"I guess you are right, then again, aren't you always? That would be the day Emily Wright is wrong about something..."

"Yeah, whatever. Amelia, you know you wish you were me," Emily teased, nudging Amelia in the rib playfully. Emily's words stung Amelia, and she grimaced in response. Quickly, she regained her composure, catching herself before Emily had the chance to notice her facial expression. Emily was right; she had a perfect life. Good grades, amazing parents, a loving boyfriend, her own car, and practically the largest house in Crimson Springs. You name it, Emily had it or would obtain it within the next couple of days. Amelia did wish for a life like Emily's, or at least a portion of it. It was wrong of her to feel that way, and she knew it. Amelia and Emily were practically sisters, and for all intents and purposes, what belonged to Emily belonged to Amelia.

They loved each other like family and had always been inseparable. Emily and Amelia were both the only children in their households, which was part of the reason the two of them were so close. Even so, from time to time, Amelia found herself envious of Emily. In her own opinion, Amelia's life was boring. She had below-average grades, a modest house, no boyfriend, or prospects for that matter. Worst of all, parents who were constantly absent from her life. It was almost as if she didn't have parents at all. *Who am I kidding, who wouldn't want to be Emily?* Amelia thought before changing the subject as they walked home from school.

"I'm absolutely going to blow Mr. Walker's homework tonight. The way I see it, I can blow at least one more assignment and still pass with a C."

"Amelia, I don't even know why you do it to yourself. You don't make it to the top of the class by skipping assignments... Amelia?" Emily turned around to see Amelia was far behind her, picking up books off the ground, aided by some handsome stranger. She hurried in their direction, looking to get acquainted with Amelia's new friend.

Amelia gazed up at the stranger as he helped her with her books. He was handsome, his hair was dark, slightly curly, and his eyes were a beautiful sea green which accented his lightly tanned skin and hair extremely well. Looking down at the books in her hands, Amelia's cheeks began to heat, blushing bright red. She didn't want to be caught staring. Little did she know, the stranger had been equally as mesmerized with Amelia as she was with him. He immediately noticed her caramel brown skin, freckles across the bridge of her nose, her reddened rosy cheeks, and her loosely coiled light brown hair. In fact, he had purposefully bumped into Amelia. He saw her in the distance and couldn't resist talking to her.

"My name is Alex, by the way. Sorry, I pretty much just knocked you over, May I ask your name?"

"My name is Amel—"

"Emily! My name is Emily. Nice to meet you, Alex," said Emily, as she reappeared seemingly out of nowhere. Emily was now standing in front of Amelia with her hand outstretched eagerly. Alex shuffled the books into his left hand and shook Emily's reluctantly with his right.

"Nice to meet you too, Emily… and you, Amel." Alex smiled at Amelia warmly after he spoke. Amelia's cheeks reddened as she was slightly embarrassed by the mispronunciation of her name. The scene unfolding had her at a loss for words, and she made no effort to correct him. Alex handed Amelia back her books, displaying another grin.

"Well, I have to get going now. It was nice meeting the two of you. Hope we see each other again," said Alex, as he walked away, looking back at them once more before completely disappearing from view. Unbeknownst to him, Emily and Amelia were mesmerized as they watched him walk away. Seeming to be in a trance-like daze until they lost sight of him.

"Wow, what a catch! I've never seen him around here before. A guy like that, I would definitely remember, dark hair, tall, tan, and dreamy? I think I'm going to have to get formerly acquainted."

"Aren't you already spoken for? What about Johnathan?" Emily had a boyfriend already, As far as Amelia could see, Emily and Johnathan were madly in love with each other. They never argued, always were there for each other, and Johnathan pretty much worshiped the ground Emily walked on. He loved her more than anything, and it was evident. Emily always joked or commented about other men, but deep down, she would never betray Johnathan. At least Amelia hoped that she wouldn't; their love wasn't one to throw away.

"Johnathan who? Whatever, Amelia, you're no fun. It's unlikely he would choose you over me, anyway. I saw the way you were drooling over him. Keep dreaming, Mel. Besides, whoever said there was anything wrong with two men? At least, as long as they don't find out about each other." Emily grinned menacingly as she rubbed her palms together with intent.

"I see you are counting your chickens before they hatch. You don't even know anything about him, and you probably don't even remember his name! Don't worry, though, as far as competition goes, I know when I'm beat, you don't have to worry about any interference from me." Emily could be so blunt at times, never seeming to care about the impact her words had on other people.

Amelia acknowledged there'd be no competition if the two of them competed for one person. Emily was beautiful in all regards. She had auburn hair, bright blue eyes that were swoon-worthy, flawless clear skin, and on top of that, she had everything. She and Johnathan were a match made in heaven. He was a tall, muscular blonde with blue eyes. Johnathan was highly intelligent, but he didn't care as much about school. He only got by in his classes, just enough to pass. Johnathan, also captain of the football team, had to maintain a certain grade point average to stay on the team. Amelia couldn't even begin to understand why Emily would ever look elsewhere.

Emily stopped walking suddenly, causing a near collision between her and Amelia a second time. Amelia stopped abruptly, looking up and realizing they'd reached Emily's house.

"See you tomorrow, Amelia, and do your homework!"

"Ok, mom." As Amelia began to walk off, Mrs. Wright, Emily's mother, opened a window and waved at Amelia.

"Oh, hello, Mrs. Wright, how are you?"

"I'm doing fine, sweetheart. Tell Amber we send our greetings."

"Will do, Mrs. Wright. I'll see you all soon." Amelia waved at Emily and her mother as she proceeded to walk home. Her house was located only four blocks away from Emily's, so it wasn't too long a trip. When Amelia stopped in front of her house, she noticed the property to her left was no longer for sale. The sale sign had been removed, and a couple of boxes were stacked neatly near the front door.

Strange, she thought. *I never even knew anyone had purchased the house. Maybe I should stop by and meet my new neighbor.* Amelia opened her door and walked inside. She decided to bake one of her signature cakes—punch bowl cake was her specialty, one of them anyway, and everyone knew her for it. Amelia had been in the kitchen since as early as 5, cooking had always been her passion. It was something she remembered bonding with her mother over.

The two of them always spent mornings together cooking. Amelia's time with her mother in the kitchen were some of her fondest memories. They were also some of her only memories of her mother. Taking her back to a time when things were simpler. Amelia may not be a scholar, but she could cook anyone under the table. *Maybe a cake is too much, don't want to seem too eager. What the hell, may as well continue since I've already started.* The cake finished baking, and Amelia began to assemble it in her parent's crystal punch bowl. Amelia created an array of strawberry flowers atop the whipped cream and flowered the edged of the bowl with cream.

"I have to say, this cake is really something." The layers were perfectly visible and separate. It looked so beautiful, like something out of a cookbook. Amelia enjoyed anything in which she had to create things, cooking, baking, writing, even chemistry. That was her gift, it was where she shined if nothing else. She may not have been an academic scholar, but she'd been blessed with other talents.

"This cake is so nice, I almost think I shouldn't be just willingly giving it away," Amelia said aloud as she slipped out her phone and took a photo for personal reference. *What if they don't even eat it? What if they aren't nice neighbors? Or worse, what if they are allergic to one of the ingredients?* Questions soared through Amelia's head as she gathered the cake and headed toward the door. What ifs no longer mattered, her mind was made up, and she would deliver the cake. It would also give her something to do instead of waiting endlessly for her parents to return home. They had left on one of their famous conventions. Amelia's parents constantly disappeared on a whim, leaving her with car keys and funds to take care of herself in their absence.

"They probably won't return home until I'm asleep anyway, as usual," said Amelia to herself as she rang the neighbor's bell in two short bursts, half-hoping no one would answer. Two minutes go by, and no one comes to the door. The awkwardness of her standing there started to make her anxious. Amelia wasn't usually great with introductions; it was Emily that was the social butterfly. Amelia felt out of place, so she gathered herself and proceeded to walk away. The door opened, and she turned around, shocked to see a familiar face.

"Sorry to keep you waiting, I was... Oh, hey, Amel!"

"Wow, who'd have thought?"

"How did you know where I lived?" asked Alex, slightly shocked.

"Oh god, I hope you don't think I'm a stalker or anything. I live right next door. I just thought I'd stop by to meet my new neighbor."

Suddenly, she felt extremely embarrassed to be bringing a cake with her. Amelia held the punch bowl behind her back, hoping he wouldn't notice.

"Ha! Stalker? That never crossed my mind. You are too beautiful to resort to stalking anyone, especially me. Oh, and you brought a cake? If the rest of my neighbors are as welcoming, I don't think I will be leaving anytime soon. Why don't you come inside? It's quite chilly out tonight, and I wouldn't want you catching a cold."

Amelia couldn't recall ever being as embarrassed as she was at that moment. It occurred to her that she had not mentioned the cake, and she thought it was perfectly hidden behind her. Maybe it had been more visible than she'd thought. Still, there could have been anything inside of the bowl. Amelia handed Alex the punch bowl cake. He placed it on the table as he went into the kitchen to retrieve some dishes. She looked around, marveling over the interior of his house. Even when it was on the market, Amelia had never been inside the house. It was beautiful, fully equipped with beautiful Victorian furniture, crown molding, high ceilings, chandeliers, the whole nine. *His parents must have extremely good taste*, Amelia thought.

"Wow, Alex, your house is really something. I could only dream of a house like this. Your parents must be very... well off."

"Parents? Haven't had those since... I digress. This furniture has been passed down over generations, and everything else I've acquired and arranged all by my lonesome."

Amelia looked at him, puzzled at his comment about his parents.

"I'm so sorry. Did your parents pass away?"

"Something like that, yea..."

"I'm so sorry I brought it up, so... You live here by yourself?"

"Yep, just me and my cat, Sir—"

"Charles," responded Amelia abruptly with conviction. She had no idea why she spurted out that name.

"Interesting… how did you know that? That's really something to be able to guess my cat's name… Of all the names you chose Charles. Interesting indeed."

Alex stared at Amelia intensely as if there was something he couldn't quite place. As attractive as he was, Amelia couldn't help but be a little weary, alone in a grand house, after hours, with a gorgeous stranger. As strange as it may sound, it made her a little uneasy. *How could I have possibly guessed the cat's name?* Thought Amelia.

"I really must get going, Alex. Thanks for having me, but it's getting late, and my parents will worry if I don't come home soon." She blushed and turned away, embarrassed by his staring and the fact that she had told a complete lie.

The truth of the matter was her parents didn't care in the slightest if she came home or not. They were always so preoccupied with work. The only way they'd realize Amelia wasn't there was if she stopped cooking dinner and leaving it on the countertop.

"Alright, Amel, I'll see you around." Standing at the threshold of the door about to exit, Amelia turned around to face Alex.

"Amelia, my name is Amelia," she said with a smile.

"Even better," said Alex as he watched Amelia walk away.

Wow, what an interesting guy. I don't think I've ever met anyone like that, and he's my next-door neighbor too. I need to come up with another excuse to go over there again.

"Mom, Dad, I'm home!" Amelia yelled through the house with no response. "What a waste of time." Amelia walked upstairs to her bedroom sluggishly and got undressed. She quickly opened her armoire and pulled out her pajamas.

"Strange," said Amelia to herself. It felt like someone was watching her. Amelia turned toward the window. Seeing nothing, she slowly peered out onto the street. The night was still; no one was outside. She stared at the flickering light post briefly before ogling a white figure down below it. Across the street under the light post was a fat white cat seemingly staring up at her window. Sensing no cause for concern, Amelia turned from the window and planted herself firmly on her bed. All too quickly, Amelia began to drift off to sleep.

Once asleep, Amelia began to have the most peculiar dream. She could sense her presence inside the body of another. It was her dream, except it wasn't her.

"Amara, my love," said a man with a shocking resemblance to Alex.

"What ails you, Alexander?"

"I want you to teach me... I want to be able to protect you from Johnathan. He is powerful, and I want to help you defeat him."

"Are you sure this is what you want? Once you embark on this journey, there is no going back."

"Despierto," said the man who looked like Alex to the woman named Amara.

Instantaneously, Amelia woke up in her bed drenched in sweat. Sluggishly, she peered over at the alarm clock, she'd slept through it and was now late for school. The sound of it buzzing repeatedly only now annoyed her. She slammed down the snooze button angrily. Amelia didn't consider herself to be the best student, but she was never late to school. Amelia took a quick shower, got dressed, and began jogging to school. Completely out of breath, she stumbled into her first period, Mr. Walkers' class.

"Miss. Moore, you're late. I guess there's a first time for everything."

"So sorry, Mr. Walker... It won't... happen again," said Amelia between breaths trying to regain her composure.

"Let's hope not. Class, turn your books to page 26, and we'll have Sarah begin the reading."

Amelia sat down in her usual seat and proceeded to take out her textbook. She turned to page twenty-six and was greeted by Emily as she pulled her notebook from her bag.

"You're late, Amelia," Emily whispered in Amelia's ear mockingly from the desk to the right of her.

"Yeah, I know. I overslept. Can you believe it?"

Everyone turned towards the door staring at the student who had walked in.

"This is our new student everyone, why don't you introduce yourself to the class?" said Mr. Walker.

"Hello everyone, I hope that I'm not interrupting the lesson. My name is Alex."

"It can't be," said Amelia to herself as she looked up at the person speaking. *This is crazy. We keep running into each other,* thought Amelia.

"Well, go ahead and choose your seat," said Mr. Walker as he returned to reading the textbook.

Alex met Amelia's gaze and smiled at her briefly. He then ogled the empty desk to her left. Alex didn't so much as give Emily a passing glance as he moved past her to sit next to Amelia. Amelia could barely contain her embarrassment.

"Well, hello there, Amelia. It seems we keep running into each other. It must be fate."

Amelia couldn't help but blush at his bluntness in suggesting their fated meetings. Emily stared at the two of them blankly, flabbergasted that Amelia was getting the attention instead of her.

Emily raised her hand, instantly drawing Mr. Walker's attention. "Mr. Walker, I can't focus with all this chatter going on in the classroom," said Emily annoyed.

"Settle down, class. We wouldn't want to hinder our best student, now, would we?" Responded Mr. Walker sarcastically.

It was apparent Mr. Walker had a slight distaste for Emily though she didn't seem to realize it. Not everyone enjoyed her self-centered personality. Some people disliked that she was so perfect. Amelia had learned to get used to it, so it didn't bother her as much.

Amelia began to write a note. She folded it up neatly and slid it to Alex while Mr. Walker's back was turned. It read, "*So it seems you are the one stalking me.*"

Alexander grinned as he read the note and began to add a sentence. "*Very observant you are. Maybe I could not get enough of you, so I just had to transfer to your school. The only high school in Crimson Springs for miles around.*"

"Perhaps you are right. If you are a stalker, I guess, under those circumstances, it'd be fairly easy to find me. After all it is a small town."

Amidst their note writing, Amelia and Alex hadn't noticed Mr. Walker began to approach them. Mr. Walker grabbed the note off of Alex's desk without warning.

"Well, what do we have here? It seems you've already gotten yourself into trouble on your first day."

Mr. Walker was notorious for reading notes written in class aloud.

"Aianm elimino," Alex mumbled under his breath. As Mr. Walker began to open the note, an expression of disbelief could be seen across his face.

"Interesting, how very interesting indeed. I could have sworn I saw you writing... Anyway, let's focus on the lesson, shall we?" Mr. Walker placed the note back on Alex's desk, and Alex slipped it into his jacket pocket.

"That was a close one. I don't know why he didn't read it. He always does," Amelia whispered to Alex.

"Who knows, maybe he is also a stalker, and he wants to initiate me into his cult."

"Whatever, or maybe we're just lucky," she responded with a smile.

It was harder than usual for Amelia to focus on the lesson. Amelia noticed herself glancing at Alex every so often, captivated by him. He was mysterious, and that intrigued Amelia. She could sense Alex's glares when she wasn't looking at him. Whatever she was feeling toward him, Amelia knew it was mutual. More so, she felt like she'd known Alex for a long time.

The class was over, and the two of them would likely be separating. Amelia had a strange feeling, that if they parted, there was a chance she'd never see Alex again. In her mind, she acknowledged how strange a feeling that was; he lived next door to her after all. Even stranger, Amelia had only just met Alex the day before.

"What's your next class?" asked Alex, interrupting Amelia's thoughts.

"I have biology. Hey, are you a sophomore as well?" Amelia felt like she was asking a dumb question. Alex did look older than her, and the fact that he lived alone, he must have meant that he was no less than a junior.

"Nah, I am a senior, actually. Ha! Didn't know you were a sophomore. You seemed a little older than that." Alex lowered his tone of voice and crouched down slightly. When he was at Amelia's ear level he whispered, "No worries, it doesn't change anything." Alex ruffled Amelia's hair and started to walk off.

"Hey, what did you mean by that?" Amelia asked as he walked off.

"You'll find out soon enough. See you later."

What did he mean by that? Is he really interested in me? Nah, that can't be it. I mean, who would be interested in me? Amelia smiled as thoughts raced through her head about Alex.

Amelia and someone else collided as she walked toward Biology in a daze. Amelia lost her balance from the impact and began falling backward. The person she'd bumped into grabbed her reflexively, steadying her and helping Amelia to regain her balance.

"I am so sorry. I should be watching where I was going, it's my fault," said the person who'd caught her; it was Johnathan.

"Hey, Johnny. It was my fault, honestly. I was daydreaming, sorry I'm so accident-prone."

"Yeah, you should really keep your eye on the road." Johnathan winked at Amelia and walked off.

Amelia had always found Johnathan to be attractive, but that was before he started dating Emily. Now he was somewhat of an older brother to her. He was also a senior and captain of the football team. On top of that, he was extremely nice. Amelia made her way into Ms. Elmhurst's class. Biology and chemistry were the only subjects Amelia enjoyed.

The lunch bell rang, and everyone exited the class in a hurry, the sight comparable to an animal stampede. The students raced through the hallways in anticipation of getting the better seats in the cafeteria. Amelia wondered where Alex was. She was anxious to see him and didn't know when they'd bump into each other again.

In the cafeteria, Emily approached Amelia. She had been waiting for her to arrive.

"I can't believe he's talking to you. When did you guys get so close? He seems so interested in you. I can't understand why..."

"I don't know... It feels like we know each other as if we've met before somewhere... I feel like we've known each other even prior to yesterday. There's something about him that I just can't place. Never mind, I'm rambling like a crazy person."

"Jeez, you're weird, which makes this even harder to believe that he is so much more interested in you than me. It's literally driving me insane."

"You'll be alright. You have a great boyfriend; Johnathan really is great. You two make the perfect couple."

"If he's so great, you date him. That way, Alex won't have to choose. You'll be taken, and he'll be up for grabs." Emily rubbed her hands together mischievously.

"Yeah, sure, as if you'd part with Johnny. You don't even know if you like Alex. You are just infatuated with him because he's a new student, and he's attractive, that's the only reason he has your attention. You may get to know him and find out you have nothing in common. Or you may find things about him that you don't like.

"I guess you are right. When did you become so wise?"

"I have no idea. A lot of weird stuff has been happening lately." Amelia grabbed her lunch tray and turned around to find Alex sitting at a table surrounded by other female classmates. That didn't deter him from spotting Amelia in the distance in almost the same instant she looked at him.

"Hey, Amelia! Come over here and sit with me," he yelled out to her, waving in her direction.

Emily rolled her eyes in disgust as she gently nudged Amelia forward.

"See you later, Mel. Don't keep your new boyfriend waiting, especially with all the surrounding leeches."

Amelia was embarrassed by his outburst and all the eyes on her as she made her way to the table. When she got closer, Amelia noticed it was Misty, the mean girl, and her minions. The girls at the table stared at Amelia with distaste. Not knowing how to react, she just stood there in front of them with her tray in hand. It was Misty who got up first, turning around to stand directly in front of Amelia. Misty rolled her eyes at her before turning back to face Alex.

"You're wasting your time with this one. She's a total loser."

With those words, Alex's demeanor seemed to shift completely. He stood up abruptly to address Misty's remark.

"That's funny. The only loser I see here is you. Putting others down so that you can feel better about yourself. Surrounding yourself with people who aren't really your friends but intimidated by you. In short Misty, I think that makes you the loser, you really should run along now. We are only allotted so much time for lunch, Amelia and I have wasted enough time on you as it is."

"What? How dare you? Who do you think you are? Girls!" Misty clenched her fists in anger and turned on her heels to walk away. All the girls who remained sitting stared at Amelia with distaste before getting up and walking away after Misty, leaving Alex and Amelia sitting there.

"I wonder what all that was about," said Alex.

"Nothing, they are just typical schoolgirls. You are the new shiny toy everyone wants to play with. I guess it's a kind of competition."

"Is that so? I'm guessing that's how you feel as well?"

"N-no, I mean... I was only explaining the situation."

"Oh, so I'm not a shiny new toy you'd like to play with?"

"Oh boy..." Alex made Amelia even more embarrassed than she thought humanly possible.

"I'm only teasing you; relax. You don't have to answer that, besides, I already know the answer. Hey, since all the girls seem to be so interested, how about we put on a show for them?"

"A show? What do you mean?"

"Here, let me demonstrate."

Amelia looked around and noticed the girls who'd left earlier still had lingering eyes. They had been staring at the two of them from the moment they left the table. Alex leaned over the lunch table and kissed Amelia abruptly, deeply, running his fingers through her hair. Everyone that'd been watching gasped simultaneously, and soon after, returned to what they were doing previously. "There, now that that's settled, it's no longer up for debate."

If only it were real... Too bad it was only for show, Amelia thought to herself.

"It felt pretty real to me," said Alex with a smile.

What!? How did he? Amelia stood up, both astonished and embarrassed.

"I have to go," Amelia ran off quickly to the girl's bathroom, leaving her unfinished lunch behind her. Amelia stared into the mirror and splashed cold water onto her face.

"What's going on with me?" she asked her reflection. Amelia gathered herself and began to walk out of the bathroom when she realized her purse was not on her shoulder. She searched around, checking the stall she was in and the counter, but it wasn't there either.

"Crap, I forgot my purse. How could I be so careless?" Said Amelia to herself.

Amelia ran back to the cafeteria but no luck. Lunch was already over, so she didn't expect it to still be there. She went to the lost and found, thinking someone had brought it there.

"Excuse me, Ms. I lost my purse recently and wanted to know if any purses have been brought in," Amelia said as she walked up to the security desk.

"What does it look like?" Asked the security guard at the front desk, her voice laced with annoyance.

"It is a black tote with gold trim and gold buckles." She took a brief look in the lost and found bin, barely a glance, and returned to Amelia at the desk. "There's nothing like that here."

Amelia rolled her eyes as the security guard looked away.

"Thanks anyway." Amelia's eyes welled up with tears as she slowly walked toward her next class. Everything was in there, her school Id, house keys, and wallet. *How could you have lost something that important?* However, it dawned on Amelia that Alex might have it. After all, they were sitting at the same table together, and she remembered having it last in the cafeteria. She hoped he hadn't overlooked it.

As Amelia wandered toward her class, she caught a glance of Johnathan, who seemed equally troubled. Johnathan looked up from his locker, briefly spotting Amelia.

Johnathan was a little bothered by an issue presented to him by a fellow teammate. His teammate ambushed him right after the game, regarding his duties as captain. They felt as though he'd been neglecting his obligations due to his needy, self-centered girlfriend. He'd missed a few meets, and to them, he didn't seem as focused. Johnathan disagreed with that, but the declaration had him conflicted, weighing down on him. Emily was his girlfriend, but the football team was his life.

"Hey, Amelia, what has you looking so down? If you don't mind me asking."

"Ah, nothing I want you to trouble yourself over, Johnny. I just misplaced my purse, and all my belongings were in there."

"Damn, Amelia, I hate to add insult to injury, but how could you manage that? I thought purses were like an extension of a woman's arm."

"Wow, Johnathan, that was almost funny," said Amelia with a smile. "What is bothering you, by the way? You don't look so good yourself."

"Eh, just some team stuff, you know. Being captain has its perks, but it is no walk in the park. I love my team; they're practically my brothers, but... they think I'm spending too much time with Em."

"That's quite the conflict. I hope you can resolve it. I get it, though. Both things are important to you. You can't just choose one or the other."

"At least someone sees it from my perspective. I hope you find your purse, Mel. We should probably get to class before they close the doors. Oh, and if you can't find it, you can always stop by my place if you need to call your parents or something. I think Em might be stopping by as well."

"You're probably right. We'll talk later Johnny, thanks for the offer." Amelia parted from Johnathan and made her way to her gym period.

Amelia walked into the gymnasium and quickly changed into her gym clothes. Not before seeing the girls huddled around Misty Mai, who seemed to be holding some type of polished stone.

"I mean, I bought it online, but it's so... mystical. It's some type of crystal. I don't remember the type exactly, but..." They came to a pause as there was a knock on the door by the gym teacher.

"You girls, hurry up. The class is starting. Whoever isn't out here in five is getting points taken off from their average."

In a hurry, Misty placed the crystal in her pocket and rushed by Amelia, knocking her purposefully into the lockers as she passed by. Misty turned around, making direct eye contact with Amelia as all the girls laughed while exiting the locker room.

"You should totally watch where you're going, Amelia. That could have been avoided. Oh, and before I forget, don't think you don't have it coming for the cafeteria incident. You may have been able to catch the new guy's attention, but you're still a loser. Let's just hope he comes to his senses sooner than later," said Misty as she joined her friends in the gymnasium.

"What a bitch," said Amelia to herself as she leaned down, tying her sneaker. Amelia already had lost her purse, now this as well. Misty had always been a bully, but it seemed to aggravate Amelia even more with the day she'd already been having. There was something else, though; something felt strange for Amelia. She reached into her left pocket and pulled out a crystal. The same crystal everyone had just been marveling over, Misty's crystal.

Amelia grasped the strange object and glanced it over in the palm of her hand. It began to glow suddenly, a deep purple hue, temporarily blinding Amelia. In the surrounding mirrors, Amelia's hair stood up on edge, and her eyes shone bright white. Lasting about three seconds. Amelia placed the crystal back in her pocket hesitantly and made her way into the gymnasium to rejoin her classmates.

"Alright, class. Today we are going to do a series of workouts leading up to tonight's cheerleading tryouts. Are any of you guys going to try out?"

Misty stepped forward eagerly with her group of minions who followed faithfully behind her.

"Of course, Ms. Fields. Cheerleading runs in my blood."

"Alright, Misty, why don't you give us a little pre-tryout demonstration?"

Misty smiled, turning around to Amelia once more.

"Maybe you should take a couple of pointers, keep your notepad handy. You and your stuck-up friend could learn a thing or two."

Amelia and Emily rolled their eyes; it was all they could do. Ms. Fields instructed everyone who wasn't participating to sit and watch from the bleachers. Misty executed her routine flawlessly. Her minions threw her up in the air gracefully as Amelia watched nearby.

"Don't choke," said Amelia under her breath.

The girls threw Misty into the air, intending to catch her in a finishing act. The crystal in Amelia's pocket seemed to be growing warm. Amelia pulled it out slightly and saw it glowing its deep purple hue. The same way it had earlier when she went temporarily blind. Suddenly, one of Misty's minions, Jane, sneezed when she was supposed to be catching Misty. In that small moment of confusion, everyone else was thrown off balance, and Misty came tumbling to the ground, twisting her ankle in the process.

"Shit! you stupid bitch!" wailed Misty at the top of her lungs. "You did this on purpose, you stupid cow. You have always wanted to be the head cheerleader!"

"Misty, I'm so sorry I didn't mean to. It really was an accident, I swear," said Jane apologetically, attempting to console her. Misty winced in pain as Ms. Fields helped her to her feet.

"Listen, for the remainder of this class, you have a free period. I must take Misty to the nurse. No one is permitted to leave until the bell rings, got it?"

The students acknowledged Ms. Fields as she began to walk off with Misty limping beside her. Amelia stared at the crystal once more. She had a strange feeling it had somehow been connected to the cheerleading incident.

"Wow, I guess Misty is finally getting some well-deserved Karma. Well, I guess she isn't indestructible after all."

"I guess, but come on Emily, have a little heart. I mean, did you see the way that her ankle buckled? Just watching it made me cringe..." Amelia sighed as she pushed the crystal further into her pocket. Her day just seemed to be getting stranger and stranger.

When school was over, Amelia immediately set off for Alex's house, hoping she'd bump into Alex along the way. He would have to be walking down the block since he lived right next to her. For some reason, the streets were empty. Amelia was the only passerby on both sides of the sidewalk, which she found a bit strange.

"Please be home and please have my purse," Amelia said to herself as she made her way up Alex's steps. The lights were already on inside. Alex didn't have curtains, and Amelia figured he must be home. Stepping up to his doorway, Amelia reached for the doorbell, and as she pressed it, he was already opening the door.

"Come in, Amara. I've been expecting you."

Amelia walked past him and then paused, realizing Alex had called her by a strange name.

"What did you call me?"

"Amelia, of course. You can't possibly believe I could forget your name, could you?" Amelia sat down on the old Victorian chair by the entryway. There was a look of uncertainty that came across her.

"Make yourself at home. I'm going to go change."

"Ok, but I didn't want to stay for that long. I just wanted to ask you if—"

He was already gone. Alex came back down the stairs shirtless, and Amelia couldn't help but admire his physique. His musculature accented his features, dark hair, green eyes olive skin. He looked like something out of a magazine, which almost made Amelia forget what she came for. Seeing him in that state left Amelia at a loss for words.

"A-Alex, have you... by any chance seen my purse? I think I left it in the cafeteria earlier..." she couldn't look directly at him and talk; she was afraid of what might come out.

"Oh, yeah, I have it here. I thought you'd come back for it, but then the bell rang, so my only option was to walk around with a woman's purse. It wasn't strange at all," said Alex with a smile. He walked over to Amelia and handed her the purse. She embraced him abruptly.

"Thank you, thank you, so much. I was so worried I'd lost my purse. I would have died if I'd lost it, My keys especially. I don't know what I would have done. You really are a lifesaver." Amelia realized she had still been hugging him that entire time. He was warm and smelled like fresh herbs, lavender, and mint. It was a noticeably light fragrance and made Amelia feel tranquil. She felt like she could stay there in his embrace forever. Alex grasped Amelia's shoulder gently and moved her slightly backward.

"As much as I'd enjoy just standing here with you, I wouldn't be properly entertaining my guest. How about something to drink? I have a lot of different varieties of tea you might enjoy. That is if you like tea."

"Sure, I'd like that... tea would actually be great, I love tea."

"I guess it's settled then, tea it is. Give me a second. I'll be right back."

Amelia sat on the couch and just admired the setting. Sir Charles, the cat, jumped up on the couch and sat beside her. Amelia began petting him as she waited for Alex to return. The cat purred as she stroked his neck. He was so relaxed that he fell asleep on her. Alex re-entered the room with a mug and saucer in hand. It was china and expensive, by the looks of it.

"It's lavender tea with a little something extra and honey, of course. Though you are sweet enough without it."

"Oh, stop it with your flattery. You're embarrassing me. Did you say lavender? That explains it. Do you grow your own herbs?"

"As a matter of fact, yes, I do. I have a large herb garden in the back. I make my own teas, salves, scents. You name it."

"Wow, all that, and you live alone? I'm barely getting through high school as it is, and you look like you have it down packed. Did you say salves? Wow... how old are you, really?"

"I'd say 500 hundred years or so, give or take a few years...." said Alex with a smile, and Amelia rolled her eyes. "Trust me, though, living alone isn't all it's cracked out to be. Being by myself all the time gets very lonely. I started the garden because it helps pass the time when I'm not in school. I'm glad I did, though. The herbs really come in handy."

"I know what you mean. My parents are hardly ever home. They're constantly away on conventions... and such. Hell, who knows what they really are up to. It's been like this since I was about eleven years old. It hasn't let up since. Sometimes I feel like they may never come back. If it weren't for school and Emily, I would be completely alone..."

"There's no need for you to be lonely ever again. If you ever want company, I am a stone throw away, always."

Amelia smiled as she took another sip of the tea. Her eyes began to flutter, and she started dozing off. The cup Amelia had been holding slipped from her hands. The last thing she'd seen before falling asleep was Alex catching the cup Alex caught the cup in mid-air without using his hands. Amelia assumed she must have already started dreaming.

The dream she'd had days ago returned to her. Once again, Amelia was no longer herself. She was within the body of the one called Amara.

"Alexander, Johnathan mustn't know that you embraced the gift."

Amara began to perform a sacred ritual in passing the gift onto him. She sat in front of her altar on her knees and hummed. Amara cut her wrist, and some of her blood was emptied into a wooden chalice. She poured a portion of the blood from the chalice over what seemed to be an oval-shaped quartz crystal. The moment the blood came in contact with the crystal, it glowed a deep purple hue. Her wound healed instantly. It was that sign that showed her the gods were watching.

"I pray to the goddess, I call upon you in this time of need, lend me your strength so that I can bless another with your divine power. Another tribune for your glory, an obedient and worthy subject. Please accept my sacrifice and grant me this request."

A lamb on her altar, alive and bound cried in anguish as it anticipated its demise. Swiftly, she slit its throat, and a flash of white light engulfed everything.

Alexander sat behind her, looking dizzy like he was about to fall asleep. Alexander was amazed; he always was when he watched Amara. Not just because she was a witch but because he loved her.

"Alexander… we must consummate the ritual. Within me is the power that you seek, but there is only one way to bestow it upon you."

Alexander looked at Amara with longing and began to kiss her, caressing her face as he did so. He kissed her deeply, passionately. Amelia could feel the kisses, the caressing, the slicing of Amara's wrist, and the warmth of alexanders touch. Amelia was experiencing it all as if she had been there. The dream she was recalling had been so vivid she felt as if she wasn't dreaming at all. In fact, it seemed more like a memory than anything else, although it seemed to have occurred hundreds of years ago.

Alexander began to undress Amara, tearing off her garments. It was extremely intense, and as if Amelia had no willpower, she could not stop it, not that she wanted to. Alexander slowly crept over Amara. She was completely naked, and Amelia had the urge to wake up. Amelia realized she didn't want this experience; it wasn't hers to have, and she felt like she was invading Amara's memories. Amelia felt her legs quiver as Alexander began kissing her neck. Suddenly he stopped, pausing by Amelia's ear.

"Despierto," he whispered in her ear, and instantly, Amelia was back in her bedroom, drenched in sweat and exhausted.

Amelia got out of bed and headed into the shower. She realized she didn't remember leaving Alex's house after she drank her tea.

"Did Alex carry me back here?" said Amelia to herself, smiling at the thought of him carrying her. She returned to her bed after the shower, but her thoughts lingered on her dream. *What could all this mean*? *Who is Amara?* One thing was for sure though, Amelia had an inkling she knew Alex longer than she'd initially thought. It made little sense to her, and then there was the crystal. She felt it somehow would connect her to Amara, whoever she was. Amelia grabbed the clear-colored crystal off her nightstand and held it close to her chest.

"I want to remember," said Amelia to the crystal as she returned it to the nightstand. She laid there, wondering why she was having these dreams. Amelia closed her eyes and shortly returned to her slumber.

Chapter 2
Amara's Arrival

It all happened so quickly. The foreigners arrived in the night, and Amara had little time to think. Everyone had been asleep, and her father, King Imari, was out with his men. She was awakened to an eerie scream followed by the smell of smoke.

Amara ran outside to search for her father. Quietly she crept around, not aware of what had been terrorizing her village. It was dark as Amara made her way cautiously through the village. Their homes were set ablaze as the villagers ran around frantically; the flames were tremendous, engulfing her entire village. The village, where she was born and raised, was now being swallowed whole.

Amara, only 15, had not been prepared for the dangers she was about to face. Her father created a very sheltered life for her, and Amara had no idea what she should do. Amara searched around in the distance, identifying a few pale figures in foreign attire speaking a dialect she could not understand. She made her way through the village, doing her best not to be detected as she maneuvered through all the chaos.

One of her father's men seemed to search around aimlessly. Amara spotted him, looking around briefly before calling out to him.

"Where is my father?" Amara whispered to him.

"I'm so sorry I had to... he was... I'm sorry." He pointed towards a bush and ran off in the opposite direction. He ran as fast as his feet could carry him, disappearing in the wilderness. The young soldier was afraid, the King had been wounded, and he left him to die. Even so, Amara did not judge him. He was overtaken by fear of the unknown. In short, their tribe was unfit to defend themselves against this terror.

Amara stood over her father in disbelief, her body trembling as she looked over him. King Imari was lying on the ground, with a fatal wound to the stomach. The damage had been made of a weapon Amara had never seen before. Amara rushed to her father's aid, kneeling beside him and resting his head on her lap.

"Father, how could you let them do this to you?" She exclaimed in anguish. "Father, you are stronger than this! I must gather the herbs, I... I can fix this. The wound isn't that..." Amara cried as tears were streaming down her face. She was not ready to lose her father, it wasn't his time. She stared at her hands in anguish; they were drenched in her father's blood. Amara knew that it would be a wasted attempt for her to try to save him. This she knew, but she couldn't stomach losing her father, not like this.

"My precious daughter, I haven't much time left in this life, I must be brief." said the king followed by a cough that spewed specks of blood. Amara sat there beside her father and listened to him intently. She wiped away her tears as she did so. "I wanted to wait... until you came of age, but there is no time for that now. You are part of a powerful ancient bloodline of gifted individuals. I cannot teach you what I know, but I can bestow upon you this very gift. Passed down from the gods themselves to man, father to son, mother to daughter over many generations, and now I pass it on to you. My child, my only daughter... be strong." Amara's father looked toward the sky and chanted something she could not understand. She had seen him do this before but never understood why exactly until now. "I pray to the gods and goddesses, with my dying breath, bestow upon my daughter your gift. She will honor and praise you, carrying out your will until she breathes her last breath. Accept me as a sacrifice…"

Amara stared at her father as he took his final breath. She didn't know what was supposed to happen. Her father had passed, and Amelia had no time to perform his burying rights.

"Father, no! Don't leave me," Amara grabbed his hand and there was a sudden burst of white light. A searing pain raced through Amara's head, and before long, she'd fallen unconscious. A group of foreign men stood over Amara next to the King and leered at her.

They talked amongst each other "Mmm, this one would fetch a fair price in the market," said the captain to the men standing beside him.

"Oh yes, her skin is fair. She's of a decent age. Yes, she will fetch a fair price indeed."

"You should know that in my frequent scouting of this village, I found some valuable information about this one. Not only is she all the above, but she is also the daughter of King Imari," said the man standing to the right of the captain. The captain seemed quite taken by Amara's status as he ran his fingers through his beard in contemplation.

"Let's get her on the vessel and start our journey back. I believe we have enough cargo for the trip," said the captain as the three walked away carrying Amara.

As the foreigners returned to their ships, screams could be heard echoing throughout what they left of the village. The great village of Motombi and the King had fallen in a single night.

*   *   *   *

Amara found herself shackled from head to toe, standing in a line amongst others. Some people she stood with were from her village, and others were from rival villages. The chains were foreign to Amara's body. She felt like she was being pulled down. They were extremely heavy for her small frame to sustain. All the faces that surrounded her were of different tribes, this made her feel alone.

The journey from Motombi was long and unforgiving. Amara remembered only bits and pieces of what she'd endured. She'd been falling in and out of consciousness ever since they took her from her village. Tears streamed down Amara's cheeks as she realized her father would no longer be around to protect her. Despite that, Amara knew she had to adjust to her new surroundings, and she had to do so quickly.

All the many voices that flooded Amara's ears were to her, unintelligible. She could tell they were in a foreign land, surrounded by foreign objects and people. Amara made out a man who seemed to be of great importance. When he spoke, all present seemed to listen intently. He was speaking so quickly Amara could not even try to understand. She stared at the mouth of the man, trying to make out what he was saying. The man looked directly at Amara.

"And next we have the princess of the village Motombi, daughter of King Imari she would make a fine addition to any collection," he said.

Amara composed herself, focusing her energy on the man and taking deep breaths as she watched him. Amara realized she could suddenly understand every word during her last inhale,

Though she quickly came to regret it. With her new understanding of the language, Amara now knew what was taking place before her eyes. They were all being auctioned off, stolen from their lands, and sold to the highest bidder. Amongst those in the crowd, Amara made direct eye contact with a young man, his piercing blue eyes watching her intensively as if he were interested in the purchase. This made her very uneasy, and she shifted back and forth in place. Others were standing around him that seemed to have just as much interest.

"Sold! To Sir Johnathan Sharpe," yelled the auctioneer with utter delight.

Amara felt extremely uncomfortable with the situation and was especially wary of Johnathan Sharpe. Johnathan Sharpe smiled as he made his way front and center. His blue eyes made Amara shiver and even more at his icy touch. Amara was loaded onto a cart with a few others, still none from her village. They whispered to her in the back of the wagon

"What tribe are you from?". Though a different dialect, for some reason, she understood clearly.

"I am Amara Imari, Daughter of King Imari of Motombi."

"Motombi? Motombi does not speak the way we speak. How do you know the tongue?"

"I... I do not know... I just understand it. It just comes to me."

The woman who asked Amara the initial question seemed to lose color in her skin. She looked as if she'd realized something dreadful.

"I know all about you people. Mothers tell their children bedtime stories of the Great King Imari and his ancestors. Horrible stories of devil worship and human sacrifices meant to keep children obedient. You and your people are devil worshippers possessed by the spirits of demons."

"Your people are the reason we are in this mess. All those years of devil worship have brought us here. The creator is not pleased with your kind. You have brought death upon us all."

The people that surrounded Amara looked at her with looks of pure hatred.

"You know not what you speak of. King Imari was a great man, loved by his people. You would speak so harshly toward someone you suspected of demonic influence?" Said Amara bitterly.

The others all displayed looks of distress, realizing what Amara had said. Anger welled up inside of Amara. She'd just lost her father, and the accusations against him made Amara's blood boil. In almost the same instant, a swarm of bees flew overhead, beginning to sting all who spoke ill of Amara's people. They screamed in agony, all but Amara, who had not been stung by a single bee. Amara smiled mischievously as she watched the others being terrorized.

Johnathan Sharpe yelled to the back of the wagon, "Quiet back there, or we will have to stop the wagon!"

The others stopped at once and looked at Amara with disgust as they neared their destination. There was no explanation for what transpired with the bees, but they had an inkling it was Amara's doing, for she bore no sores from the bee attack.

Amara sat in silence as she took in their harsh words. The wagon pulled up to an enormous property, different from what Amara had been accustomed to. It was a grand plantation, acres upon acres of land, which seemed to be tended by people who looked more like Amara. They were dressed raggedly, in tatters, a sight which Amara found horrific.

The blistering sun shone brightly against the workers in the fields. She watched as they labored in the blistering sun. Amara realized that this would be her fate as well, an unwilling laborer on this property. The slaves were led out of the wagon while Johnathan Sharpe lifted Amara from it.

"What a fine specimen you are indeed. Come at once; I must introduce you to father. He should be pleased with this purchase."

His eagerness to show her off detested Amara. She was not some fancy new piece of cloth to be displayed. Yet this is how she was being treated, and it made her feel like a possession and not a human being. Johnathan hastily walked Amara to the property's main house. Amara couldn't help but wonder why the gods had brought her here why take her father away.

"Good evening Mr. Sharpe," said a woman dressed in finer clothes than the others Amara had seen as she greeted him at the door. "Shirley, where is my father?"

Johnathan was eager to show his father what he had purchased. He thought for once, his father would be proud of him.

"He's in his office, sir," responded the woman called Shirley bitterly, as she turned toward Amara, giving her a warm smile. Reflexively, Amara smiled back at the woman called Shirley. With no time for further greeting, Amara was pulled off in whatever direction Johnathan was headed.

Johnathan led Amara up the stairs to his father's office. The door was already unlocked, so Johnathan pushed it forward and led Amara in after him. Amara wondered why he was acting so strangely with her why she was being separated from the others.

"Father, I present to you princess Amara of Motombi."

Expressing no interest at all, Johnathan's father said "Fine, put her with the rest of the slaves. I'll have Shirley put her to work first thing tomorrow," Johnathan's father said coldly, not even glancing in Johnathan's direction; he didn't care too. In his mind, everything and anything else was more important than interacting with his son.

"You aren't interested at all?"

"Why would I be? As if the slaves weren't defiant enough, you come waltzing in here with one claiming to be some type of royalty? You should take heed not to address her in such a way, especially when she is present.

Our primary goal is to detach her from the childish ideas of her upbringing. It holds no value here—princess, doctor, architect, I care not. If she plans to live here, she will learn to put those things behind her. Have you not learned anything from me? Now get out. You are interrupting my concentration. Unlike you, I have some very important matters that need to be dealt with. I'll leave the slaves to you."

Johnathan, infuriated, stormed out of his father's office. Seemingly with no regard to the shackles on Amara's arms as he yanked her furiously after him. Johnathan brought Amara to the slave's quarters. Even with all his rage, he hesitated when it came time to leave her there. Johnathan decided she wasn't fit to sleep with the other slaves and started dragging her off toward another location. For whatever reason, Johnathan felt the need to keep a close watch on Amara. His father may not have had any interest in her, but he did. Johnathan thought to himself, *I've never seen a slave as pretty as Amara.*

He intended to get better acquainted with Amara. He meant that in every sense and intended to do so, whether it was by force or her own volition, he cared not. Amara was rightfully his property, and he felt he could do with her as he pleased. His thoughts shocked him, for he'd never had the urge to lie with a slave girl before.

Johnathan made his way into his candlelit bedroom, placing Amara down into a seat near his bed. Johnathan knelt in front of Amara as he removed the shackles from her wrists. He stared at her with much intent, studying her. Johnathan admired the beauty that sat before him, her tightly coiled brown hair, light brown eyes, the curvature of her body, the shape of her lips. Amara was not like any woman or slave he'd ever seen, she was unique, and he had to have her.

"Well, get on with it," said Amara with distaste as she'd noticed how intently he'd been staring.

Amara knew what Johnathan was craving, and she wanted him to understand that. However, Amara's statement prompted Johnathan to change the conversation. Though his interests remained the same, Amara giving him permission was off-putting for Johnathan.

"Y-you can speak. Where did you learn English?"

"I learned it on the way to this... plantation."

"Impossible! You must have learned in your village in some way. Perhaps your father, the King taught you—"

"Don't you dare speak of my father!" Amara sneered at him cutting him off during his sentence.

Johnathan was taken aback by her comment. Her aggression toward Johnathan only aroused him further.

"We will excuse your rudeness this time, but the next time you speak out of turn, there will be consequences. Now, I must know, how could you possibly have learned English that quickly?"

Amara searched for the right words as she examined Johnathan strenuously. Amara couldn't quite understand it, but something told her he could be trusted.

"I'm a witch."

Johnathan laughed loudly, looking up to find Amara sitting there staring at him with not as much as a smirk.

"A witch? How intriguing, but I am going to need some convincing, I'm afraid. It's not every day one runs into a witch not only that but the daughter of a King as well."

Amara stared at Johnathan as the temperature in the room elevated drastically. Johnathan tugged at his shirt, feeling the air get hotter, his palms started to sweat, and he found himself unbuttoning his shirt. It was late December, and weather like this wasn't normal. He got the picture loud and clear.

"Ok, enough of that, I get it. How did a person such as yourself wind up on the auction block? Couldn't you have evaded capture or something?"

As Johnathan began the conversation, Amara's concentration was broken. The temperature ceased immediately, returning the room to its normal climate.

"I'm new to all of this. It comes and goes. I don't really have it all under control. It's bizarre. I get memory flashes of spells and some things I can just do naturally. Everything I've learned was passed on to me from my father when your people killed him. I don't quite understand it myself everything will reveal itself in time, I suppose."

Johnathan looked at Amara with fascination, to meet someone so interesting and a slave at that.

"I'm sorry about your father, Amara. I—"

"I'm tired," said Amara. "If you aren't going to do anything, may I go to sleep?"

Embarrassed by her remark Johnathan led her to his bed to sleep. Now, with no ill intent, he watched her as she slumbered.

*   *   *

Johnathan had been watching Amara every night, attentively sitting in during her ritual practices. Even allowing her to set up her altar in his bedroom. He was in love with Amara, and he knew she knew it. He didn't want to push her into anything. Johnathan wanted Amara's feelings to develop on their own. Though he knew she cared for him, to what extent he didn't know. Johnathan vowed he would make Amara fall in love with him, no matter what it took. This was all an unfamiliar experience for Johnathan; he'd never had so much as a girlfriend.

Shirley, a middle-aged house slave, knocked on the door. His father had a particular liking for Shirley and sent her out running his errands. Anything of importance he left up to Shirley, sometimes putting her before Johnathan. This infuriated him, but he also didn't particularly like Shirley either. There was no doubt in his mind that when he inherited the plantation, he would sell her. Shirley had also been with child; she had been wearing larger dresses, trying to hide it. Johnathan could tell, and he knew why she'd want to hide it. She was embarrassed to be carrying his father's child. He knew it was the only plausible explanation. She was not intimate with any of the other slaves.

Johnathan did not want to answer the door, but Shirley continued to knock, knowing Johnathan was in his room. Amara turned over in her sleep, not slightly disturbed by the persistent knocking at the door.

"What do you want?" Johnathan asked sounding extremely irritated.

"Y-your father, Master Sharpe, is requesting the slave girl you brought to him yesterday."

"Then go get her," Johnathan responded rudely.

"Yes, well, everyone knows she is in here. All except for your father, I thought I'd do you the favor of coming to fetch her. To avoid your father having to do it," responded Shirley confidently. Shirley knew Johnathan hated her. It brought her great joy finding him in bed with a slave, something he pretended to detest. Moments like this made Shirley's days a little easier. Because secretly, she despised Johnathan as well.

Shirley had been tasked with taking care of Johnathan when he was a child. He had a special place close to her heart, and he was the sweetest child. All until Shirley began to take care of another child, her sister Angela died during childbirth. In her sister's passing, Shirley became a caregiver to James, her flesh and blood. She raised the two of them, favoring Johnathan more was necessary because he was the master's son. For Johnathan, that wasn't enough; he wanted to be the only child Shirley cared for and lashed out accordingly. By the age of five, Johnathan's antics became unbearable for Shirley. He would steal the young slave's playthings, start small fires, and attack James without provocation. Johnathan was a large five-year-old, and James was only two at the time.

There was not much Shirley could do to protect James from Johnathan, which prompted Shirley to commit an act out of disparity. Shirley made her way to Johnathan's father's office and practically begged him to task another with caring for his son. The reason she'd been so bold as to ask him directly was that she knew he fancied her. On occasion, Shirley would catch him staring at her with much interest.

Master Sharpe agreed to appease her. However, he wanted something in exchange, and that night his visits to Shirley began.

These events created the relationship the two currently shared. Growing into adulthood, Johnathan became bitter, and Shirley couldn't help but blame herself for part of it. She left Johnathan high and dry as his biological mother did before him. Shirley knew he depended on her, and the love they'd once shared for each other had dissipated entirely. Though she felt like she did something much worse, Shirley left him for his father in Johnathan's eyes.

To Shirley, it was all a game. The relations with Johnathan's father were only a ploy to uphold her standing in the main house. The hatred for Arthur Sharpe was a mutual feeling that, despite everything, she and Johnathan shared. Johnathan closed the door on Shirley, feeling embarrassed that she knew he'd been harboring Amara in his room. It seemed accurate enough his father was always the last to know, preoccupied with his endless tasks.

Amara was awake now. Having heard the conversation, she got ready to leave. Amara noticed the look of worry on Johnathan's face. In requesting Amara's presence, Johnathan was afraid his father wanted the same thing with her as he had wanted with Shirley. As far as he knew, Arthur Sharpe had only been involved with Shirley. However, Shirley was getting older. Amara was new, young, and extremely pretty. Johnathan did not want his father to even look at Amara, but he didn't know what he could do to prevent it. Johnathan felt helpless and wanted to accompany Amara to his father's office.

"What's wrong, Johnathan?" asked Amara with concern. She knew that he was worried for her.

"Nothing, don't you worry. Come, let's go see what my father wants." Johnathan decided he would accompany Amara regardless of what his father wanted.

They stepped out of the room together, and Shirley tried to hide her grin, having her suspicions confirmed.

"Sir, I believe your father wants to see her alone."

"I am aware and have no intention of letting her go in there alone. Furthermore, I don't recall requesting your opinion on the matter. Truthfully, I don't require your opinion on any matter, Shirley, but you should begin your tasks for the day. I can handle it from here," said Johnathan, who practically spat the words at her.

Johnathan thought, *how dare she! Thinking her opinions matter to me? If I oversaw this plantation...* Johnathan had malicious intent for Shirley. He didn't know what he would do, but he knew he would do it whenever the opportunity presented itself.

Shirley walked away hesitantly and started for the kitchens. Amara sensed the tension in the air between Shirley and Johnathan. His rudeness towards her made Amara a bit uneasy, but she dared not ask anything of it.

Shortly after, the two of them reached Johnathan's father's office. Johnathan stood at the front door and sighed deeply. He turned the knob slowly and saw his father sitting at his desk. Arthur Sharpe looked up, seemingly annoyed by the sudden intrusion. He assumed a slave had stumbled into his office unannounced and was even more annoyed to see his son. Arthur also noticed the timid slave girl standing directly behind Johnathan. The outline of her skirt was the only thing that gave it away. Otherwise, he'd have thought only Johnathan was there.

"Oh, well, I wasn't expecting you to be here. No matter. Have a seat, Johnathan, and you. Come over here and let me have a good look at you." Arthur Sharpe stared at Amara, looking her up and down in a sort of inspection.

He found himself very much intrigued by her overall presentation. Arthur hadn't been able to have much fun with Shirley lately, not that he wanted to with her being with child. To him, it was a nuisance, and he had no time for it. Arthur Sharpe had been looking for someone new to satiate his desires, and he felt Amara would fit the bill.

Amara approached Arthur hesitantly. She could sense his intentions. Arthur pulled Amara close to him abruptly and smelled her hair, stroking her behind as he did so. Amara's body grew rigid as she stood there uncomfortably.

Johnathan suddenly stood up from his seat as if he wanted to say something but couldn't find the words. Arthur released Amara.

"Is there a problem, boy?"

Amara was extremely uncomfortable and appreciated the distraction. Still, although Johnathan was outraged, he could not find the words to express how he felt.

"So, it seems you have already taken a liking to this one? Very well." Arthur smiled, looking pleased with himself. "Anyway, there is another reason you have been brought here today. We do not allow freeloaders here. Everyone works for their share of luxuries."

Luxuries? What is this man thinking? Being a slave living in squalor is a luxury? Amara thought to herself and held herself back from smirking or spitting at him, for that matter.

"Your new name will be Sarah, and hmm... I think you would be well suited for the kitchens. Since your keeper is here with you, he can escort you there. Frankly, he probably would anyway without me saying so." Arthur Sharpe laughed briefly at his joke before getting back to what he was saying. "When you get to the kitchens, Shirley will explain everything that is required of you. She won't have any problem putting you to work, and I'll make sure you are well... encumbered. Do you have anything to say, Sarah?"

Amara said nothing and just stared at him blankly.

"So, we have a slave who doesn't speak? How interesting, and you are in love with her? I wonder how that's working out for you. Nevertheless, you will do well to learn English quickly. It will help you realize your place amongst the rest of the slaves. Until then, you are dismissed... both of you."

"Oh, and Johnathan?" Johnathan stopped on his way out of his father's office. Amara had already let ahead of him.

"What?"

"Be sure to break her in for me, will you? I like a slave that knows what she's doing... If you understand what I'm getting at," said Arthur with a smirk.

"You're disgusting," said Johnathan as he eagerly left the room, not caring to close the door behind him.

As the two walked off, they could hear Arthur Sharpe's disgusting laughter. He seemed to be pleased with himself. Amara wanted to know why his father kept him longer, but she felt it was out of her place to ask. She was still adjusting to the environment and how that extended to her and Johnathan. *Did he feel like she was his property?* Amara wondered.

Johnathan could not believe his father tried to make an advance on Amara right in front of him. "I'm sorry he put his filthy hands on you like that." Johnathan made a look of pure disgust, recalling what his father had done to her.

"Don't worry, I'm fine. I was not hurt, and I will be alright."

Johnathan pulled Amara toward him in an embrace as they neared the entrance to the kitchens. The feeling of her body against his caused Johnathan's heart to race, and his hands began to linger slightly. He quickly made himself aware of what he was doing and recomposed himself, pulling away from Amara. Now was not the time, and he wanted Amara to be with him because she wanted to, not because she felt obligated to. Especially after what just took place in his father's office. Johnathan was afraid of Amara, thinking that he and his father were the same.

Amara placed her hand on Johnathan's shoulder as if to console him when it was, she who had been violated. Johnathan smiled and planted a kiss on Amara's forehead. He didn't want to leave her alone in the kitchens with the other slaves. For whatever reason, Johnathan didn't see Amara as a slave but something else… He couldn't quite place it and didn't know why. All he knew was that he didn't see her fit to work the kitchens, she should have a much higher position in his eyes.

"If you need anything, or anyone says or does anything to you, come to me at once."

"Don't worry, Johnathan, I will be fine." Amara smiled at Johnathan, trying to reassure him, appreciative of his concern. Though she felt it was a little excessive, it was nice to have someone who cared about her, especially in a place like this. Amara proceeded to enter the kitchens. She could feel Johnathan staring after her, not wanting her to go.

"What you doing in here, girl?" Shirley greeted Amara inside the kitchen.

Amara hesitated briefly before deciding it was okay if Shirley knew she could understand her.

"I was sent here by Master Sharpe. He instructed me to let you know I was to work in the kitchens. Master Sharpe requested you show me how to perform my tasks adequately."

"Where you learn to speak like that, girl?" Shirley asked, staring at Amara in disbelief.

Amara didn't answer. She only stared at the area behind Shirley, where the others were already working.

"Well, let's get you to work then, missy. What the master say we call you?"

"Sarah, but that isn't my name. If it isn't any trouble, I'd rather be called by my name, Amara."

Shirley looked at Amara with confusion. She wondered why master Sharpe would name a slave Sarah; it was his wife's name. Shirley didn't want to think about it any longer, but she felt she might be replaced. She couldn't bring herself to call Amara Sarah; she didn't think she ever would.

"Ok, miss Amara, I will show you how to make the bread."

Amara learned the ways of the kitchen quickly. Soon she fell into a routine. Wake up, head to the kitchen, cook all day, return to Johnathan's room, perform her honoring of the gods, and repeat.

Amara woke up that morning and headed to the kitchen as usual. Shirley smiled when she saw Amara's face on the threshold. Reflexively Amara smiled back and began her daily chores. There was someone different in the kitchens that Amara hadn't seen before. He smiled at her when he caught her looking at him. Amara looked away, embarrassed that she'd been caught staring. The man was very handsome, and he looked only a few years older than her.

"Who's that?" Amara asked Shirley in a hushed tone making sure he didn't hear her.

"Oh, get over here and introduce yourself," said Shirley in response to Amara's question.

"No, that isn't necessary—" before Amara could finish her sentence, the man was already there.

"My name's James, and I'm Shirley's son. What's yours?"

"Amara…"

"That's a pretty name… did master give it to ya?"

Amara didn't answer, not knowing if she should or not.

"Enough with the questions," Shirley approached James. "Here, take this basket you came for and get out. Make sure no one sees you with it, no one important."

"Sure, Ma. I'll see you later, and nice to meet you, Amara."

Amara blushed and returned to the work she was doing.

"What ya think of James?"

"What do you mean, Ms. Shirley?"

"Mhm, I see the redness in those cheeks. You aren't foolin' me."

Shirley had an ulterior motive in having James meet her that morning. He worked the fields with the others and had no real reason to be in the kitchens. The night before, Shirley told him to stop by the kitchens for a few things for himself and the others in the fields. She knew how handsome her nephew was and wanted to work toward getting the two of them together. This was in hopes of swaying the master's interest in her; if it happened, Shirley hoped it would be enough to discourage him. It was apparent how interested Johnathan was in her, and she wanted that to be broken up as well. She'd gotten to know Amara and found her to be a sweet girl. It was her intention not to allow Amara to become accustomed to Johnathan and his wickedness. It would change her personality for the worst, and Shirley wanted to prevent that. With her attempted matchmaking, she knew it might cause problems in the long run for her and James. If Johnathan or Arthur Sharpe wanted something, especially from a slave, they were sure to get it.

Everyone in the kitchens continued to work as usual. Before long, it was already nighttime, and Amara had been working diligently throughout the day. Keeping busy to avoid the subject of James, who Shirley kept seeming to bring up. It was soon time to wrap up for the night, and the others dispersed, leaving only Shirley and Amara in the kitchens.

"Goodnight, Ms. Shirley. I'll see you in the morning."

Shirley looked up at Amara and smiled.

"Before you go, take this girl, but you'll have to finish it on your way up. Don't want you being seen by anyone. They'll go right back to Master Sharpe and tell him you are stealing from the kitchens." Shirley had tossed Amara a warm biscuit with sliced strawberries in between it.

Amara placed it in her dress pocket inconspicuously before giving Shirley one last smile and heading out of the kitchens. Amara made her way through the dimly lit halls and paused when she reached the staircase. She had a strange feeling that made the hairs on the back of her neck rise. Hesitantly, she made her way up the stairs, only to be stopped by a hand on the back of her shoulder. Amara turned around to come face to face with Arthur Sharpe and she knew it would be trouble.

"Where are you off to, girl?"

Amara could smell the liquor on his breath. Arthur Sharpe made his way atop the stairs blocking Amara's path as he stood in front of her. Arthur grabbed Amara by the waist and stroked her the same way he had in his office a few days prior. Amara attempted to shake away, but his grip on her got even tighter. She didn't want to fidget too much and lose her balance on the stairs. Arthur grabbed Amara's dress and lifted it as he began to slide his hand up her thigh.

"Leave me alone!" Amara closed her eyes and screamed. She was full of emotion and tried to extend her energy outwards.

A sudden gust of wind brushed past Amara and sent Arthur flying over the railing. He hit the ground with a thud, and Amara opened her eyes and ran straight up the stairs. She didn't take the time to check if Arthur survived the fall. As Amara ran toward Johnathan's room, she could see candles emerging in the hallways. The slaves were coming out to investigate what had happened.

Amara ran into Johnathan's room and closed the door behind her. She leaned against the door, trying to catch her breath.

"What's the hurry?"

Amara gasped for air as she started explaining what had transpired. "Your father made an advance."

Johnathan bit his lip angrily. He couldn't take him putting his hands on Amara any longer. He would not stand for it. Johnathan walked towards the door out of the room with his hands clenched into fists, and Amara grabbed his arm.

"No, it's taken care of. I'm not sure if it was my doing, but I didn't do it on purpose."

Johnathan stared at Amara, both interested and confused. "What happened?"

Amara looked down at the floor in embarrassment as she explained the events. "Your father made an advance again, and in protest of your father's actions, I screamed, which caused a sudden gust of wind. I felt the wind, but it didn't shift me. Your father, however, lost his balance and toppled over the stair railing. There were no windows open, no breeze coming through, and I think... no, I'm sure it was magic. I can't explain it; I just have a feel—"

Johnathan pulled Amara in close and kissed her passionately, not letting her finish her sentence. Amara shocked at the sudden affection, didn't know how to respond. Johnathan didn't know what came over him at that moment. Something about Amara and what she'd just done sparked an even greater desire than before.

At that moment, Johnathan realized it wasn't just Amara he wanted, he wanted power, and she had plenty of it. He felt as though with her by his side, they could conquer the world. Her run-in with his father was only further proof of what she was capable of.

"What was that for?" Amara asked, blushing but also confused.

She didn't know how she felt about the kiss, about Johnathan, about anything. It was all a tricky situation for her, and Amara didn't know how she felt about anything.

"I don't know. Let's not think about it right now."

"What if your father comes for me in the morning? He knows what I did. He will have me beaten, hanged, sold, or worse..." Amara shuddered at the idea of being in the presence of Arthur Sharpe.

"We can stop him, erase his memory, something, let's do it," said Johnathan with anticipation.

Amara could erase his father's memory. She didn't know what fate would await her if she didn't. She didn't want to be taken away from Johnathan. He seemed like the only friend she had in this new world. If he could even be considered a friend, under the circumstances.

Amara began burning incense, chanted a couple of words, and pulled out a piece of parchment. Amara cut her finger, and with a bird feather, she began to write down her request in blood. Forwards and then backward, she repeated it until it was done. *In the morning, you will forget, in the night we never met.* A phrase which she said aloud, clearly followed it, and with intent, *Aainm memoria erasure.*

Amara burned the parchment in the flame. The orange flame turned purple and then blue before it blew out on its own. It was done, and all Amara could do now was sleep and see what awaited her the next day. Johnathan laid beside Amara, resisting the urge to force himself upon her. With each passing day, his urges grew even more difficult to control. The events of the night had brought forth something within him; it took every fiber of his being to resist. He could hear Amara's light snoring and knew she wasn't tasked with the same problem. Johnathan stared at Amara as she slept, which was all he could do. He turned over and placed an arm over her waist. Taking care not to wake her as he did so. Before long, he, too, had fallen asleep.

Morning came, and Johnathan woke up to find himself alone in his bed. Amara was already gone, and Johnathan couldn't help but fear that the worst had happened. Amara's spell had not worked, and his father remembered. *How could I have not heard him enter? Or her leave?* He rushed out of his room and to his father's office.

Johnathan barged into the office to find his father looking at him with as much annoyance as he normally had.

"What's the meaning of this? Can't you see I have tasks to attend to?"

Johnathan saw his father sifting through his paperwork. He thought to himself, *What possible paperwork? A bill of sale!*

"What have you done with Amara? I demand to know where she is!"

"Someone is in a mood, I see. Your beloved is probably where she usually is. Doing what any good slave would do, their job. I suggest you leave my office. You are upsetting me."

"What about last night?"

Responded Arthur, pausing briefly to rub a knot on his head. Johnathan hadn't noticed his father's injury until that very moment.
"What are you referring to? Did something transpire you aren't telling me about?"

"No nothing, I wouldn't want to task you with anything else since your paperwork is so important."

Johnathan left his father's office, closing the door behind him. His father seemed to have lost his memory of what happened the night prior. The only reminder was a large knot on the front of his head. Nevertheless, Johnathan was elated; the spell had worked, and Amara wasn't being sold. She was merely in the kitchen where she was supposed to be. He should have checked there first, but he was frantic.

In the kitchen, Amara swept the floors, gleefully smiling to herself as she did so. She felt oddly happy about how the previous night played out. No one had come to get her in the morning, so she was sure her spell had been successful. Amara thought of her father and how proud he must be looking down at her from the heavens. She missed her father more than anything, but she was glad he didn't have to make the journey with her to this dreadful place. Though it wasn't all bad, the place seemed to be growing on her, all thanks to Shirley and Johnathan.

Shirley was beginning to like Amara very much. Spending much of the days working alongside Amara, she was getting to know her. Amara reminded Shirley of her deceased sister Angela; they were quite alike in personality and even slightly in looks. The two shared an understanding of each other, and Amara understood why Shirley felt the way she did about Johnathan. She didn't agree with everything, but it gave some insight as to the person he became. Shirley felt relieved being able to converse freely with Amara; she had not had confidence until this point to share her problems with anyone else.

Getting to know Amara made Shirley understand why everyone seemed to be so infatuated with her. Shirley didn't consider herself unattractive. In fact, she felt she was one of the better-looking slaves. Amara surpassed even Shirley in beauty and had a certain mystery about her, which had even Shirley intrigued.

"Amara, what happened on the stairs last night?" Shirley asked her suddenly.

"I don't understand what you're asking Shirley." Amara frowned.

Shirley pulled a slightly smashed biscuit from her dress and placed it on the table in front of Amara. Amara tried to hide the look of shock on her face as she realized she'd dropped the biscuit.

Johnathan barged into the kitchen and grabbed Amara by the arm gently.

"Come with me, Amara. We have some things to discuss."

She let out a sigh of relief as Johnathan led her out of the kitchens. Amara followed Johnathan into an area she had not been before. They walked through a corridor into an empty unfurnished room. No one was around, and it was quiet and secluded. Johnathan grabbed Amara and began to kiss her passionately; this time, Amara kissed him back. Maybe it was the impending sale or possibility of murder that had her emotions all over the place. There was also now the danger of Shirley discovering her secret.

"You had me so worried. I thought my father sold you, or worse. I don't know what I would have done if you—" Johnathan's eyes began to water, and he looked away. Amara reached for Johnathan's face and held her hand against his cheek.

"It's okay, I'm fine. Did you have no faith in my magic?" Johnathan smiled and pulled Amara in close, embracing her lovingly. Amara still could not understand her feelings for Johnathan. She didn't know what she wanted from this, was she in love with him? How could she know? Amara had never been in love with anyone before and didn't even know how it felt.

Johnathan leaned in once more to kiss Amara, and she kissed him back once more. Johnathan moved Amara toward the back wall and leaned into her. He began to kiss her neck as he traced the lines of her body. Amara gasped slightly and began to feel a bit overwhelmed.

"Johnathan… I'm not ready for this, not yet…"

"Fine Amara… whatever you want," said Johnathan in a low whisper by Amara's ear, which sent shivers down her spine.

She slid from under him. As she began to make her way past him, Johnathan grabbed her arm. He let go and smiled as he watched her walk out of the room. Feeling flustered, Amara made her way back to the kitchens. her thoughts lingered. She thought of her father and wondered how he would feel about her falling for one of her captors. After all, Johnathan, though not directly, was part of the reason her father was dead. Her village was destroyed, families torn apart, and villagers abducted and forced into slavery. She couldn't forget the circumstances that brought her to this place, no matter how much she cared for Johnathan.

Back in the kitchens, Shirley confronted Amara once more.

"Look, you don't have to explain to me what happened... I can kind of figure it out for myself. How about I keep my mouth shut, and you take this basket here to the field? James will be waiting for you when you get there. Just hand it off to him and come right back, you hear?"

It seemed like a simple enough task in exchange for Shirley's silence. Amara picked up the basket and made her way out into the fields. The heat was unbearable, and she couldn't believe how they were made to work in these conditions. As she walked deeper into the fields, she searched amongst the others. She found James all too quickly, and when she did, she couldn't help but admire him working. James stood shirtless with a sack on his back filled with pieces of cotton. Sweat ran down his chest as he continued to work. Amara sensed a presence and noticed the overseer making his way around. He hadn't yet spotted her, but he was rapidly approaching.

"Amara, what are you doing out here?" asked James in shock.

"Shhh, keep working. Pretend this is normal." Amara helped him pick cotton as the overseer rode by them, seemingly unbothered by the sight.

When he was no longer visible, Amara stopped and pulled the basket from behind her. "Well, what brings you out into the fields?"

"Shirley asked me to bring you this." Amara handed him the basket and turned to leave.

James grabbed her wrist as she tried to walk off, causing her to turn around and face him.

"Thanks," said James as he let go of Amara.

Amara nodded before she ran from the scene. She fanned herself with her hand as she ran back toward the main house. Partly due to the heat and being so close to James. The way he looked at her and even the way he spoke sent chills through her. Amara felt that she was developing feelings for James, but she feared what may happen if Johnathan became aware of them. She knew she couldn't pursue anything with him, and if she did, it would have to be in secret.

*   *   *   *

This day Johnathan had a prior engagement, horseback riding with two of his friends, Alexander and Carter. He wanted so badly to take Amara with him, he didn't want to leave her to work in the kitchens. His father wouldn't allow a slave that didn't work, no matter what the circumstances were. He could always just defy his father as he'd done before, but he feared that might only cause problems for Amara. Another reason he decided against bringing Amara was that he didn't want his friends ogling her. One of his friends in particular, Alexander, intimidated Johnathan. Johnathan felt he was a lot better looking than himself. He didn't want Amara to be exposed to any of them unnecessarily.

Alexander Francisco and John Carter arrived at the entrance to the Sharpe plantation. As Johnathan readied his horse, he couldn't help but notice Amara looking out from his window. He smiled warmly at her before realizing it wasn't him, she was looking at. She seemed to be making direct eye contact with Alexander. This infuriated Johnathan, he could feel his blood come to a boil. Angrily he took off rapidly on his horse, Alexander and Carter following close behind him. Alexander sped up his horse to where he was now beside Johnathan.

"So, it would appear you've purchased a new slave?" Alexander asked curiously as they rode through a wooded area.

"What business is it of yours?" Sneered Johnathan still angered from what transpired between Alexander and Amara.

"No need for the hostility. It was only a question."

Johnathan calmed his temper a bit, realizing his outburst was ungentlemanly. He just didn't appreciate the way Alexander was looking at Amara.

"Besides, I can always just ask her myself," said Alexander confidently as he sped off on his horse.

Johnathan caught up with him keeping his composure as he began to respond to Alexander's comment, "Maybe you'd be able to converse with her, but she doesn't speak the common tongue, completely illiterate for lack of better words."

"Some things don't require any speaking at all. I'm sure you've figured that out by now, Johnny?" Said Carter mischievously.

"That isn't any concern of yours, what I do or don't do with my slaves. My affairs are my business and mine alone."

"This conversation is becoming rather taxing. Let's continue our riding, shall we?" suggested Alexander.

Though he was in no way bored, Carter had already gotten the answer that Alexander was looking for. Based on Johnathan's response, Alexander was quite certain that he had not been intimate with his new slave. For he knew Johnathan's character very well, he was somewhat of a braggart. Had he been intimate with his new slave, Johnathan would have seized the opportunity to brag about the ordeal to Carter and himself. Alexander would make it his mission to get acquainted with this mysterious new slave woman; he was certain of that. There was something about her, and even without meeting her, Alexander felt like he was being pulled toward her. The way she stared at him made him feel something he'd never felt before. The three of them continued to ride, silently racing each other through the fields.

That night, Johnathan returned from his day out with his companions and made his way into his bedroom. He found Amara already there, rearranging parts of her altar. Johnathan wanted nothing more but to confront Amara about her interaction with Alexander that morning. The way they stared at each other made him uneasy, a feeling that clung to him throughout the day.

"What did you find so interesting about Alexander? You seemed to be quite taken with him the way you stared so longingly."

"I wasn't looking at him in that way... I was only curious. He doesn't look like you, or your father, or any of the other men I've seen in this land."

Johnathan was relieved to hear that was all it was. "That's because he's not like my father or me. He is a Spaniard. His family is from Spain," Johnathan said, relieved.

"Spain?"

"Yes, Spain, his father is a slave trader, which is why they are here in America."

"Is that so?"

"Yes, if I'm not mistaken, slave trading is a nasty business, I'm told. The voyages are very long and brutal. I couldn't fathom being away from home that long."

Amara cringed at his statement. She longed to return to her home to be amongst her people. Amara missed her old life but was starting to learn how to navigate her new one. Johnathan noticed Amara's reaction to his statement, also spotting the awkward quietness that engulfed the room.

"I'm sorry... I'm going to head off to bed, Amara. You're welcome to join me whenever you're ready," said Johnathan as he got into the bed and shut his eyes.

Amara lit the candles on her alter and began to write something down. She was writing on a dried leaf, not a spell but a request. Amara said aloud what she wanted, *To find purpose in this land.* Amara lit the leaf on fire and watched as it was reduced to ash. As if led by a guiding hand, the ashes sailed out of the window into the night air.

Arthur Sharpe sat in his office patiently in preparation for the arrival of his house guests. He'd made plans a few weeks prior to host a small get-together in his home. He watched as Shirley made the arrangements. She set the table, prepared the dinner as well as the liquor to accompany it. Arthur enjoyed having slaves to do as he wished. He lived a carefree lifestyle, able to dedicate his time to his business. Having slaves allowed him to focus on tasks he felt more important, and Shirley was invaluable.

Arthur knew his son would not be attending, probably too preoccupied with the new slave, Sarah. Not that he wanted him to be there. Arthur arranged his office with its finishing touches. "There, that's perfect." He had Shirley at the door awaiting the arrival of his guests.

Arthur's office door was suddenly turned open to reveal Christopher Francisco, Jane Francisco, his wife, Henry Carter, Elizabeth Carter, Maryann Smith, and her husband. They all walked in one after the other. Arthur met the Carter's during his own Childhood, he grew up with Henry Carter. The Smiths were more recent friends who Arthur met on a hunting trip two summers prior.

He had met Christopher Francisco as an adult during one of his business ventures. He and the Francisco's became friends immediately and have been for all of Johnathan's childhood. Which was the reason his son was friends with their children.

Arthur was known for having lavish parties from time to time, and during those parties, the children present would intermingle with Johnathan. Johnathan had never been a friendly child, but, both Carter and Alexander took a strong liking to him for some reason.

Everyone gathered around Arthur's dinner table. They were served dinner and began their festivities. The men stayed in Arthur's office, and the women toured the house looking for other things to get into.

"So, who's up for a game of Poker?" Asked Henry Carter, sitting back with his feet propped up on the table.

"Well, you know I'm undefeated at poker. You don't want to do it to yourself," responded Christopher Francisco.

"How about you both forget about winning? It is going to be me this time," said Arthur.

"Yeah, sure, you are yet to win a game," said John Smith, Eliza Smith's husband.

"I bet my best slave on it. I will win, I have a feeling." Arthur took a shot of whiskey from his flask, and with that, the four of them began to play their game of poker.

To no one's surprise, Christopher Francisco had won the game.

"Your best slave, eh?" questioned Christopher victoriously.

Arthur slammed his cards on the table in defeat.

"It was only a joke. I had no intention of giving you my best slave, it was just talk. You weren't supposed to win."

"Nevertheless, Artie, a bet is a bet. I'm open to financial compensation if that's more to your liking."

"Fine, you can have a slave of your choosing. Come by in the morning, and you shall have your pick," responded Arthur bitterly, ashamed of his defeat.

"I hear you have a slave that doesn't speak? Fairly common, I suppose but less common is she's some type of royalty?" asked Henry curiously.

Arthur displayed a look of shock ever so briefly. He'd first wondered how Henry could have possibly known about that, but then it dawned on him. Arthur had a conversation with Eliza Carter earlier in the week, during which he had told her about the new slave Sarah. Arthur raised his hand to his head in disappointment. Eliza had trouble keeping anything to herself. As far as he knew, the entire town was probably aware of his predicament.

"Well, I probably can't tell you anything new. That wife of yours has a mouth on her. The way I see it, if ever I needed everyone to know something, I only must tell one person, your wife."

Everyone in the room smiled at the comment, knowing it to be a true statement. All the men, at one point or another, had confided in Eliza only for her to turn around and relay it to those who would listen.

"She doesn't talk, but she's beautiful. She seems to comprehend very well, though; she doesn't have me fooled. Wait until I get my hands on that one, the things I would do," said Arthur.

"Why not get yourself a proper wife and stop fraternizing with the slaves?" Asked Christopher.

Christopher didn't appreciate that Arthur forced himself on his slaves. Bad enough they were slaves, having to deal with the likes of him was too much.

"Who are you to tell me what I can and can't do with my property? Frankly, it's none of your business."

"It becomes my business when you boast about your intentions. If you don't want any opinions from others, you shouldn't make mention of such indecencies."

The night took an unexpected turn, and all the other guests became uncomfortable. "Well, I think there has been enough activity for the night. Thank you for a wonderful evening. I will be on my way," said Christopher as he walked out of Arthur's office.

"I'm not finished with you just yet," said Arthur, practically spitting out the words.

"That's fine, but I am finished with you."

Arthur stood up and walked after Christopher, He staggered and stopped abruptly. Arthur was intimidated by Christopher. He was taller and more muscular. Arthur was sure it would not be a fair fight they would be engaging in. Deciding that letting him exit unscathed was the best choice.

"We must be off as well. What a wonderful evening Arthur. We will have to do this again soon," said Henry Carter as the men exited to meet up with their wives.

In his guests' absence, Arthur sat in his chair drinking his bottle of brandy. No longer interested in using a glass, he chugged it down in gulps.

"Shirley, come in here at once. Don't make me have to repeat myself," Yelled Arthur slurring his words as he spoke.

Arthur propped his legs on top of his desk and unfastened his belt. Shirley heard his calls from the entry hall as she closed the door behind the final guest. With a roll of her eyes, Shirley headed upstairs. It surprised her she had been able to avoid him for as long as she had. Shirley gagged on her way to Arthur's office. She knew what was to come, and she already dreaded it.

Johnathan woke Amara up the following day.

"What's going on?" asked Amara as she sluggishly put on her clothing for the day.

"My father requested I round up the slaves. He hasn't told me why, but I wish I didn't have to bring you as well. However, leaving you up here will only cause suspicion and draw more attention to you."

"Maybe he wants to lash someone... though, I hope not. I couldn't bear to watch that again," said Amara.

Arthur Sharpe was a cruel man, and Amara was worried for the other slaves. Johnathan hoped that was what it was. For one, he knew it would not be affecting Amara, and he also enjoyed hearing the slaves cry out in agony.

Amara followed Johnathan outside and joined the lineup of slaves; Johnathan stood by his father. He spotted Alexander at the gate. Johnathan had not made any plans with him, so he wondered why he was there. Alexander was let in and walked up to them casually.

"I see your father was too embarrassed to return after his outburst last night?"

"On the contrary, he wanted to spare you the embarrassment of having to face him. After your unfortunate statement last night that ended your dinner. Then there was also the fact that he had a few prior engagements. Since I was free, he sent me instead," responded Alexander, seemingly unbothered by Arthur's remark.

"What's the meaning of this?" asked Johnathan.

"If you must know, I lost a wager to Alexander's father during a game of poker. His reward was his pick of any slave that he pleases." Johnathan's father said with an awkward smile as he looked in Amara's direction.

"Your relationship with that one is unhealthy. How can you expect to find a proper wife when you are meddling with the servants?"

"You are one to talk! Amara is not a servant, and she isn't for barter."

"I thought she was purchased as a slave. Not a servant, you say? You sound as if you'd rather take her place. I don't default on investments; I will not have a slave that doesn't pull their weight, ever. Because of you, maybe we shall double her work duties when all this is over. If she isn't selected, that is."

"You can try it. Amara will be my personal slave. She won't have to answer to the likes of you."

"Is that so? All these demands, fraternizing with the slaves, sounds like you are finally becoming the son I raised."

Secretly, even Arthur was afraid of losing Amara. He had not been able to be with her yet. Something told him Amara was a virgin; he had not experienced a virgin since his ex-wife, Sarah. Arthur thought to himself, *An unwilling slave girl may be even more satisfying...* He wanted at least that before just freely giving her away, and even then, would he want to? Arthur had wanted to get rid of Shirley for some time now. She was getting older but especially being that she was with child. Alexander walked up and down the array of slaves confidently. His father had given him the right to choose. He pretended to be interested in various other slaves, though he only had an eye for one.

Arthur Sharpe pushed Shirley forward, "This one here will be of great service to you. She is fit, speaks English very well, and is also quite the cook. Though you are free to choose whomever you would like, this one would be a great choice."

"Is that so? Hmm… I wonder," Alexander looked Shirley up and down as if interested in selecting her.

He did not want to seem too predictable. He was enjoying himself gearing up to his preconceived selection. Alexander made eye contact with Amara, purposefully so, and smiled at her. Amara smiled to herself as Alexander walked off.

She sensed a kindness in Alexander that Johnathan did not possess. He might've been kind to her, but Amara knew in his heart he was not kind to others. She'd tried to overlook that, but in meeting Alexander, she realized it wasn't normal.

Alexander was not big on slavery, but his father was, it was free labor after all. However, the Francisco's had different methods in rearing their slaves. Alexander never imagined that he would be out picking a slave to take home. Nonetheless, he was there now, and he had made his decision. Granted, had his father been able to do it, maybe it would not be Amara that was taken.

"Such an array you have in front of me today, yet I've made my decision. I will take that one there," Alexander said, waving a hand in Amara's direction as if in the revelation of something.

"No! She is not up for your idiotic wager. You can't have her."

Arthur Sharpe agreed with his son, he did not want to give Amara away, but a bet was a bet. This Johnathan knew and yet was completely prepared to do whatever it took to keep Amara. Johnathan Sharpe stepped forward, ready to initiate confrontation if Alexander still wanted to take Amara.

"Johnathan, it's alright. I am going to go of my own volition. Let's not create any conflict over me."

Johnathan's father and Alexander were flabbergasted. Arthur had not heard a word from Amara since she'd arrived. Not only could she speak, but she didn't sound like any slave he'd ever encountered. She was well-spoken, even more so than Shirley. *She may even be more articulate than me,* thought Arthur to himself. Had he known she was so well articulated, he too would not have allowed her to be a part of the wager.

Amara started toward Alexander, ready to embark on her next journey. Johnathan stared blankly, not knowing what to do. He couldn't lose Amara; he was in love with her. His emotions were running wildly, his blood was boiling, and fists clenched. All he could do was stand there and watch her walk away. He didn't understand why Amara wanted to go. After all, he treated her well, and up to a point, he was certain she had feelings for him too. His stomach turned at the thought.

Amara stared back at Johnathan as she made her way in front of the carriage alongside Alexander. Amara had never seen him like that before. She wondered, could he really have been that upset that she was leaving? Amara felt as though she was free to make her own decisions, even as a slave. Still, it saddened her to see Johnathan that way. Johnathan truly had deep feelings for her, but she didn't know if she felt the same way.

Alexander lifted Amara into the carriage and sat directly in front of her, "Pleased to meet you, my dear.

My name is Alexander Francisco. What is your name? A pity we hadn't met sooner."

"A pity? Why? I am Amara."

"Why?" Alexander laughed.

"Must there be a particular reason? You interest me, Amara, quite a beautiful name. I just would have liked to meet a person such as yourself earlier if you must know. I've wanted to meet you officially since I ogled you in the window the other day."

"Is that so?"

"Indeed, you do recall seeing me the other day?"

"How could I not? We made direct eye contact. Also, you stand out amongst your friends."

"I stand out? Do explain what you mean."

"Well, you are taller than the others, you have darker features, and you are also more handsome than the two of them," Amara said bluntly.

"More handsome, you say? Hmm... good to know," Alexander smiled.

He knew he was more handsome than his two friends, but it was nice to hear it from a woman. Especially one as beautiful as Amara.

Alexander had seen his fair share of slaves, but never one quite like Amara.

"Alas, we are almost at our destination, The Francisco Plantation. You should know, my parents don't treat slaves traditionally... Aside from the labor required of you, they will treat you as somewhat of an equal. I think slavery is a nasty business but, it keeps my family's business afloat. I imagine you will be treated a lot better here than you were at the Sharpe plantation."

"Why is that? Since I've been in America, I've found that the only people that are people are the ones that look like you. Why should they treat us any different?"

"Don't think like that Amara, everyone in America doesn't have the same mindset. There are many varying opinions on how slaves should be treated. A dark-haired woman emerged from the house along with a darker-haired man. They had a striking resemblance to Alexander, so Amara figured that they were his parents.

"Hello, we have heard so much about you. Let's get you inside so you can get settled. I think you will enjoy your new home."

"This isn't my home. My home was with my father in Motombi."

"Well, that's understandable, but you are no longer in Motombi," said Alexander's father bluntly.

"I would be had your people not invaded my village, stolen my people, and murdered my father."

The woman seemed ashamed at Amara's exclamation, looking down at her feet before returning Amara's glare. The woman placed a gentle hand to the side of Amara's face.

"I'm sorry for your loss. I'm sure you miss your land very much. I wish there'd been different circumstances, at least in acquiring the slaves. I don't think anyone needed to be murdered. Surely there must have been a more civil way," said Alexander's mother, still with her hand placed on Amara's cheek.

Amara jerked away from her touch in disbelief. She couldn't believe the statement which she'd just heard. *Better circumstances regarding acquiring the slaves? Not that slavery is wrong, but the way that we were captured...* thought Amara.

Noticing the mood shift, Alexander changed the subject, "Well, it is pretty late. I will be showing Amara to her chambers at once."

Alexander's parents stepped aside, making way for Alexander and Amara. Alexander led Amara to the main hall in which there was a bedroom that would be hers, next to his. Alexander wanted her in proximity, so he could keep a close watch. Amara saw the grand bedroom equipped with magnificent arches, crown molding, large windows, and a bed much too large for her alone. Immediately she thought, *this is hardly a room fit for a slave.* Though Amara was not going to complain, the slaves had treated her with distaste since finding out what she was; all accept Shirley and James.

Shirley was kind to her, and Amara couldn't help but wonder what she'd be getting into without her present. Then there was James... Amara hadn't had the time to gage her true feelings for him. Now she felt she would never get the chance to either.

Amara turned around toward Alexander at the threshold of the room.

"I hope you do enjoy your stay here. At the very least, we strive to be a bit more civil than at the Sharpe Plantation." Alexander smiled.

Johnathan's bedroom was nothing like this. The fact she had her own room already surpassed her stay at the Sharpe's plantation. Alexander closed the door, slowly watching as Amara faded out of his view. Amara flopped down onto the bed and stared at the ceiling with a sigh. She didn't feel completely right that she was treated with so much more respect than the other slaves.

Amara felt as though she was lying on a cloud as soon as she hopped on the bed. She spread her entire body across the bed and closed her eyes. Taking in the sounds of her surroundings as she lay there, her mind became flooded with thoughts of Johnathan and his wellbeing after she left. With her mind racing, she eventually drifted off to sleep.

The following day was Sunday which was a day of worship for those on the Francisco plantation. All except Amara, she was dedicated to the worship of the gods she had known. She didn't want to be forced to worship anyone else's gods.

Amara opened the door promptly when she heard a knock. She was wearing one of the gowns left in the room for her. Alexander couldn't help but lose his train of thought, staring at her silhouette.

"Good morning Alexander, or would you prefer I call you master? Johnathan's father seemed to enjoy the title."

Alexander pondered the question a bit, he felt being called master by Amara would be delightful, but he thought better of it. The other slaves called him master out of habit, but he never demanded the title. Hearing it from Amara made him feel a different way.

"I would not like for you to do anything that you are uncomfortable with. I'm fine being called Alexander if it isn't a bother. However, I'm here for a different reason, I'm here to escort you to church. Today is our plantation's day to honor the Lord. Everyone participates in the sermon, and I'd enjoy it if you accompanied me."

"No," said Amara bluntly.

"No?" asked Alexander in disbelief, Alexander was taken aback by Amara's response. It was unexpected, but he quickly recomposed himself. He didn't want Amara to recognize any discomfort. "I'm afraid I must insist, did you not attend church on the Sharpe plantation?"

"No, I was never forced to. I have no interest in worshipping your gods. I have gods of my own."

"Understood, but at least accompany me? As a sign of good faith, I am not asking you to partake in the service, just attend. Everyone here on this plantation is Christian. You are the first I've encountered with a different belief. Maybe on the walk, you can tell me something about your gods." Though Alexander did not inherently agree with Amara's practices, he did not want to deter her.

Amara found herself smiling as she turned from Alexander to change her clothes. Amara was delighted for the opportunity to enlighten Alexander of her customs as much as she could, anyway. She removed her garments, completely disregarding Alexander's presence. Amara had subconsciously gotten used to changing in front of others due to her living arrangement with Johnathan. Alexander blushed as Amara seemed to have no concern for changing in the presence of a man. Alexander turned away and stood outside the door, waiting for Amara to finish. Noticing his exit, Amara finished up and followed shortly after him.

"Is everything all right? I noticed your absence."

"Everything is just fine. Just waiting for you to finish changing is all."

"You didn't have to leave to do that."

Alexander was surprised by her response. Even so, he was brought up differently and felt that women deserved privacy. Amara walked out and started down the stairs, Alexander following closely behind her. Amara seemed to know exactly where she was going, but Alexander hadn't ever shown her the way.

Alexander couldn't help but watch Amara as she walked with him to church. He felt like a sinner for looking at her lustfully, especially on a day such as this. Not only had he never been with a woman before, but Amara had an otherworldly beauty. Alexander watched her in admiration, taking in all her details. The way the sun shone off her hair highlighting its light brown color and how smooth her medium brown skin was. To him, she was a woman without any flaws; nothing was out of place.

The two of them proceeded to church and listened in on the service. Alexander noticed that his parents were not present, which was unusual. They usually were always there on Sundays to listen in on the sermon. Amara pretended to be interested though the whole time. She found herself reminiscing of her time back home. Listening in on her father's speeches, she was always present by her father's side. She still couldn't believe he was gone, and she was left to face the world alone. Even here in this foreign land, Amara felt as though her father was with her, watching over her and guiding her decisions.

The church sermon was over. Amara and Alexander proceeded to exit, but Alexander stopped in the main house. One of the house slaves handed him a letter from his parents. Alexander tore the envelope open and started to read its contents. Revealing his mother's dainty handwriting, the note read:

My dearest Alexander, your father and I have left to handle some important affairs. There seems to be an issue on the port that must be rectified immediately. In our stead, you are to oversee the house. Your father and I trust you will keep everything orderly until we return. Adios Mi Amor.

Alexander folded the envelope and placed it neatly in his pocket. "Well, the sermon has concluded, and it would seem my parents are off on business. What do you say we do with our time Amara?"

Amara didn't respond. She began wondering off toward the animal pen. She was, daydreaming about life at home. She had had many animals back at home in Motombi and interacting with them always made her feel at peace. Her favorite animals were two hyenas her father had obtained before she was born. They were by her father's side for as long as she could recall. She thought a hyena's average life span was around 12 years and realized they must've been older than she was. Her father told tales of being a boy and having Abdu and Ade by his side. She'd never thought it strange until this very moment, but her newfound abilities gave her a bit more insight. Maybe there was more to the world than she had once thought. Amara began to wonder about Abdu and Ade's whereabouts; she'd not seen them the night she'd been abducted.

Suddenly a searing pain raced through Amara's head, blinding her as she plummeted toward the ground headfirst. Amara's vision was taken over, and she was back in her village the night of her capture. The flames engulfed her village as fleeing figures ran past her. One of the villagers headed straight toward her, and Amara tried to move out of their way, but she was too slow and closed her eyes. After a moment, she opened her eyes to find herself completely unharmed. The villager seemed to pass directly through her. Amara was being pulled in a direction by some strange presence. A familiar figure lingered in the shadows that Amara placed immediately. Her father, flanked by Abdu and Ade protecting him as he made his way through the village in ruin.

King Amari came face to face with two foreigners, weapons drawn ready to fire. The King seemed to radiate blue energy that engulfed the two foreigners. They were seemingly paralyzed as Abdu and Ade lunged toward them, screaming in anguish as the two hyenas sunk their fangs into the foreigner's throats. Causing them to topple over backward, completely lifeless.

"Father!" Amara cried out as another of the armed foreigners crept up behind her father and was upon him in an instant.

As if he'd heard Amara's cry, he seemed to look directly at her as a loud boom went off behind him. He had been shot in the back. As Abdu and Ade noticed it, they charged after the foreigners. They disappeared into the distance, and the sound of two shots followed shortly after. King Amari fell to the ground beside a bush, the same bush Amara would find him later. The King clasped his hand to his wound in pain as a white light resonated from his hand. He fizzled out the light with a brief wave of his hand. Amara understood at that moment; her father wanted to die. He had the opportunity to heal himself, and he refused to.

Tears welled up in Amara's eyes as she began to fade back into reality. Alexander caught Amara during her fall and sat in the grass with her across his lap. He had tried to wake her up to no avail, however, he could feel her pulse. Alexander knew she was alive but did not know what came over her. Suddenly, Amara's eyes fluttered as she gracefully regained consciousness.

"You had me scared to death, I'm glad you're alright."

Amara smiled ever so slightly as tears streamed down her face. Alexander wiped the tears away, puzzled as to why she was suddenly crying.

"I very well understand I am in no position to deny you anything, you... own me, after all. I just... I know you'd like to know what is wrong, and I just can't answer that now... Please do not force an explanation... please," pleaded Amara.

Alexander frowned as he looked down upon Amara, saying, "As you wish, I will not force anything upon you against your will."

Amara smiled again, straightening out her dress as she got up. Wanting to take Amara's mind off whatever it was, Alexander suggested Amara follow him with a hand gesture. He'd discovered something in the woods a while back and had never shown it to anyone else.

Amara followed Alexander sluggishly. They wandered off into the woods. It seemed to Amara as if they were walking aimlessly. She could tell Alexander wasn't exactly sure where he was going. Alexander tried to recall where he had spotted the oddity. When they finally stumbled upon it, Amara recognized it immediately. Deep in the woods on the Francisco plantation was a deserted altar. It looked as though it hadn't been used for some time.

"In my 18 years of life, I've never seen such a thing, and on my property, nonetheless. I think it was used to practice witchcraft. I haven't set foot over here since I discovered it. No one else knows it exists."

"That's exactly what it was used for," responded Amara.

"I wonder who built it, and these inscriptions are not of the English language or Spanish for that matter."

"It's a tribal language, but it is not of my tribe," Amara began to walk toward the altar, tracing her hand across the engraved letters.

"You shouldn't touch that!" said Alexander, his voice laced with concern. "You don't know what kind of evil surrounds it. They speak about things such as this in church, and only evil can come of it."

"Is that really what your church tells you? That couldn't be further from the truth. It seems like your people like to demonize what is beyond their comprehension."

"How can you be so certain it isn't dangerous? Pardon me if I offended you. I just… never mind."

"This is part of my… religion. This is part of what I used, to worship my gods."

Alexander stared at Amara blankly, not knowing how to respond. Amara was right, he was taught to demonize such things, and he did.

"Are you the one who built this?" Saying it aloud, Alexander thought himself as foolish to consider such a thing.

Amara hadn't been on his plantation long enough to fabricate such a thing. Also, the distance between his plantation and the Sharpe's was considerable. It wouldn't make sense for her to make her way to the Francisco plantation to build an Altar and abandon it.

"No, but I know how to use it nonetheless."

"This is Devil worship. They've spoken about this plenty of time in church. Amara, I forbid you to practice any of this."

"This is not Devil worship; far from it. You learn to worship your way, and this is how I learned. We do the same things, mostly. You pray to your god, and I pray to mine, except I receive results. Can you name the last time you prayed to your god and were granted that what you requested? I didn't think so, don't patronize me for my practices, and I won't rationalize yours."

Although astounded by the way Amara spoke to him, Alexander wasn't angered by her. However, he felt slightly embarrassed for not having anything to say in defense of himself or his religion. To some extent, Alexander felt she was right. Though he did not know her religion, his didn't present very many results.

Alexander recalled asking his mother as a child why God was not listening to his prayers, often getting frustrated when his prayers went unanswered. His mother quelled Alexander in telling him, "Sometimes, our prayers go unanswered because they are being saved for a later date. Everything happens in its time, maybe not today but tomorrow, the possibilities are endless. One must have faith in our Creator, and in due time, your prayers will all be answered."

Alexander replayed the memory in his head, thinking life was a lot simpler during childhood. Amara began rearranging the altar to suit her needs.

Amara had not found the time to make offerings since she left Johnathan's plantation. He allowed her to worship her gods, even permitting her to build her altar in his bedroom. Alexander stood there in contemplation, wondering if he should stop her. He watched her as she performed her offering to her gods.

A white haze began to arise from her alter. Alexander stared in amazement as the grayish figures began to form shapes. The figures danced around Amara, who was seemingly unscathed. Praying to his Creator, Alexander had never witnessed such a sight. The smoke figures suddenly vanished. Amara ceased chanting, and only the two of them remained. Amara stood up and walked over to Alexander, and she began to cry once more.

Tears streamed down her cheeks as thoughts of her father overwhelmed her mind. His death weighed on her, even more so that she witnessed how it happened.

"What's wrong?" Alexander grasped Amara in his arms.

Amara didn't respond. She only looked up at Alexander with teary eyes. Alexander stared into Amara's large brown eyes and felt sympathy for her. He couldn't imagine how she must feel being taken away from her village and brought to a land surrounded by strange customs and foreign people. She was so young but faced with things that some older than her couldn't handle. He lifted Amara and carried her through the woods. Amara felt weightless in Alexander's arms as he brought her back to the main house.

Alexander walked up the stairs and brought Amara back to her bedroom, laying her down on the bed. He turned away and began to walk out when Amara grabbed his arm.

"Stay with me?" She pleaded as she stared up at him.

Amara did not want to be alone, her emotions were racing, and her mind felt heavy. Alexander obliged her request and sat on the bed beside her. Amara eased toward Alexander and placed her hand against his chest. He looked at Amara, curious as to what she was doing. Amara now sat directly in front of him, staring into his green eyes. Alexander could feel the air getting thicker and started to act on pure instinct. Alexander grabbed Amara around her waist and began kissing her passionately as he untied her gown. Amara had never been with anyone before, neither had Alexander.

Alexander kissed Amara starting from her lips, down to her ankles. She had never felt the way she did with Alexander with anyone. Not even Johnathan. She couldn't help but feel a little sad, realizing this was what Johnathan wanted from her. Only now did Amara find she truly did not share the same feelings for Johnathan as he had for her. Johnathan was more of a brother to Amara or a very close friend. Being there with Alexander,

Amara's feelings finally became clear. Alexander made his way on top of Amara, sliding down her undergarments as he did so.

"Are you sure about this, Amara?" asked Alexander consensually.

"I... I'm sure," responded Amara as she gripped the sheets.

*   *   *   *

Alexander and Amara had been together for what seemed to be six weeks. Alexander's parents had not yet returned. They were to be gone for exactly one month. Alexander had become so preoccupied with Amara he'd forgotten his parent's absence.

Alexander gazed out of his bedroom window to find a carriage pulling up to his entrance. Slipping on his shoes, Alexander made his way swiftly out of the house to greet his parents. It seemed they'd finally returned from their adventure at the port. However, it wasn't his parents but a courier with a letter addressed to "Sir Francisco, heir to the Francisco estate." He read the title aloud and choked on his words. The letter didn't seem like it would bring any good news.

Amara walked outside to Alexander; intuition had told her what the letter contained.

"Don't read it," warned Amara.

She knew what the grief the loss of a parent or parents would bring. Alexander opened the letter anyway and began to read it, "Good day to you, sir. I regretfully inform you that your parents have passed. They were hit by another carriage on the way back to their estate, and the impact sent them off a cliff. Please be aware funeral arrangements will be made at your request."

Alexander balled up the letter and began to walk back into the house.

"Mr. Francisco?" called the carriage driver as Alexander walked away.

"Please leave him be, sir. He needs this time to grieve."

The carriage driver stared at Amara, confused by being addressed by a slave. He grimaced, shrugging off the response and leading his carriage away from the grounds.

Alexander retreated to his room to wallow in his emotions. Despite that, he did not want Amara to witness him cry. He thought to *himself, My Lord must be evil and unjust to take away my mother and father. They had done no wrong. Who am I to worship a creator such as that? The creator that allowed my parents to be killed, watching idly and choosing to do nothing. Isn't the Creator supposed to be all-powerful? And yet did nothing when my parents needed him most.*

Alexander knocked the candelabra off his dresser, sending it flying. His mother had always thought so highly of their Lord. His father, not so much. Sometimes Christopher Francisco didn't even attend service. He was a man of logic, a man of science. Alexander imagined his father probably suggested they leave Sunday without attending church. Alex thought, *maybe father is the reason they are no longer here, but to punish the wife for sins of the husband? It is too cruel to fathom.*

Amara followed Alexander. She knew now was not the time to be alone. The door to his room was left unlocked, so Amara made her way in after him. He sat on the foot of his bed, with his face planted in the palms of his hands. Amara watched him by the threshold of the room. She'd developed deep feelings for Alexander in the time they'd shared. She stared at him from the threshold, unable to bear seeing him in that state. Amara wondered if there was something she could do to ease the grief.

An idea sprung upon Amara, and she set off toward the animal pen. Amara made her way to where the birds were being held and removed one of the chickens. There was a plump black rooster she felt would be an excellent offering.

The night was especially dark as Amara made her way through the woods. The rooster protested, making it a slightly more difficult trek. Amara severed the roosters head and drained the remaining blood into a wooden chalice.

"Please, goddess, I call upon you to grant me a request." Amara requested the grief be lifted from Alexander, the sadness be removed, and only the memories remain. A way to lift the sadness without erasing the memories altogether.

"Accept this offering and grant me this request" said Amara as she lit the chicken ablaze.

Amara grew suddenly tired and fell asleep soon after performing the ritual, even if she didn't find it to be particularly draining.

Alexander sat in his room, lost in his thoughts about his parents' awful fate, when a feeling of extreme warmth took over him. Suddenly, his thoughts were flooded by the affairs on his plantation. Alexander had a sudden realization he had no interest in governing the slaves. Or slavery at all, for that matter. He'd never quite cared for it as his father had. Partly to slight his father, He decided that he would grant all the slaves of his plantation their freedom the following day.

Alexander had no intention of becoming his father, or anything close to him for that matter. He resented him for his mother's death. He felt she genuinely didn't deserve her fate.

Alexander didn't wish to continue growing rice, cotton, and sugar cane on the plantation. He had enough money inherited that he did not care for more. In fact, there was only one thing that Alexander wanted, and that was Amara. He couldn't understand how he could think like this only moments after finding out about his parents' passing. It was hard for him to believe, but he no longer felt grief.

Alexander left his bedroom to look for Amara. He had a feeling he knew where she went. Alexander stumbled through the dark woods and found Amara lying on the ground beside her altar. He couldn't help but admire how beautiful she was while asleep. Although he didn't want to disturb her, he couldn't leave her outside in the cold. Alexander picked her up and brought her inside. Placing her on the bed in her room, Alexander stared at her, sleeping peacefully. She seemed to light up the room with her presence, and she was brighter than the rays of the sun.

Am I in love with Amara? Alexander thought to himself as he stared at the radiating beauty. Alexander noticed she had opened her eyes.

"How are you feeling?" asked Amara sheepishly as she gazed up at him.

"Surprisingly... I feel as I did the day prior. It's quite strange, actually. I know my parents are no longer here, but..."

Alexander had a feeling Amara had played a role in the way he was feeling, but he would not complain. Amara kissed Alexander's cheek, and he grasped her chin, staring into her eyes as he did so. Alexander kissed Amara deeply, and she kissed him back passionately. Alexander undressed Amara, tossing her garments on the floor as Amara unfastened his shirt, revealing his bare chest. She then whispered in his ear, "Someone is at the door."

"The door can wait, Amara."

Alexander moved on top of Amara and began to kiss her neck. Amara moaned, and the knocking grew louder.

"Fine, just fine, I will answer the door," responded Alexander in frustration.

Alexander, shirtless, proceeded downstairs. He opened the door to come standing face to face with Johnathan. Alexander had not seen Johnathan since he took Amara from his plantation. Johnathan was taken aback by Alexander's appearance, which he found odd, but he decided not to comment on it.

"I'm sorry to hear about your parents... I can't imagine how hard that must be. You have my condolences," said Johnathan.

Alexander acknowledged his comment, but it seemed Johnathan was preoccupied with something else. Johnathan was adamantly searching behind Alexander. *He must have another purpose in coming here*, Alexander thought.

"If you'd like to see Amara, I can arrange for her to come down and greet you."

"Where is she?" asked Johnathan eagerly.

Amara grabbed the first article of clothing she placed her hands on. It just happened to be Alexander's missing shirt. Amara, not realizing the significance, in a rush to greet Johnathan, tossed on the shirt. Amara proceeded to make her way down the stairs. She heard Johnathan's voice and was honestly eager to see him. It had been so long, and she'd longed to talk to him again, to see how he was.

Johnathan walked away from Alexander towards Amara. Amara looked slightly in disarray; her clothing was not fitted properly, and her hair was rather messy. Upon closer inspection, Johnathan made an observation he immediately dreaded. Amara seemed to be sporting Alexander's missing shirt.

Johnathan looked at Alexander with rage and hatred as he realized what had been going on. Johnathan raised his fist to strike Alexander, but he rolled his eyes in annoyance. Johnathan knew he was no match for Alexander. Nevertheless, he attempted to provoke him, as they'd fought each other on countless occasions growing up. Johnathan was a bitter child who always wanted to take his emotions out on whoever he pleased, which caused many altercations between the three Alexander, Johnathan, and Carter. Johnathan was more muscular, but he was slow and predictable. Alexander had a muscular but fit build which allowed for quicker movements.

"Careful now. You wouldn't want to start something you won't be able to finish," said Alexander affirmatively.

Amara rushed in between them before blows could be exchanged.

"Stop! How could you be so heartless, Johnathan? He just lost his parents."

Johnathan stared at Amara in disbelief. His face grew suddenly tender as he looked at her. Johnathan placed his hand against her cheek softly.

"I understand. Is that the only reason why you're sleeping with him? Out of pity... his parents just died after all."

Amara pulled her face away from his hand and looked down to the side of her. Amara's face was red in astonishment. Though she couldn't find it in her to respond, she felt whatever she said would only escalate the situation.

"Did the time we spent together mean nothing at all to you? How could you do this?"

All Amara could do was look away, staring into space as Johnathan spoke at her rather than to her.

"Remove yourself from my property at once. She's made her choice. Now it's your turn, leave or be thrown out," said Alexander bitterly.

"Not without her. Amara, come with me... please. You can't seriously want to be with him as opposed to me. I can forgive this indecency if you leave with me at once," Johnathan pleaded.

Amara stepped forward in his direction as if contemplating the choice but then stopped. She knew she'd hurt him, but her place was with Alexander. Johnathan stared in disbelief as he retreated backward. He took one final look at Amara and Alexander before entering his carriage and driving away.

Johnathan stormed into his bedroom, tears welling up in his eyes. In one swift motion, Johnathan knocked Amara's altar off the shelf and onto the floor. The items made a loud noise as they hit the floor. He then had an idea, *Maybe I can perform a sacrifice to the gods to grant me the power to destroy my enemies, to destroy Alexander. With him out of the picture, Amara's head will be cleared, and she will realize she loves me... that she always has.*

Johnathan walked to the pen to pick out an animal for the slaughter. There was a distant sound of a child crying. The sound redirected Johnathan as if being pulled by an ominous force. One of his slaves had recently given birth. Shirley had given birth to his father's child. He couldn't bring himself to call it his brother. In his eyes, it was merely another slave. Johnathan detested Shirley and thought now was his greatest opportunity to destroy her. He planned something more physical in the future. Johnathan needed a sacrifice, and he knew with a human sacrifice, the gods could not ignore him.

"Shirley bring me your son, immediately." demanded Johnathan as he barged into the house she'd been staying in since she had the baby.

She looked at him in fear as she was too weak to protest, but she knew that something was amiss with this request. Johnathan's voice was bone chillingly calm which told her all she needed to know. He had nothing but malicious intent for his brother.

"Your father doesn't know about this... why do you want him?"

"When do you question me, Shirley?"

Shirley went silent in anticipation. Johnathan went to the baby's crib, where it laid, looking up at him. The baby began to cry when approached by the unfamiliar face. Johnathan grabbed the baby by the neck and started to walk off with it. Shirley pleaded and pleaded, but it fell on deaf ears. She grabbed Johnathan's arm in protest, causing him to turn around.

"Please, Johnathan... he's your brother."

Johnathan grimaced at hearing those words uttered aloud.

"I know we have our disagreements, but I promise the baby will not be harmed. Father asked me to retrieve him," said Johnathan with a menacing smile.

Shirley was not sure if she believed him, but all she could do was stare in Johnathan's direction as he carried her baby off into the night. She bellowed over in tears as she had an unshakeable feeling she wouldn't be seeing her child ever again.

James came into the house shortly after Johnathan had left. He looked to Shirley, who was huddled on the floor, crying a pool of tears.

"Ma, what's wrong? Where the baby?"

"Johnathan... took him..."

"That evil... I will go get him back."

Shirley grabbed James' arm as he attempted to exit, "No... James, I will not lose you as well. Don't leave me alone in this dreadful place. I couldn't bear it. Please..."

James felt utterly defeated as he helped Shirley to her feet. He placed her back into the chair she'd been sitting in previously.

"Fine, Ma... but we have to get out of this place. There has to be somewhere better than here."

Shirley nodded and leaned her head on James' arm.

"We'll escape this place one day..."

James thought of Amara and smiled when realizing she'd escaped the Sharpe plantation. Even though it was to another plantation, it had to be better than where they were. He hoped it was and that she never had to go through anything like this.

Johnathan proceeded to his bedroom and locked the door behind him. The baby cried the entire way there and still cried as Johnathan placed the baby on the altar.

"Hush now. This will all be over soon," Johnathan cooed to the baby. "I call upon the gods and goddesses. I give you this offering in exchange for the power to destroy my foes!"

With one clean motion, Johnathan slit the newborn's throat, and the crying ceased. The candles in his room blew out at once, and the room was pitch black. A surge of immense power raced through Johnathan's body.

"I think it's time I test out my new abilities," said Johnathan as he proceeded through the hall toward his father's office.

All that was visible in the dark hallway was Johnathan's glowing red eyes.

Chapter 3
I Need You to Remember

Amelia had been trying to steer clear of Alex. Between the cryptic dreams and him calling her Amara, it was just too confusing. She skipped Mr. Walker's class that morning just to avoid him. It was the only class she shared with Alex, and she was not yet prepared to face him.

Amelia stood at her locker and stared blankly into it. As she stared into her locker, her mind began to wander. Ever since the dreams started, Amelia found herself dreaming while awake. Suddenly, she was snapped out of her trance by a familiar voice.

"Hey Amelia, have you seen Emily?" asked Johnathan.

"You are her boyfriend, you tell me." Amelia wondered if this was the Johnathan mentioned in her dream. Now that she thought about it, they did bare a resemblance.

It couldn't be, Amelia thought, *there's no way*. Just then, Alex walked up to Amelia

"Hey, Amel... get away from her, you devil," he sneered at Johnathan, his eyes full of rage.

"Whoa, what's your problem, dude? I was only asking her a question; you need to chill."

"Why are you being so rude, Alex? What's the problem?"

Alex realized that either Johnathan was playing dumb, or his memory had not returned to him yet. He decided to go with the ladder, but that didn't stop him from wanting to kick his teeth in. Alex decided he'd rather him understand why he was attacking him before he initiated the confrontation. He didn't feel like engaging with Amelia as to the cause of his actions. He needed her to remember already. He needed to figure out how to trigger her memories.

Alex mumbled something Amelia couldn't quite understand, "Aainm accidentis."

"Amelia, I'll catch you later. If you see Emily, tell her I'm looking for her,"

"Alright Johnny, will do."

Johnathan sped off, headed to his next class as Alexander watched in anticipation.

Johnathan overlooked the puddle that suddenly appeared in his pathway, causing him to slip and land face first. His lower body landed in the remnants of the puddle, soiling his clothes in the process. The students in the hallway began to laugh uncontrollably at the sight. Amelia ran toward Johnathan, reaching down to help him off the floor.

A surge of energy rushed through Johnathan, and his face went blank. He came to and ripped his hand away from Amelia's, picking himself up off the ground. Johnathan had felt like he'd been electrocuted and began to develop a searing headache. He looked at Amelia with confusion

"I... I have to go."

Johnathan stormed off, leaving Amelia in his dust as he made his way out of the school. Alexander couldn't help but laugh along with the rest of the students in the hallway but not Amelia. Amelia rushed over to him and helped him up instead of laughing with the rest of the student body.

"Leave it to Amelia to be kind even to this scum." Alexander couldn't put his finger on it, he knew he hated Johnathan, but he couldn't understand why. That portion of his memory hadn't come back to him either, but in time, he imagined it would.

"Watch where you are going!" Johnathan screamed at Emily on his way out of the school building, not realizing it was her. When he'd realized who he bumped into, he found himself even more annoyed. For whatever reason, his eagerness to find her earlier completely dissipated. "Oh, hey, Emily."

"Hey Johnny, I've been looking for you all day. Come on; we are going to be late for chemistry."

"Can't make it, Em. Go on without me. I'm heading back home; My head is killing me, and I don't feel well enough for class."

"But, Johnny, what about our date tonight?"

Johnathan grimaced at her self-centeredness. He wished she could be more like Amelia. He couldn't understand why he was thinking about Amelia.

"Forget our date, you little bitch. I'm tired of your fucking shit. Find someone else to annoy. We are through."

Emily stared at him in disbelief, her jaw agape at his sudden outburst. Johnathan walked away, leaving the school and not looking back. Emily had never been dumped before, and it angered her to the core.

Emily didn't care if he had a headache. She didn't care if his leg was broken, he didn't have a choice but to take her on their date, and after school, she planned on making that known. Emily proceeded to chemistry alone; she had a lot to tell Amelia.

Amelia had no idea why Alexander verbally attacked Johnathan. Maybe she was right; maybe Emily's Johnathan was the Johnathan from Amelia's dream after all. *This is insane! None of this is making any sense. What the hell is going on?*

The lunch bell rang, and Amelia proceeded out of the class. She was intercepted by Emily, who grabbed her arm and pulled her towards the bathroom.

"You won't believe what this asshole said to me."

"Let me guess. I'm tired of your fucking shit? Annoy someone else? Quite frankly, so am I, Emily. I'm fed up with your antics. I have enough going on with myself to be worried about your relationship drama. Go fucking figure it out yourself and leave me the hell out of it!" Amelia stormed out of the bathroom, leaving Emily again, flabbergasted she had been broken up with twice. Emily would not stand for this, someone had to apologize at once!

"Hey, Amelia, come back here!" Emily ran after her grabbing onto her shoulder from behind.

"Leave me alone!" Amelia screamed, and suddenly the water fountain faucet became unhinged and popped off, flying straight towards Emily.

Emily tried moving out of the way, but she was too slow for the faucet. It raced toward her at an incredible speed, hitting her in the stomach, which knocked her backward, planting her on her butt. Amelia looked back in disbelief as she ran off out of the cafeteria. She had to get out of there; school was becoming more unsafe with each passing second, and Amelia felt like she was the cause.

Amelia ran home. Upon her arrival, she found her mother sitting at the island in the kitchen, drinking a cup of coffee.

"Mom, I need to talk to you. There's been so much going on. I don't even know where to start. There's this guy at school who's been talking to me. I think I really like him, but I feel like we have known each other. Do you believe in reincarnation? It's crazy I know, there's something strange about this entire ordeal. Then there's Emily. I think her boyfriend plays a role in all this as well. The guy I told you about has it out for him, and I don't know why. I know it's a lot mom but there's more."

"Is that so? Why not tell your father?" Amelia's mother had not heard a single word and didn't care too either.

Amelia walked away angrily upstairs to her bedroom, slamming the door behind her. On her bed sat Alex's cat, Sir Charles.

"How did you get in here?"

Sir Charles stared at Amelia blankly.

"Well, maybe you should lock the window next time," an unusual voice said.

Amelia jumped backward, bumping into her dresser as she did so.

"Who said that?" Amelia looked around, trying to find out if someone else was in her room.

"Obviously, it was me. We are the only two in this room, last I checked anyway."

Amelia looked down at the cat. She saw his mouth moving and heard what was coming out of it but still couldn't believe he was talking.

"How are you talking? It's official. I'm crazy."

"Indeed you are."

"Please stop talking, or how are you talking? How is this possible? What are you?"

"Well, if you'd stop bombarding me with questions, I might be able to answer you. I am Sir Charles, the familiar at your service Princess Amara."

"Who is Amara?"

"You are Amara, obviously. You just haven't realized that yet. The spell you cast is powerful indeed."

"What spell?"

"Your memory spell. You cast it on Alexander, Johnathan, and yourself before you died."

"Died?" Amelia swallowed hard.

"Well, more like sacrificed yourself for your love. You see, Johnathan came to destroy Alexander so that the two of you could be together. You intervened and got hit with a lethal blow. Johnathan became corrupted by hatred and became a product of dark magic. He resorted to human sacrifice, a true evil that only bred a greater evil. Even in your dying breath, you still had hope for Johnathan, whom you cared for even after the evils he committed. Alas, I don't want to divulge too much information. The rest you must find out on your own."

"Wow," said Amelia as she plopped down backward onto her bed. "Amara seems like a really selfless person. Honestly, I would have toasted him. Maybe I'm not her, after all."

"Well, I guess we know how you differ from Amara. You are her; don't you doubt it for a moment. But you are also you, if that makes any sense at all. You have part of Amara's soul, but you are not Amara in a literal sense. For all intents and purposes, you are Amelia, in this life. I digress, I am here as your spiritual guide to help you unlock your true power. We can start by showing you how to set up your altar. Your altar is the source of your power. Technically, the power comes from within you, but your altar harnesses that power and makes your spells stronger. When you make sacrifices to appease the gods, you can be granted certain powers in exchange. Sometimes when a spell is too powerful, or you just need guidance, you can pray to the gods for aid. Are you following?"

"Sorry, I'm a little overwhelmed at the moment. This is a lot to take in at once."

"You're a fast learner. You'll get it; you are Amara after all."

"Me, a fast learner? Yeah, tell that to my schoolteachers."

"No need. You are an extremely fast learner when you put your mind to it. I've seen it in action. Back to what I was saying, having the altar charged keeps you current. I almost forgot, that crystal in your pocket is very powerful; do well to guard it. Having it on your person strengthens any spells you cast. Just hold it in your palm when you are casting."

"So, to keep the altar charged, I just have to… make animal sacrifices?"

"I imagine that should be fairly easy."

"Oh sure, I'm staring at an animal right now," responded Amelia laughing aloud.

"Very funny, but let's not get any ideas. Besides, I am of more use to you alive than dead."

"So how did Alex and I meet? Or Alex and… Amara?"

"Hmm, I don't know if I should tell you. How about I summarize, you were bought as a slave by Johnathan's father. Johnathan fell in love with you, shortly after that you were lost in a bet to Alexander's father. That's how Alexander's plantation got possession of you, and there you fell in love with Alexander. That's all that I will tell you, for now, no more spoilers."

"That sounds like an interesting love story. Amara must have been quite the catch. She had two men fawning over her. I can barely obtain one boyfriend. So, what you are saying is Johnathan and Amara were never a thing?"

"Not at all. However, he may tell the story differently. You should talk to Alexander. He is just as confused as you are. Well, less confused, but still confused nonetheless."

"What does he know?"

"Pretty much everything except jumbled up. He has an inkling that you are Amara. He knows he is a warlock. Also that whoever Amara was, he knows he was madly in love with her. He is aware that he has a deep hatred for Johnathan, but he doesn't know why."

"Why not just tell him everything then? If you are aware of the entire story."

"Because, my dear girl, what fun would that be? Besides, I promised Amara I would not tell either of you anything, and I've already told you quite a bit."

"Well, considering I'm practically Amara, I command you to tell me."

"Nope, my lips are sealed."

With that, Sir Charles jumped out the window, headed back to Alexander's house. *Wow, my head is spinning with all this information. Who would have thought, me a witch... and a powerful one at that? I'm glad I had Sir Charles for some clarification.*

Amelia headed downstairs, making her way to Alex's house. She stood at the door, sensing a presence. Upon opening the door, she found Johnathan on her doorstep with his arm in the position to knock.

Johnathan stared at Amelia for a second in admiration. He had never noticed before how pretty she was. It felt as if until this point, he had been seeing her through dirty glasses. Johnathan couldn't imagine now more than ever how he had chosen Emily over Amelia.

"Hey, Amelia. I just wanted to talk about some things. I don't know what's going on with me, and I feel like you can help. I don't know why I feel like you can help me. Emily and I were perfectly happy this morning, and then... I don't know. I just got fed up with her. Then there's you; I'm starting to have these feelings about you that I can't explain. I've never felt this way about you before. It was always just Emily—"

"Sorry, got to go!" Amelia locked her door and ran past Johnathan off to Alex's house next door.

She didn't know how she felt about Johnathan yet, and after her conversation with Sir Charles, she wasn't ready to be around him. Alex opened the door, already knowing that Amelia was there, and she ran inside.

"Whoa, what's the matter, beautiful? What brings you running into my arms?"

"I was already on my way here, but I ran into Johnathan. He's at my house now, and I'm not ready to deal with that chapter yet."

"I'm going to go handle this guy once and for all."

"No, stop, leave him alone." Amelia grabbed Alexander's arm and turned him toward her, kissing him.

He was surprised by the sudden affection but went along with it, anyway. He kissed Amelia back and ran his fingers through her hair. Alexander got caught up in the moment and began to unbutton his shirt.

"No, stop. I'm not ready for that yet," said Amelia turning away.

As she turned, she got a flash of memory— Amara kissing Alexander and then them in the woods discovering an altar. Alex noticed Amelia staring off blankly.

"Amelia? Are you alright?"

"Yeah, I'm fine. I should get back home, and we have school tomorrow. We'll talk later."

Amelia walked away from Alex and toward the window of his house, looking out to see if Johnathan was there. Sure enough, he was, sitting on her stairs waiting for her to return. He looked angry, feeling as if he was losing Amara to Alexander all over again. Alexander came up behind her, placing a hand on her shoulder as he spoke to her, "You can stay here tonight if you want. I can sleep on the couch."

"No need, this is your house. I'll sleep on the couch."

"No, I must insist, you will not be sleeping on my couch tonight. I will. It's not up for discussion."
Amelia smiled, and Alex led her upstairs to his bedroom. His bedroom was beautiful, like something out of an interior decorating magazine. Victorian bed frame, gray painted walls, large windows. It made Amelia

embarrassed at her own bedroom. The room was so large Amelia felt like she was getting lost just standing there. She imagined how lonely it must be for Alex to be in this large house. No one to talk to or care for him, aside from Sir Charles. Alex kissed Amelia on the forehead and began to walk away.

"Stay?" Amelia did not know what made her want him to stay there, but whatever it was, it gave her a feeling of déjà vu.

Amelia did not want to be alone, and Alexander obliged her request. He sat beside her in his bed. Eventually, they both drifted off to sleep.

Johnathan gave up. He could see Amelia wasn't coming back, and that pissed him off even more. His memory was coming back. Slowly but surely, it began to flood his thoughts. Taking over the person he thought he was and replacing it with whom he actually was. *How could Amelia leave me again! After what it caused in the past! It should have been mine! She should have been mine. I cannot lose her again. I will do whatever it takes.*

You shall have your chance once again. Our vengeance will be swift and unavoidable.

The voice in Johnathan's head startled him, it was his, but it wasn't at the same time. The voice in his conscious was deeper, darker, and undoubtedly evil. Johnathan figured his imagination was just getting the better of him.

Johnathan waited, hoping for another response from the ominous voice. When nothing transpired, Johnathan stormed off in the night. He was prepared for the long walk home. Upon Johnathan's arrival, standing at his doorstep anxiously was Emily.

He couldn't help but admire her determination, as she waited for him, the same way he'd waited for Amelia just moments ago. Even so, he had no interest in her; he'd make her understand. Johnathan's blood grew warm, and the voice he'd anticipated began to surface once more.

You must not let this one slip away from you. She will make a very fine offering indeed.

Who are you? Thought Johnathan to himself. He knew that whatever he'd been communicating with could hear his thoughts.

I am known by many names. You may refer to me as Gruhnekzahl. At last, we have reunited... Johnathan. You've been asleep for a long time. I am glad it's over.

Emily turned around to walk away, almost bumping into Johnathan as she did so.

"Where have you been, Johnathan? I've been waiting here for at least 5 hours!"

A lie, and Emily knew it, but that's who she was. Exaggerating was a part of her character, which annoyed Johnathan even more.

"Come inside. It's cold out here. We wouldn't want you catching a cold now would we Em? I know how you must be feeling. I've been a total... well, you know, but I promise I'll make it up to you."

Emily smiled coyly though she was overjoyed, Johnathan had realized the errors of his ways, and she had her Johnny back. She followed him inside, taking off her jacket and turning on the light. Johnathan trailed off into his kitchen, all the while silently contemplating how he would kill her. For some reason, he felt his sacrifice to Gruhnekzahl would be best received if Emily was in a state of complete bliss. This would bring Gruhnekzahl more favor which translated to more power for Johnathan, and he required it if he was to defeat Alexander once and for all.

*   *   *

Everything seemed like it had changed for the better. Amelia and Alex grew closer with every passing day, Emily and Johnathan were back together. Even Amelia's grades were improving somewhat, yet something was bothering her. Amelia had a gut-wrenching feeling that something was amiss and didn't know what could be causing it.

Amelia made her way to her third-period class for the day, Mrs. Jones Chemistry which was a class she was in with Johnathan. As she made her way to the entry door, Misty brushed past her, knocking Amelia off balance and causing her to drop her books.

"How clumsy are you, Amelia? Let me help you with those," said Misty with a smile as she planted her foot on one of Amelia's books and leaned down to her so that Amelia could hear what she was about to say. "I want my crystal back. I don't know how you managed to steal it, but I know you have it. At the very least, you know who has it. I'll tell you what, you have until lunchtime to produce my crystal, got it?"

Misty didn't stay and wait for Amelia to respond. Instead, she lifted her foot off Amelia's book and made her way to her seat. Misty glared at Amelia reassuring her of the threat she'd just made.

"Amelia, gather your things and take your seat. I'd like to begin the lesson if you would be so kind."

Misty smiled mischievously from her seat.

"Ok, class, we are going to turn to page 31, the properties of Selenium—" Mrs. Jones seemed to be completely frozen in place as if time had stopped.

Amelia looked around the classroom frantically as, one by one, the students fell asleep in their seats. Amelia saw Johnathan mumbling something. He was reciting a spell which Amelia picked up on immediately. Only, for some reason, she was completely unaffected. In the left pocket of her pants, she could feel the crystal warming. Her memories had begun to return though she was getting only bits and pieces. She dug around in the recesses of her mind to try to find something she could use to reverse Johnathan's spell. It was to no avail; Amelia still could not recall enough to protect herself from him.

Amelia braced herself for what would happen next. Johnathan seemed to have free movement as he got up from his seat. Amelia could not move, but she was completely conscious. The classroom grew oddly dark, for it being midday; the sun had been beaming only moments ago. Amelia couldn't see her hands in front of her, but she did see something that sent chills through her body. Glowing red eyes slowly approached her. They were Johnathan's, and Amelia had never seen anything like this before. Fearful, she realized she had not yet begun practicing and couldn't rely on her magic to save her from whatever fate awaited.

Johnathan walked over to her and appeared to be smiling, though it was not entirely visible in the darkness. Johnathan was ecstatic; he was finally getting the chance to have Amelia all to himself. With no interference, no Emily, no teachers, and her precious Alex was in another class.

Amelia could only see him through the movement of his eyes. Johnathan began unfastening her blouse forcefully as Amelia cried out. Johnathan grabbed her face by the chin to see her better though the room was pitch black. He could see perfectly clear despite the circumstances.

"Johnathan! You don't have to do any of this. Please." Johnathan was visibly startled at Amelia's sudden outburst.

"I guess I must be a little rusty. You are supposed to be completely paralyzed as well as unable to speak. Maybe it's better that you can make a little noise. Don't worry, my love. No one can hear you. It's just the two of us. For once anyway, you will be mine, Amelia. Whether it happens willingly or not is up to you, but I no longer care; I've waited long enough. I may not have been able to have Amara, but I will have you."

Amelia heard Johnathan talking, but it sounded as if his voice wasn't his own. This sounded deeper, darker, and it sent chills through Amelia's body. She was genuinely scared, but she knew she had to do something to save herself.

"You are a creep. I see why Amara was disgusted by you." Amelia spat the words at him.

"Disgusted? The hell would you know!"

"I am Amara. After all, I know how she felt about you. She despised you, pitied you even. My thoughts are joined with hers," Amelia lied to Johnathan in an attempt to get him away from her.

"Lies, you are a liar, Amelia. Amara loved me! I know it! If it wasn't for Alexander!"

Alex walked into the room, not seeming to be affected by the spell Johnathan had created.

Alex closed his eyes briefly and seemed to conjure an energy ball out of his palm. The energy ball soared into Johnathan, knocking him into a wall nearby.

The room returned to normal though everyone was still frozen, including Amelia frozen in place with her blouse unfastened.

"What were you trying to do, you freak!" Johnathan picked himself up off the ground dusting off his uniform.

Alex hopped over the desks coming face to face with Johnathan. Planting his fist right between Johnathan's eyes. Johnathan became disoriented, and the class returned to normal. Johnathan gathered himself and returned to his seat next to Emily as if none of that had even transpired. Alex stood in front of Amelia as she hurriedly buttoned her blouse. Amelia was embarrassed, ashamed, but also relieved Alex came to her aid. Amelia didn't want to fathom what may have happened had he not arrived when he did, or worse if he hadn't come at all.

Mrs. Jones resumed the class exactly where she had left off before Johnathan interrupted. Alex had cast a spell as well. Mrs. Jones and the class were completely unaware of his presence.

Alex sat down beside Amelia to keep watch over Johnathan. He would not be trusted alone with Amelia, that was for sure. Alex still didn't completely understand why, but he was madly in love with Amelia. He planned to do whatever it took to protect her, even if it meant putting an end to Johnathan against her will.

Johnathan sat back in his seat and stared back over at Amelia. Alex noticed immediately and returned the glance with an evil stare causing Johnathan to return to his textbook. When lunchtime came, Alex and Amelia separated. Amelia knew he wouldn't be gone for long, especially not after the incident with Johnathan. This gave Amelia some comfort, knowing someone was looking out for her.

As Amelia made her way into the cafeteria, she was abruptly yanked backward. Amelia stumbled as she was dragged into the empty hallway by the unknown. The person turned around to reveal themselves; it was Misty yet again. Amelia rolled her eyes briefly and sighed as she contemplated what she'd tell Misty.

"I told you I would give you until lunch to retrieve it, I paid a pretty penny for that thing, and I want it back. Now Amelia."

Amelia opened up her mouth to speak when she felt the crystal grow warm in her pocket once more.

"Misty, I want you to tell me honestly, why are you such a brat? I've never done anything to you. What's really behind all of this?" Amelia immediately realized what she said and covered her mouth.

Strangely Misty's face softened as she looked at Amelia. Her eyes began to tear up.

"I... I... it's just that... I was raised by my aunt. We were inseparable for a long time until she passed. Now, I live with my mother, and she's never home. I mean, I don't think she cares if I live or die. I pretty much raise myself and my little brother Jake by myself. It's hard, you know? I try to be the strong one for him, but... I feel like I'm falling apart, and I guess I pick on you because you seem to have it all together. I mean, two men are practically fighting over you, you're beautiful, and you have an awesome best friend. What more could one ask for? I... I have no idea why I just told you all that. You know what... I didn't care much for that stupid crystal anyway. If you find it, Amelia, you keep it. I guess I'm sorry for how I've been treating you."

Amelia reached out and brought Misty in for a hug. Misty returned the hug as tears streamed down her face.

"Misty, I want you to know that if you ever need anything, I will be here for you. If you ever want to, you know... talk about anything, ok?"

Misty smiled as she pulled away from Amelia's embrace.

"Woah, there now, this is moving way too fast for me. Just because you know my life story doesn't automatically make us best friends. I'll see you later, Amelia," said Misty as she walked off, smiling to herself.

As Amelia made her way back into the cafeteria, she was immediately bombarded by Emily.

"Hey, Mel, what's the deal with you and Johnathan?"

Amelia was taken aback by the question. She hadn't known Emily was aware of it. She didn't want to give too much away or say anything that Emily didn't know.

"What exactly are you talking about?"

"Well, it's probably nothing, but I've been catching him staring at you. Like in admiration or something, and it's really creeping me out. I wish he wouldn't do it, especially in front of me."

"You are overreacting, Emily; it's nothing. I'm sure Johnathan wants nothing to do with me, nor do I with him."

A blatant lie because Amelia could feel Johnathan staring at her from across the cafeteria at that very moment. It made Amelia's skin crawl. She wished he wouldn't do it as well.

"Yeah, I guess you are right. It's probably nothing. I'm just a little worried because things have been so great lately. I'm just hoping I don't ruin it; you know? I really love Johnathan, and I hope he knows that."

"Yeah, he needs to get a clue, you are the best thing in his life right now, he shouldn't take you for granted. I hope he realizes it soon. You know, maybe you guys need a little time away with each other, like a short vacation or something. Go somewhere nice this weekend; maybe the alone time will put him in perspective."

"Wow, Mel, that's actually a great idea! I'm glad I confided in you for help. I think I definitely will do that. I know exactly where I want to go!"

"Glad I could help. I hope you two enjoy it, and if he doesn't realize you are the only one for him, you deserve better. Don't put yourself through it, Em."

Amelia left Emily and walked over to Alex. He had been waiting on her to finish her conversation. Alex had been watching her closely since they separated earlier. Not only because of the impending danger but also because he enjoyed looking at her. She was beautiful, and he couldn't help himself. He enjoyed watching her walk, talk; everything about her sparked his interest. Amelia sat down in front of Alex, placing her lunch tray beside his.

"Johnathan seems to be becoming a serious problem. We can't continue this for much longer. I don't want you getting hurt, and I don't trust him around you. It's bad enough you two have a class together."

Amelia smiled, "You're sweet. I appreciate your concern, really, I do, but we can't just get rid of Johnathan. No matter how much you might want to, he's still human, though he seems to have forgotten that."

"Yeah, but look at him now, and his memory isn't even fully returned. Imagine how he will be when it does."

"You are right, but what can we do? None of our memories have entirely returned yet. Maybe when they do, we will all be stronger. Regardless, I think now is the time to start practicing my magic."

Alex nodded in agreement with Amelia. She needed to practice in order to protect herself when he wasn't around. Although Alex planned too always be around.

"I promise you, I will always protect you from him, no matter what." Alex meant every word of it; promises were not something he allowed to be compromised.

"I know." Said Amelia as she stared into Alex's eyes. They stared at each other for some time before returning to reality. "We'll start your training immediately." Alex kissed Amelia's forehead and the two of them ate their lunch in silence.

Chapter 4
Sir Charles, the Familiar

The days that passed by since the run-in with Johnathan had been peaceful. Everyone was gone. All the slaves, Alexander's parents, everyone.

Amara and Alexander couldn't have been happier. They grew more in love with each day, hour, second even. They were inseparable; God, have mercy on whoever tried to break them apart.

Amara walked over to her altar one day, and there, sitting atop it, was a fat white cat. He had an interesting facial marking a gray diamond shape on his left eye. Amara picked him up, figuring he was some type of gift from the gods, and one should never turn away a gift. She brought the cat inside to meet Alexander.

Alexander never liked cats. He had a slight allergy, but other than that, he found them to be a nuisance, as well as dogs, for that matter. Since Amara brought it, he could not argue; he would let her do whatever she wanted.

"Why don't we give him a name?" said Amara to Alexander.

He immediately noticed the diamond-shaped birthmark on the cat's eye.

"Is it a male or a female?"

"Male," said Amara.

"Sure, how about Sir Fat Cat?"

"Stop. A serious name, one fit for a servant of the gods."

Alexander gave it a serious thought. He recalled having a wooden cat as a child that he was fond of. He'd named it Charleston, which gave him an idea of what to call the cat.

"How about Sir Charles?"

"I like that. We hereby name you Sir Charles," said Amara with delight as she raised Sir Charles into the air and gave him a spin.

"I like the name as well. It sounds very regal. A very fitting name indeed for one of my... stature," said Sir Charles.

Alex fell out of his seat when he heard Sir Charles speak.

"What a delight, he is a familiar," said Amara

"A familiar?"

"Yeah, he is a spiritual guide in an animal's body. Familiars come into your life to aid in magic practices."

"Yes indeed, I was sent here as your guide on your journey into enlightenment. You should know, young lady, you have the gods' favor. Usually, a familiar is passed down through families; some practitioners never receive a familiar. You had your familiar personally selected. Tomorrow we will begin your lessons in the craft."

Amara smiled and set Sir Charles down on the floor.

"You never cease to amaze me," said Alexander to Amara.

That night, the romance between Amara and Alexander was greater than ever. Alexander only wanted Amara to be happy. He did everything possible to keep her that way. She wanted that time to be memorable because the very next day, she would devote herself to her lessons.

In the coming weeks, Amara excelled at her lessons. Never having to be shown anything more than once. Alexander and Sir Charles were in awe at how quickly she progressed. Amara had been thinking of Johnathan more than usual; she wondered about his wellbeing. Amara felt that she was causing him anguish and wanted to see how he had been. She didn't want Alexander to know she had planned to visit Johnathan. For she knew he would oppose, thus she gave him no opportunity to do so.

Amara left Alexander asleep peacefully in his bedroom one morning. On her way toward the exit, Amara performed a glamouring spell. She only extended it to the driver of the carriage. That way, her traveling to Johnathan's plantation would not cause any suspicion. Closing the door quietly behind her, Amara signaled the carriage and told them her plans, "I'm off to the Sharpe plantation. I have a few matters to attend to there."

"Of course, we will set off at once," responded the driver.

The vehicle came to a stop as it pulled up to Johnathan's plantation. Amara stepped out of the carriage and received many awkward stares from the slaves and Johnathan's workers. She looked among the faces trying to pick out a few that she knew. But she did not see James or Shirley. The slaves looked at her with awe; they weren't accustomed to seeing slaves riding around in a master's vehicle. At least never alone.

Amara proceeded to enter when a familiar face stopped her. Shirley seemed disheveled and out of breath but began to speak rapidly and franticly, "Amara, don't go in there. Something is wrong with Johnathan… otherwise I would be happy to see you, but you have to get out of here. You don't belong amongst us anymore. Leave while you still can… please."

"Why would you say such a thing, Shirley?"

Shirley stood in silence as she saw Johnathan looking out from the window directly at her. Shirley knew if she uttered another word, she might end up like her baby or his father.

"Please be careful, Amara. You are a dear friend to me."

"I will, Shirley. Don't worry about me."

Amara couldn't understand why Shirley was so shaken up. Without another word, Shirley pursed her lips and scurried away. Amara sensed something unsettling about the house; something wasn't right. Amara walked up to the door and knocked twice. Upon the third knock, the door swung open. Amara looked around, not able to find the person who opened the door.

"Come in," Johnathan said, but his voice seemed different, somehow sinister.

Amara couldn't see him. His house was unusually dark to be in the middle of the day. The air was putrid, it smelled of rotting meat. With the flick of her wrist Amara created a lighted pathway. It clearly depicted a few bodies strewn about the room. Amara shuddered when she came to the realization of what occurred on the Sharpe plantation.

"Where's your Alexander?" Johnathan called out in the distance.

"Not here. I came… to see you… alone."

Amara choked on her words; she could taste the air with every word. It took everything in her not to vomit.

"Is that so?" responded Johnathan.

"Where are you?" asked Amara

he proceeded to step forward and realized she was frozen in place.

"What's the meaning of this?" she asked as it dawned on her that Johnathan was using magic.

"Surprised? It was pretty easy to do. I watched your rituals attentively. I wanted to be like you, I was going to tell you, but then Alexander took you away."

Johnathan proceeded towards Amara, and Amara saw his eyes glowing red. She knew this was no ordinary magic; this was dark, evil. Johnathan had committed to human sacrifice. Amara swallowed hard, not wanting to believe it.

"Impressed? I'm a little impressed myself. So many powers... things I didn't even know to be possible."

Johnathan conjured a bright orange energy ball in his hand and toyed with it as he neared Amara. Amara said nothing. She was in shock. Amara couldn't believe Johnathan had gone to such lengths.

"How could you murder another human being?"

"It was easy, a newborn baby quick and painless it isn't like anyone will miss him. Besides, he served me a greater purpose dead than alive. Oh, and my father... He had to be punished for the way he treated you. It was easier than breathing. The other bodies, well, those were just fuel for the fire if you catch my drift. Honestly, I'll show you how easy it can be when I murder your precious Alexander."

"How could you? Your own father? And… your baby brother? Shirley's baby… Johnathan, no…"

A tear began to roll down her cheek. Amara now understood why Shirley didn't want her to enter. Johnathan had killed her baby like it was nothing. Slaughtered like a chicken to be made into a sacrifice, his own blood.

"You won't lay a hand on Alexander. This isn't you, Johnathan; you have to fight this possession. You are stronger than this…"

"Oh, no, that's where you are wrong, my lovely Amara. I am completely myself. I mean, sure, I am possessed, I've been quite aware of that. All my actions, though, have completely been my own. This is what I want; I enjoy being like this. You should join me, then the two of us would be unstoppable."

"I could never! You have become a monstrosity murdering innocents. How could I love a man who can commit such atrocities?"

Johnathan grabbed Amara by the waist and started to lift her dress, kissing her neck.

"Whatever you do to me, it won't have been willingly."

Johnathan stepped back and put his hands on his head as if he was experiencing immense pain.

"Amara, get out of here. I'm s-sorry."

Amara couldn't move, and suddenly there was a flash of white. Sir Charles jumped on Johnathan, clawing at his face. Amara was unbound immediately and fled the scene with Sir Charles following closely behind her.

They ran into the carriage and sped off. Amara glanced back at the house in the distance to see

Johnathan looking out through the curtain. Amara couldn't believe what she had just experienced. She felt Johnathan was trapped inside of this monster. He couldn't have been in his right mind, the Johnathan she knew wasn't capable of these things. At least, that was what she believed. However, Amara knew the toll human sacrifice would take on Johnathan.

There was no coming back from this, and Johnathan had to be stopped before he committed anymore heinous acts.

"That was a close one, Amara. What could you have possibly been thinking to go there alone? Though, there was no way for you to have known that he possessed such dark power."

"Was that really him?"

"I'm afraid so. He has been taken over entirely by something evil."

"Something happened in there, though. I'm not convinced he can't be saved. He... told me to get out. It was like he'd detached himself from himself for a brief moment. No matter the degree, there has to be some of him still in there."

"It's a peculiar thing indeed. He has been taken over by something dark he isn't himself, and he is. For the entity to latch on successfully, there had to have been evil there, to begin with."

Amara shook her head in disagreement. They were back at the Francisco plantation. Amara did not want to face Alexander.

"Oh, don't worry," said Sir Charles. "I already told him where you were before I left. He knows."

Amara felt even worse; she should have told Alexander herself. At the same time, he wouldn't allow her to go, or worse, he'd insist on coming with her. Alexander would not have been able to defend himself under those circumstances. Amara couldn't face losing another important man in her life.

She entered the house and was greeted at the door by Alexander. His face was an array of emotions—angry, afraid, confused, and relieved all at the same time. Alexander pulled Amara in for an embrace.

"Why would you go over there alone, Amara? You had me worried sick. I'm glad you are okay but promise me you will never go to such lengths again."

Amara felt her eyes watering as she began to sob in Alexander's shirt. Alexander patted Amara's hair and sighed. He didn't know how he could help, but he wanted too, more than anything.

"Tell me what happened, Amara," Alexander asked with concern

"Johnathan has magical power, granted to him by way of human sacrifice."

Alexander stood in silence, not knowing how to respond. He felt that Johnathan would now be an even bigger problem.

"Did he hurt you?"

"No, he tried to..." Amara didn't want to finish the sentence.

"We need to do something about him. I need to do something, and I will not stand for this!"

That night Amara and Alex proceeded to Amara's altar.

"Amara, my love," said Alexander as he took Amara's hands in his own.

Amara could sense something was off about Alexander. He wore his emotions on his face, and she could see discomfort. "What is the matter, Alexander?"

"I want you to teach me all that you know... What happened today, can't ever happen again. I want to be able to protect you from Johnathan. He is powerful, and I want to help you defeat him."

"Are you sure this is what you want? Once you embark on this journey, there is no going back."

"I've never been this sure about anything. Let me help you, Amara. Let us be together in all aspects, please."

Amara began the ritual. They made love passionately that night, and it was the most powerful thing Amara had ever felt. The energy flowed between the two of them freely. Alexander was now just like Amara.

The weeks that followed would be filled with training for Alexander to prepare him for Johnathan. Amara and Alexander both knew that as they trained, so did Johnathan. Trying to master his power. Johnathan's sole purpose was to eliminate Alexander. He was prepared to do whatever it took to destroy him. Johnathan was not aware of Alexander's newfound abilities. He was preparing for Amara to be an obstacle. He needed a way to ensure she remained away from the confrontation. *She loves me, and she will realize that when I get Alexander out of the way. He's the problem, once he's gone... I just have to get rid of him, that's all. I need power, more power.* Johnathan decided it was time to pay Shirley a visit.

Alexander was enjoying all of his new abilities. Amara and Sir Charles admired how natural Alexander was with his new abilities. They didn't have to show him more than once for him to grasp it. He enjoyed being like Amara, and he wished he had agreed to it sooner. Amara was happy that she shared an even deeper connection with the one she loved.

Amara and Alexander sat in the grass and stared up at the stars. They endured a long day of spell work with Sir Charles and were greatly exhausted. Sir Charles sat in the entryway, keeping a watchful eye over the grounds. Amara rolled over on top of Alex.

"I wish we could remain like this forever... in love and at peace."

"Peace, I can't promise you, but we will always be in love. At least, I will always be in love with you. Amara, I will love you until the end of time, in this life and the next."

Amara smiled and kissed Alex lovingly on the neck.

"Keep that up, and you know what happens next."

Amara continued to kiss Alex, and he flipped her over onto her back.

"You asked for it."

Alexander began to tickle Amara, and she laughed uncontrollably. Alexander stared at Amara for a while before rolling over beside her. They silently watched the stars once more. Even in a time of such joy, they both shared thoughts regarding how they would deal with the threat of Johnathan and when he would try to attack. For, Johnathan could arrive at any moment, and they had to be ready.

Amara didn't want to think of what would happen to Johnathan if he attempted to murder Alexander. She didn't want to hurt him, and she knew that Alexander would stop at nothing to protect her. Amara was afraid of that. Though she wasn't in love with Johnathan, she still did care for him. In an attempt to win her affection, he decided to resort to human sacrifice. Amara knew a person like that could only be a detriment to society. He would eventually have to be stopped before he could commit any more unspeakable acts. She thought of the events that took place at Johnathan's house previously and thought she might be done for if not for Sir Charles' intervention. Having a familiar seemed to be a necessity, especially if it happened to be Sir Charles.

"Come now, let's go to bed. We will face the coming days as they arrive. For now, all we can do is rest and, in the morning, prepare. No use worrying over possibilities. Que sera sera, what will be will be."

With that, Amara took Alexander's hand, and they proceeded to walk inside Alexander's massive house. Amara thought to herself, *Father would have enjoyed an environment like this. Peace, complete tranquility, no villages to govern over, just worship and relaxation. I wish he were still here.*

Amara had wondered if her father would have approved of Alexander. On her 16th birthday, there was to be a ceremony for Amara to be selected a husband. Gladly that ceremony did not come, for she would have never met Alexander. Amara was a strong believer in fate and thought that everything happened for a reason. Though had she remained in her village, Johnathan would have never become a threat to begin with.

To some extent, Amara felt some guilt. She felt as though she was the one who created Johnathan. He did learn everything he knew from watching her practice, and then not loving him was also a factor. *Is it my fault I am not in love with him?* She thought to herself. *No, that can't be right. I can't force myself to feel something that I do not. His actions are a direct result of the person that he is. I can't be to blame for this, at least not completely.*

Alexander was sound asleep, but Amara had been having trouble sleeping the past few nights. She figured it must have been due to everything that had occurred and what was to come. Johnathan weighed heavy on her mind. Amara tossed and turned in bed, removing the sheets from over her. The room grew hotter suddenly. She turned toward Alexander, who was seemingly unbothered. Amara sprung out of bed, searching blindly for the waste bucket. When found, she hunched over and vomited inside of it. *I must have contracted some type of sickness,* thought Amara as she made her way back into bed, Alexander still unbothered. Amara made sure not to get to close to Alexander. She feared he might contract whatever it was she had.

Sir Charles made his way into the room, laying at Amara's feet his tail brushed against her. Sir Charles jumped at the surge of energy that came over him when he touched her. He attributed the pain to that of getting hit by an energy ball, one that was supercharged.

"Amara is something the matter?" asked Sir Charles in a hushed tone.

"I... I don't know. I am feeling a bit ill. I am not sure the cause either."

"Well, I think you should get some rest for now. We will deal with whatever it is in the morning."

Amara pet Sir Charles and he did his best not to react to the painful touch.

In the morning, Amara woke up to find that both Sir Charles and Alexander were not in the room. Amara got up from the bed cautiously, grasping her stomach as she bellowed over with a gasp. Amara suddenly felt overtaken by immense power. At that moment, she felt stronger than she ever had before. Amara made her way through the house and found Alexander and Sir Charles speaking in hushed tones in the kitchen.

"Amara might be what exactly?"

The two of them had not realized Amara was in the room as well. Amara picked up Sir Charles. Sir Charles jumped to the ground and motioned as if he had been struck by lightning.

"What's the meaning of that? Is it my doing?"

Amara knew something wasn't quite right with her. She felt slightly fatigued, and Sir Charles reacting to her picking him up confirmed something was out of place.

"Yes, and no," replied Sir Charles.

"That is what I was speaking to Alexander about. The same thing happened last night when I slept at your feet; when I touched you in the night, I felt a surge of energy. That same surge I felt just then."

"What does it mean?" asked Alexander with concern.

"It can only mean one thing... Amara is with child, and about the symptoms, what she's carrying is extremely powerful. Maybe even more so than she."

Alexander and Amara stared blankly, not looking in any particular direction. Alexander found himself grinning gleefully as Amara placed her hand over her stomach.

"Are you absolutely sure?" asked Amara in disbelief.

Though it made sense to her after all. She and Alexander had been intimate with each other often. Then there was the power she'd been feeling, sleepless nights, fatigue. Her mother had gone through the same symptoms when she was with child. However, Amara's mother died during childbirth. Her father told her many stories of her mother. How Amara was brought into this world. He'd told her just how powerful Amara would be, stronger than himself. Amara never quite understood what her father had meant until now. He had done a great job keeping her in the dark during her upbringing. Now, here she was, going through the same symptoms as her mother before her. All she had to draw the connection were the stories he'd once told.

"Positive," responded Sir Charles.

Amara could tell Alexander was extremely happy, but Amara didn't know how she felt about this. For one, she didn't want to have to face Johnathan like this; she feared she'd be putting the child at risk. Alexander picked Amara up and spun her around in his arms. Even in a time of joy, Alexander seemed to be thinking the same thing. He would not allow Amara or the unborn child to face Johnathan. He had already decided he would be facing Johnathan alone.

"I know what you are thinking. And I can't let you face Johnathan alone. I do not know how I would face this world without you, especially now. I… I lost my father, I was taken from my home, and your parents… I just can't fathom anything happening to you, Alexander… not now and not ever. We must stay together for the sake of our child."

"Whoever said you would be without me? I plan to face Johnathan and win. Have you no faith in me?" Alexander smiled, pulling Amara in close.

"I have all the faith in you. It's Johnathan who I don't have faith in. He will stop at nothing to gain my affections, and he has the power of evil backing his every move. It would be foolish to anticipate victory before the battle has begun."

"Rightly so, but you are in no position to aid me in battle. I didn't want you to before, and I absolutely forbid it now. Whether I win or lose, whatever the outcome, I need you to be safe. I'm prepared to face whatever he throws at me, but it would be easier if I didn't have to worry about you as well."

Amara buried herself in Alexander's chest; she didn't know how to respond. She knew that arguing would bring no victories, but she had no intention of letting Alexander face Johnathan alone. No matter what condition she found herself in, this was not only Alexander's fight, and now more than ever, Amara had to ensure they were victorious.

Amara grasped her stomach, and Alexander placed his hand over hers. Amara knew when this was over, they would be at peace, to live the life they wanted without any interference. Alexander could not read her mind, but he knew exactly what she was thinking, and he agreed.

"Soon, this will all be over, and we can begin our family. You, the child, and I."

Tears began to stream down Amara's face. She couldn't help herself, for she knew there was a possibility that one of them would die. Johnathan may defeat them both. She had never faced a foe before, especially one with dark magic. The proper thing to do would be to prepare for multiple outcomes, and that was exactly what Amara planned on doing. In a perfect world, everything would work out, Johnathan would be defeated, and the three of them would live happily for the rest of their existence. Amara couldn't shake the feeling that this would not be the case.

Chapter 5
A Trip down Memory lane

Amelia had been practicing magic often and was improving her skill greatly. Sir Charles was always there supervising her every move and making sure she did everything as he instructed. Amelia was a natural, just as Amara had been before her. Who would have thought? *Amelia C student, a wizard at magic. If only there were a class for that.*

Amelia was so excited it was Saturday, no school, no drama, and most importantly, no Johnathan. Emily had taken Amelia's advice, a brief vacation with Johnathan, and Mexico was their destination. They'd return late Monday, missing a day of school. Emily ran it by her parents a week prior, knowing they couldn't say no to her. Emily's parents really did let her do whatever she wanted.

Amelia decided today would be a great day for a walk. There wasn't any training scheduled with Sir Charles, and she wanted to take a personal day. She got ready quickly, throwing on a pair of joggers and a T-shirt. She walked downstairs to the kitchen, and to no surprise, her parents were already gone. As she stepped out onto her porch, Alex was already on his way up.

"Just the person I wanted to see. I'd hoped to catch you before you made any plans."

"Yeah, I can see that. What's going on?"

"Nothing really just wanted to see if you were free for a walk."

"You read my mind. That's exactly what I came out here for."

Amara proceeded down the stairs and began to walk with Alex.

"No sign of Johnathan today?"

"No, and I'd like to keep it that way. I get enough of him during school to have to worry about him after school as well. Besides, he's in Mexico with Emily. They took a vacation."

"A vacation? Hey, follow me. I want to show you something before we take off."

Alex led Amelia back toward his house. He brought her inside, and he proceeded to take her to a room she had not yet seen. Alex opened the door slowly as if to build up suspense.

"Well, open it up already," Amelia said anxiously.

He opened the door to reveal an altar—Amara's altar. Amelia had seen it in her dreams before.

"Why show me this?"

"I don't know. I thought it might trigger something."

"Well, it didn't."

Amelia walked toward the altar. It displayed beautiful wooden carved artifacts in mint condition. There was a chalice, decayed flowers, jars of burned remains from spells cast, everything preserved as if untouched. Slowly, Amelia reached out toward the altar, hoping that she, too, would get some type of reaction. When she touched it, she immediately felt a surge of energy, memories began rushing in, and Amelia's eyes went completely white.

"Are you okay?" Alex pulled Amelia off the altar, fearing that something detrimental may have been happening.

The memories stopped as soon as she was removed from the altar. Amelia grasped the altar again, trying to retrieve the rest of her memories.

"What happened?"

"I remember."

Alex stared at Amelia.

"What do you remember?"

"Almost everything. I remember when I arrived in America, I remember being purchased by Johnathan, I remember you, being in love with you. How is this possible? How could we have lived so long ago and now? I don't understand."

"I don't really know either, but I think everything will reveal itself soon. With all of us getting our memories back, it's inevitable."

"Oh, Alexander... I'm sorry I didn't remember you." Amelia ran up to Alex hugging him tightly, sobbing in his chest.

"It's okay Amelia, what kind of man would I be if I held that against you?" Alexander grinned at Amelia as his comment made her stop crying.

Alex kissed Amelia, and they were together again like it had been before. Sir Charles heard the exchange between Amelia and Alex, which prompted him to find other things to get into. Deciding to venture out and gather information on Johnathan. This was something he did in his spare time. The fact of the matter was that Johnathan could not be trusted. Alex and Amelia may not have known why, but Sir Charles did. His plan was always to be one step ahead of him. Sir Charles was also aware that Johnathan had gotten a portion of his memory back. Knowing that, Johnathan would have no interest in

Emily. This was a cause for concern for the cat, for there was only one reason Johnathan would be interested in Emily. Sir Charles suspected Johnathan would attempt to sacrifice her.

Sir Charles climbed up Johnathan's house to view him through the window.

"Well, that's odd. He's not home," said Sir Charles to himself and proceeded to make his way back to Alex's house.

Amelia sat on the couch beside Alexander placing her hand in his. They stared at each other lovingly. Alex wished he could have experienced the same memories as Amelia. He enjoyed the visions of the past. They showed him parts of his true self. Amelia suddenly became extremely tired, as though something was drawing her to sleep. Amelia began to dream of the past as usual. Since her memories began to return, all she ever dreamed about was the past of her former self.

It had been three months since they found out Amara was with child. Her stomach had been growing at a rapid rate; it seemed like the size increased daily as opposed to monthly. They were truly happy but weighed down at the same time. Amara and Alexander did not know when Johnathan would strike, and it could be at any time.

"Maybe he will wait until the baby comes. That will give us time to figure out how to hide our child. That way, we can get rid of him. There is more of a chance of success if we do it together," said Amara.

"Wishful thinking, my love, but he is unaware you are with child. Though I think he wouldn't care, either way, he may choose to strike sooner. Or worse,

I'm afraid if he knew you were carrying my child, he would seek actions to terminate it."

Alexander grew angry as he spoke. He knew what he'd be capable of if it came to protecting Amara and his child. Amara felt like there was still hope for Johnathan, which angered Alexander even more. He knew it would be hard for Amara to fight him if she felt like he was still human. Alexander knew it was passed that he now was something less than human, something dark, evil, and hopeless to being saved.

Alexander placed his hand on Amara's stomach, his second time doing so since finding out she was carrying. Alexander shivered, feeling the same jolt of energy that Sir Charles had felt before. This time it was different; it wasn't one jolt of energy, but two simultaneously, which indicated Amara was pregnant with twins. Alexander's eyes began to water as he realized that his parents were no longer there to participate in his children's upbringing. They would never have the opportunity to meet their grandparents.

"What's the matter?" asked Amara

"I think you are having twins. It would explain why your stomach has grown so much in only three months."

"How can you know?" Amara asked excitedly.

"Well, when I touched your stomach, the same burst of energy Sir Charles felt, I felt as well. But it was different this time; I felt two bursts of energy. It's hard to explain."

"Trust me, I understand perfectly," Amara said, grinning, but her smile quickly faded.

There were so many more lives at stake. This joyous news was also dreadful to her.

Amelia woke up feeling dazed, confused, and saddened. She stared at Alex for a while before finding the words to speak.

"Amara was pregnant with twins." Alex didn't know how he should respond.

"What happened?" asked Alex, just as confused.

"I don't know. I didn't get that far in the dream; maybe I woke up to soon."

Amelia wasn't completely honest; she had an inkling that whatever happened had something to do with Johnathan. Truthfully, Amelia was positive he had something to do with whatever happened to Amara's children. Amelia knew she couldn't suggest anything to do with Johnathan; she'd be sentencing him to death. Since she'd touched the altar, Amelia realized she was harboring feelings for Johnathan as well. Before getting her most recent memories, she hadn't felt anything romantic toward him whatsoever. Since the incident during the chemistry class, the mere thought of him repulsed her. However, her new memories also came with some of Amara's emotions and feelings.

Amelia realized she didn't want Johnathan dead. He'd been a good friend to her before all of this, and he was Emily's boyfriend as well. It was still hard for Amelia to believe what he'd become. There had to be hope for Johnathan; this was a new life after all.

"Is everything alright, Amelia?"

"Yeah, everything is just fine, just lost in my thoughts, is all."

"What do you think happened to the children?"

"Honestly, I don't know, I hate even to fathom this, but maybe she miscarried?"

"Yeah, I guess that is possible. Being a powerful witch and all, you don't think she'd be able to reverse the effects or something?"

"I don't think even witches can cheat death, Alex."

Sir Charles strolled in casually, looking surprised to see Alex and Amara still together in the living room.

"Where have you been?" asked Alex with suspicion.

"Just out for a walk. Did you happen to know that Johnathan was not home? I passed his house during my stroll and decided to snoop a bit. Keep an eye on him and such, but alas, no one was home."

"Is that so?" asked Alex

"Yes, indeed."

"Well, Johnathan and Emily are on vacation. They took a weekend in Mexico, should be back sometime Monday."

"Emily and Johnathan are alone?" asked Sir Charles with concern.

"I wouldn't think anything of it, even in this current state, Johnathan loves Emily. He just needs some time away from all this to remember that. They'll be fine, don't worry, Charlie," responded Amelia.

"Charlie? Oh heavens, what is this?"

"Ha, I think it fits," said Alex as he tussled Sir Charles' fur. Amelia's face suddenly grew more serious.

"Charles, what happened to the twins Amara was carrying?"

Sir Charles turned silent, and his face went blank as if the question caused him distress.

"I-I can't answer that. I'm afraid you must discover the answer on your own."

"It figures you wouldn't tell us. It was pointless even to ask."

"Sorry."

"Well, Charlie, answer me this, aside from the obvious as in other witches, are there any other threats we should be aware of?"

Sir Charles grinned through his teeth, "I thought you'd never ask dear Amelia, and yes, there are quite a few. There are vampires, zombies, though some may argue they are the same thing goblins, werewolves, and most importantly, hunters."

"Hunters?" asked Amara and Alex in unison.

"Yes, hunters. They go as far back as the first supernatural beings. Hunters are to be feared above all other mentions; all species can fall prey to the hunters. The goblins are almost completely extinct on their account. They waged war against supernatural's and humans a millennium ago, which created the hunters' the human's first line of defense. They are ruthless killers, and once they begin pursuit, they are nearly impossible to evade. I only know of one case of a witch pursued by hunters who escaped into hiding. Her name was Lucinda; no one knows what happened to her. She fell off the face of the earth. Who knows, maybe she was finally caught. You can only run from the hunters for so long. I digress; you should also be aware. Poison can also kill a witch, and the hunters utilize some of the most lethal poisons. They carry serrated daggers laced with poison, one of their most lethal, dragon's blood. If ever cut by this blade, I fear the gods themselves couldn't save you."

"Wow, that's a lot to be wary of."

"Not necessarily. Usually, vampires are allies of witches, zombies are more like thralls. Werewolves, on the other hand, are very reclusive. They keep to themselves, preferring to inhabit the forests of the world. Don't be fooled, though; they aren't your typical Hollywood creatures."

"So you mean to tell me, all of these things are running around undetected by mankind?"

"Yes and no. Every movie or book that you've read about these things had to have a factual backing. However, mankind has a passion for filling in the blanks; whatever they don't understand, they create. Therefore, a lot of the stories are muddled with misinformation."

"Interesting enough, it's getting late. I'm going to head home. Alex, I'll see you later?"

"Of course, you will."

Alex kissed Amelia's forehead, and she proceeded to exit his house. Sir Charles beat her to the door, "Amelia, I insist you must contact Emily at least periodically throughout this vacation. I don't trust Johnathan one bit, and who knows what he is capable of when he gets all his memories back."

"Yeah, I guess you are right, Charlie. I'll check on her, but I assure you, they are fine."

Amelia swallowed hard on her words. She, too, didn't know what Johnathan was capable of. Amelia had to make sure she was alright. She owed her that as a best friend. If Johnathan did anything to harm her, Amelia would never forgive him.

"Easier said than done," she said to herself as she proceeded inside of her house. "Mom Dad! I'm home," she yelled through the house, not expecting anyone to respond. "Probably at another one of their so-called conventions..." said Amelia mockingly.

Amelia walked around her house casually. As she walked past the living room, something glistened in her peripheral vision. Amelia turned towards the threshold of her living room and entered slowly. She ogled a mysterious object on the coffee table. Something compelled Amelia to pick up the silver vial filled with a bright orange liquid with an inscription on the side, Sangre de Draconis.

"Too bad I don't speak French," laughed Amelia. "Must be a part of mother's expensive fragrance collection, sure sounds like it."

She placed the vial back on the table and proceeded upstairs, not noticing that the vial she touched now displayed a marking of purple fingerprints where she held it.

Her parent's room was across from Amelia's. As she made her way to her room, she noticed a handwritten note on the door. She could tell it was her mother's handwriting by the penmanship. Her father's notes were illegible; he had the oddest form of chicken scratch handwriting. It sometimes took Amelia several days to figure out what he had written. The note read, *"Dearest Amelia, your father and I are out on a convention. Our boss is once again requesting our attendance for a matter of extreme importance. You are aware of how this goes. An allowance has been left for you in the top drawer of your armoire. The refrigerator and freezer are fully stocked, and you are welcome to use the car should you need it. Sadly, we are not aware of how soon we can return. Please do not spend all the allowance in one day. Sincerely, Mother.*"

Amelia stared at the note for a while, reading it over again to herself. This had been going on over the course of Amelia's 15 years of life. However, she still was unaware of her parent's profession. They never discussed their work at home. They were always away, and when they were home, it was no different. Amelia folded the note neatly and placed it on her dresser. She opened the drawer to find a thick manila envelope that must have weighed a ton. Amelia opened the envelope slowly to find several outrageous stacks of money, totaling approximately $15,000.

"How long are they going to be away?" Amelia asked herself as she placed the money back in the drawer as if it had been cursed.

Amelia pulled her altar out from under the bed. It was spread out atop a blanket carefully. As she examined it, one of the candles seemed slightly out of place. A brief thought crossed her mind whether her parents had been in her room. Amelia decided it must have been her that moved the candle. She couldn't imagine how her parents would react to finding out she was a witch.

"They probably wouldn't even believe me if I cast a spell right in front of them. Evidently, my affairs are too tedious for them to involve themselves."

Amelia plopped down in her bed and gazed up at the stars on her ceiling. There was so much on her mind, Emily's safety, Amara's twins, the money her parents left, how she felt about Alex and Johnathan. Amelia picked up her cell phone and dialed Emily. The phone rang once, and immediately switched over to voicemail.

"Hey, this is Em. Sorry, I couldn't answer your call but don't worry, I will get back to you shortly."

Emily's voice was so cheery. It was hard not to like her, though she had a lot of unfavorable traits. She was stuck up, self-centered, a braggart, to say the least, but Amelia loved her, like a sister. They had always been best friends since preschool. She could remember it like yesterday, how they became friends. Emily had noticed Amelia liked to play alone, and she took the initiative to play with her. Emily walked right over to her one day and told her, "I'm Emily, and you are going to be my best friend." She was so enthusiastic and strong-willed, and Emily always got what she wanted. The two of them had been inseparable ever since.

On the second call, Amelia left a voicemail, "Hey, Em, I don't want to bother you on your vacation. It's only Saturday, but I thought I'd check on you. I hope all is well. I miss you, and even though I'm the one who gave you the advice, I kind of regret it. Sorry, I worry too much. Love you, always. Enjoy your vacation."

Odd, Emily always answered her phone. Emily's phone was a part of her.

"I'll try again tomorrow. Honestly, I probably wouldn't answer my phone if I was on vacation. Maybe it's nothing. Sir Charles just has me all worked up, is all."

Amelia changed into her pajamas and returned to the bed. That same night around 3 am, Amelia woke up in a cold sweat. Something was bothering her, and she had a feeling something very wrong was about to happen. The doorbell rang. It was unlikely, but maybe her mother and father were back early, maybe their convention was canceled. Amelia got up sluggishly and made her way downstairs.

Amelia could make out a tall figure at the door. It couldn't have been her parents. *They must have come to the wrong house,* thought Amelia as she opened the door to greet a tall, extremely handsome stranger. *This town seems just to be getting better and better.*

The man was Native American, his jet-black hair tied back into a ponytail and was wearing a long black trench coat with black leather gloves. He was also very muscular, almost intimidatingly so. There wasn't a hair out of place, which made Amelia a bit uneasy.

"May I help you?"

"Yes, you may. What a pretty little witch you are." he responded.

Amelia stepped backward, taken aback by his comment, and someone grabbed her from behind.

"Let me go!" Amelia screamed as she fidgeted, trying to get out of their grip.

There was a sharp pain in Amelia's arm; the person restraining her had injected her with something.

"Quiet now. We wouldn't want to wake the neighbors now, would we? That would be quite… unfortunate."

Amelia could feel herself falling asleep; She tried to shake it off, but it was completely out of her control. As she quickly slipped into unconsciousness, she managed to mumble one last word, "Alex."

"Put her in the van Zak and let's get going."

"Sure thing," responded Zak as he carried Amelia toward the van.

Jared made his way back to the driver's side. Zak placed Amelia in the back holding cell of the van tying her hands and legs. Zak covered her mouth and made sure she was tied up securely enough in case the serum wore off on their drive back. Not that it would change anything, the van was armored inside and outside it was impregnable a small girl would never get out without assistance.

Alex woke up from his slumber abruptly and ran down the stairs and outside with no shirt or shoes. He sensed something was wrong as he could suddenly hear Amelia call to him in his dream. Alex could see a black van in the distance driving off speedily. With his feet bare, he ran after the van as if his life depended on it.

"Aianm confuto!" Yelled Alex with a wave of his hand in the direction of the hunter's truck. "Nothing happened…"

Alex stopped running, unable to catch up with the van, and taken aback that his spell was deflected.

"Fuck!" Alex cursed himself.

He couldn't believe his spell failed and at a time when it was most needed. Alex ran back to his house, he had to round up Sir Charles, and they had to find Amelia and bring her back by any means necessary.

Sir Charles was outside on the steps waiting for Alex's return. He had witnessed the entire ordeal and did not intervene. Alex was infuriated with himself and Sir Charles.

"What the hell? My magic doesn't work, and you are just sitting here as useless as ever!" Alex practically spat the words at Sir Charles, disgusted with himself, as well as Sir Charles, who he deemed useless.

"Hear me out. There is a reason I could not aid. I am as furious as you are that Amelia was taken away. Please understand, there is nothing either of us could have done. Your magic was rendered useless because Amelia was not abducted by ordinary strangers. They were hunters..."

"Hunters? How could they even know where she was? Or that she is a witch?"

"I'm not sure... we should maybe stop by her house and look for some clues."

Alex and Sir Charles proceeded towards Amelia's house. On their way upstairs, they passed the living room and saw a flicker of silver. They proceeded towards the object to find a silver vial with a glass chamber and purple fingerprints. Alex went to pick up the vial.

"No, don't touch it!" warned Sir Charles as he rolled the vial over to reveal an inscription—Sangre de Draconis was what was inscribed. "This is a trick vial, used to detect witches. Dragon's blood is a dangerous poison if touched, ingested, or injected into a witch. It's potent enough that through the glass, it can identify witches, hence the purple fingerprints. I can touch it because though I am a familiar, I am also just a cat. By the looks of things, someone planted it here this was probably an inside job. Amelia came home and noticed no intrusion, did not find the vial odd enough to bring it to us, and went on about her night as normal. I hate to even harbor a thought so menacing, but I believe Amelia's parents were involved. God only knows what the kidnappers plan to do with her, and all we can do is wait."

"What do you mean, wait? I have to go after her!"

"Understand this—your powers are useless. You cannot use a locator spell to find her as they are protected by wards and spells. These hunters have years of tactical training and would destroy you before you even made it to the front gate. I'm sorry, but there really is nothing we can do. There's hope, though... we have to believe her parents wouldn't allow any harm to come to her."

Alex slumped down onto the floor. It felt as though he was losing Amara a second time. All Alex could do was wallow in his defeat, his powerlessness made him feel like he was worthless.

Chapter 6
Viva Mexico!

The plane ride was lovely, all aside from that rude flight attendant. Emily saw her ogling her Johnny whenever she got the chance. Besides, she was old enough to be his mother, gross, what a hag. Emily was always exaggerating; the flight attendant was no older than 25, and Emily knew that. Here she goes again staring at Johnathan for what seemed like the 40th time as she walked through the aisle. Emily leaned over to her left, where Johnathan was sitting, and he looked back at her to see what she was up to. At that moment, with the flight attendant in sight, Emily kissed Johnathan passionately. He kissed her back, feeling nothing and also seeing through it. She was jealous, another one of her many traits he was getting tired of.

Having his memories back, Johnathan only had eyes for one woman, and that was Amelia. Johnathan had only agreed upon this trip to get rid of Emily. He attempted to break up with her, but that didn't work. At least this way, he wouldn't have to worry about seeing her ever again. *I wonder what Amelia is up to right now; I wonder if she misses me. I'm certain she's in love with me. She is just suppressing her feelings,* he thought to himself as he sat there staring out into the clouds.

Johnathan had been listening to music the entire flight to avoid talking to Emily. It worked, to an extent.

Emily pulled out one of Johnathan's headphones, "What are you listening to, babe?"

"Nothing that you would like."

"Ok, I'll take that. Wow, only 10 minutes to landing, I hadn't noticed. Great, I'm tired of this plane already. Ready for Mexico?"

"Yeah."

"You don't seem like you are enjoying yourself, babe... is it me? Is it Mexico? Do you not like flying first class?"

"I couldn't care less about all that. Let's just enjoy our time together, okay? Pretend this is the last vacation we will ever be on. Let's make it memorable."

Emily smiled. It was moments like this that showed her how much Johnny truly cared for her.

"Okay, baby. I'll try to be a little less annoying."

"Thanks, I appreciate it, and trust me, you will be rewarded."

Later that evening, Johnathan and Emily arrived at their hotel. LA GRAN FIESTA was the name of the hotel they'd booked online. It was a cheery name for a hotel so dimly lit without much of a party vibe.

"Buenos tardes bienvenidos a La Gran Fiesta," said the man at the check-in desk.

He looked up at the two guests giving them a once over before realizing they were American.

"Welcome to La Gran Fiesta. I'm guessing you are Mr. Sharpe and... Ms. Wright? The only Americans who have booked with us this day."

"Let me take care of this, babe. Go ahead and get settled in the room," said Johnathan.

The concierge handed Emily a key card in return. Emily took it and planted a kiss on Johnathan's cheek, "Okay, love, I'll be off."

Emily walked off to the room. She wondered why Johnathan stayed behind at check-in, she figures it was most likely for some extra towels or something.

Emily felt like someone was staring at her. She turned to the left to find the housekeeping woman staring at her. It disturbed Emily slightly, and she pretended not to notice. The woman began to walk toward her as Emily struggled to unlock her room door.

"Shit, this stupid key is jammed."

The woman was right next to Emily now and proceeded to speak to her, "Hola, como estas?"

"Lo siento señora, mi español es muy mal."

The woman smiled warmly, which calmed Emily down some.

"Can I help with that?" she asked Emily, and Emily was relieved she spoke English.

"Oh, that would be great. I'd really appreciate it."

Emily handed her the keycard, and the woman whispered something.

"Huh? Sorry I didn't quite catch that."

"You have to hold the keycard in the slot for three seconds before you remove it. Sometimes the machina breaks when you remove the car too quickly."

She opened the door, handed Emily the key, and proceeded to walk away.

"Gracias por su ayuda!" She yelled to the woman.

What a strange woman, but at least she helped me get this stupid door open. Now for a hot shower while I wait for Johnathan. Emily turned on the water and left the bathroom as it heated up. She rummaged through her suitcase to find a pair of lingerie she purchased just for this vacation.

"Make this vacation memorable he says. I'll give him something to remember all right." She grinned as she pulled the red and black polka-dotted lace lingerie out of her suitcase, knowing Johnathan would not be able to resist it.

"And what's my name?" Johnathan asked the man at check-in. Johnathan had glamoured himself to appear as someone else.

"Andre Forrester."

"Good, and don't you forget it. I'm going to need some extra toiletries. If it's no trouble, I'm going to need fresh chamomile, lavender, some rose water, a rope, a plastic sheet, sage, and a blindfold. I would like all these items brought to room 312 around 1 a.m. sharp. Don't be late," Johnathan said, sliding him some rolled up $100.00 bills which totaled $500.00.

"You're into some pretty kinky stuff, Mr. Forrester, but I can dig it; your girlfriend's a babe. Sorry, I don't want to offend or anything like that."

"None taken. After I finish, you can have her."

Johnathan walked off toward room 312, opening the door and walking in. Emily was lying in bed provocatively. Making sure Johnathan was fully aware of the lingerie she was wearing, but he could not care less.

"Do you like it, babe? Bought it just for you."

"Yeah, sure."

Hurt by his disinterest, Emily began to sob. The way Johnathan had been acting couldn't have made it clearer that their relationship was on the rocks.

Johnathan rolled his eyes, annoyed with her childishness as he turned to face her

"Baby, what's wrong? Why are you crying?"

"Y-you… don't want to be with me anymore."

Johnathan felt like rolling his eyes again, but he decided instead to appeal to her. He figured it was the least he could do as this would be their "last" vacation, together anyway.

"Don't say that babe, I love you, and you know that. My mind has just been wondering lately."

Johnathan walked over to the bed and got in with Emily. He knew what she desired, and Emily always got what she wanted after all. He climbed over her and began to remove her lingerie.

"There's my Johnny."

Emily kissed Johnathan passionately, and he kissed her back. Johnathan grabbed Emily's wrists and pulled them above her head.

"Baby, that hurts. You're too rough."

Johnathan heard her, but he didn't care. He was in a daze imagining Amelia in Emily's place and shutting Emily out completely. Removing Emily out of the equation would bring him one step closer to Amelia, his end goal. Emily felt the passion dissipating and could tell Johnathan's mind was somewhere else. Emily started to regret the vacation altogether.

Their lackluster moment of intimacy was over, and Johnathan was now sound asleep. Emily stood up, got dressed, and headed out for the bar. She was going to enjoy her time in Mexico with or without Johnathan.

"Fake ID, here I come," Emily smiled as she made her way outside.

The place was extremely lively, which was not what she was expecting. She understood why the hotel was called La Gran Fiesta; it seemed to live up to its name in its nightlife.

"Now, this is a vacation I can get used to."

People were dancing, barbecuing, drinking, and there was even a live singer. Barely 10 p.m. and the fiesta was at its peak. Emily paused before she ordered anything from the bar, she didn't want to seem like she'd never drank before. She opened up her mouth to speak when the stranger beside her cut her off.

"Let me get a shot of vodka, straight and a long island for the lady."

The bartender handed the stranger his drink and slid a long island over to Emily.

"Thanks. I appreciate it."

"Don't mention it. What's your name, by the way?"

"My name is Emily. What's yours?"

"I'm Andres. It's a pleasure to meet you. What brings you to this particular hotel?"

Emily was contemplating whether to mention Johnathan. She could tell in the bad lighting how attractive this stranger was, and his accent was to die for. Emily felt like she was melting from hearing him speak.

"Well, to be honest, I'm here on vacation, and well, this hotel was merely by chance. I saw it online, and it had seemingly decent reviews. I'm glad I decided to book it, though."

Andres smiled warmly at Emily's blatant attempt to flirt, "You're here by yourself?"

"Yeah, just me on a very brief vacation."

"That's too bad. I guess we'll just have to make the best of it, huh?"

Emily could feel her cheeks warming up and hoped he didn't notice her blushing. Though the lights were dim, his vision was precise, and Andres noticed every detail. He could see the cockroach on the floor in the corner being devoured by ants, Emily's beautiful red cheeks, the faces of the people furthest away, the bat camouflaged with the bark of the tree. More importantly, Andres could smell the blood of every guest at the party. He was interested particularly in Emily's, the sound of her beating heart, and the pulsing of her veins. She was beautiful, more so than anyone else there. But he would not eat her; his mother had already taken an interest in her and forbade any unnecessary interaction. However, he didn't plan on letting that get in the way of his fun.

Andres had been studying Emily. He knew she was under-aged, that she wasn't alone at the hotel, but, most importantly, he knew she wanted to sleep with him. He was an excellent judge of character. Something he picked up from his days on the street.

While at the bar, he watched as Emily downed five bottles of Long Island Iced Tea. It was safe to say she was more than drunk.

"How do you say we get out of here, Linda?"

"I'd love to, but I-I—"

"You what? Have a boyfriend? I already knew that."

Emily didn't know how to respond. She wanted to go with Andres, but she also didn't want to embarrass or disrespect Johnathan. *I'm drunk in Mexico with a beautiful man, screw Johnathan,* Emily thought to herself, remembering how he also mistreated her.

"Come, let's go. We wouldn't want you changing your mind now, would we, Linda?" Andres grabbed Emily's hand gently and began to walk her back into the hotel.

Emily wasn't able to notice until now, but Andres had beautiful eyes. They were bright grey and clear, his hair was dark and wavy, and he was muscular but slender, built like an athlete.

"Y-your eyes are beautiful," said Emily. "Are you into sports?"

"Something like that. Quiet love, don't talk," Andres said, leading Emily into a dark corridor of the hotel.

"Where are you taking—"

"Shhh, don't speak." They stopped walking suddenly, and Andres eased Emily against the wall.

Emily's body started to warm up, and Andres could see the blood rushing through her. He began to kiss Emily slowly, on her neck. She didn't protest. Mexico was coming to a great start in her book.

Emily ran her hands down his body, tracing over his abdomen. He was extremely fit, and Emily's body quivered against him. She continued to trace his body with her hand until she reached his crotch. Emily could feel his erection, and Andres wanted her too. Had it been any brighter and Emily less drunk, she would have noticed his sharp canine teeth.

Andres kissed Emily once more. She tasted metal. It was light, but at this point, Emily was too drunk to care. Andres leaned Emily onto the floor, placing himself on top of her. Andres lifted her dress, slowly building up anticipation for himself. He went down on Emily, lowering his body to where his head was between her legs. Andres moved her right leg to the side so he could get a better angle. Bearing his fangs, he bit into her thigh, one of her main arteries, and began to drink. Emily fell into a trance. She imagined that she and Andres were having sex, better than anything between her and Johnathan.

Emily moaned quietly to herself, completely dazed. Andres chuckled slightly. Part of it was the excessive amount of alcohol, but other than that, the trance was induced by Andres. A toxin produced in his saliva could manipulate his victims. When hunters hunted Andres' kind, it was usually for this toxin. They used it to poison their weapons. Andres wiped his mouth on Emily's dress, picked her up, and proceeded to room 312, where she had been staying. A streak of blood ran down her right leg.

Andres placed Emily down in front of the door and kissed her on the forehead. He knocked on the door and disappeared into the night, not waiting for a response.

To his surprise, Johnathan opened the door and found Emily sitting on the floor in front of it. Johnathan could smell the alcohol lingering off of Emily, and he was disgusted by it. He lifted her gently and noticed she was bleeding.

"Gross, Emily," said Johnathan aloud as he placed her in the bathtub.

She was sound asleep. Johnathan didn't want to deal with her accident. She would have to get up and shower in the morning.

Johnathan climbed back in bed and got lost in deep thought, *Tomorrow is the day Emily would meet the end*. Johnathan was ready, and it was all he had been able to think about.

Does she deserve it?

No, there is no going back now. You have to do it.

She's my girlfriend. I can't just—

You can and you will!

Johnathan's thoughts were conflicting, a war waged in his head since his first sacrifice. He had come too far. The sole purpose of this vacation was to end her life, and there was no going back.

Morning came, and Emily started to come to, her head pulsating with pain, *Oh, was I that drunk? How did I get in the tub?* She looked down at her legs and noticed her right leg was covered in dried blood. *Shit, my cycle isn't due for another two weeks! This is crazy.* Emily started to undress so she could shower and get rid of her soiled clothes.

"That's odd," as she washed herself, she noticed she wasn't on her period. Running her hand down her right leg, she felt a sore area, "Jeez, that hurts."

She could feel two small indentations in her leg. *What is this?* Emily didn't know what she had been stricken with, but she figured the mysterious man from last night might have a clue. *Oh man, did I sleep with him?* Emily could vaguely remember what transpired the night before. A feeling of guilt washed over Emily as she believed she'd cheated on Johnathan with Andres.

"I have to find him," Emily crept out of the bathroom and saw Johnathan lying fast asleep.

He had always been a sound sleeper, so she was safe. She got dressed quietly and made her way to the door.

"Where are you off too?" asked Johnathan.

"Oh, I just got my period. Going to get some toiletries."

Johnathan rolled over in his sleep, and Emily left the room.

She headed outside to the bar to see if she'd run into Andres once again.

"Buenas dias," said Emily to the bartender. "Have you seen a man about 6'1, grey eyes, black hair?"

"No, someone like that I'd definitely remember," responded the bartender with a laugh.

Emily decided it might be better to look for him herself. She remembered being in a very dark corridor, like a basement. It was darker than the other parts of the hotel.

"Maybe he's in the basement."

The hotel was very dimly lit, and the light coming in from outside didn't help. The setting felt very eerie. Emily could sense someone was following her, watching her, but when she turned around, no one was there. Even scarier, she was headed to the basement, an area with even less lighting.

Luckily, Emily brought her cellphone with her. She turned on the flashlight and proceeded through the dark hallway.

"Andres, I need to talk to you."

No response. She roamed through the hall until ultimately turning back. As she walked by a door she hadn't noticed before, something reached out and grabbed her arm roughly, pulling her inside. Emily was so frightened she forgot to scream.

"Why are you looking for me?" asked Andres, sounding slightly irritated.

"Who's at the door?" Someone called out from within the dark room.

"No one, Andrea. Continue your resting."

"Did you bring us a snack?" asked another person in the room.

Andres pushed Emily backward until they were both outside of the room. He closed the door behind him to keep everyone at bay.

"Who are all those people?"

"That isn't any of your business. What do you want?" Andres sneered at her.

Emily didn't understand why he was so harsh with her now. He was so gentle the night before, now he was just a jerk, like Johnathan.

"I-I just... I have this mark on my leg. I thought maybe you'd know what it was."

The doorknob began to rattle, and Andres held it closed, "I suggest you get out of here, Emily, this is a dangerous place for little girls. However, if you really want to know what that mark is, stick around, and you'll find that out. Now, run, little mouse."

Andres smiled as Emily was glaring the flashlight in his face. This time, he wanted her to see his menacing toothy grin. Emily dropped her phone in shock when she saw Andres had fangs and ran toward the stairway, the fastest she had ever run in her life. She was on the third floor in no time at all. Someone bumped into Emily as she turned the corner. The elderly cleaning lady from the night before, came face to face with her. She looked like she was in some sort of frenzy.

"Please, hear me out. Your life is in danger. The man you came here with... he... is evil, possessed by a great evil. You mustn't be near him any longer. I'm afraid he harbors malicious intent for you. Please, please, for your own good, don't return," the cleaning woman begged Emily.

This is getting weirder by the second. Mexico was a mistake... Johnathan is the last thing I should be afraid of! We have to get out of here... Emily pushed past the woman roughly and ran until she reached room 312.

Emily hesitated, standing at the door briefly, as the old woman's words lingered in her mind. She knew her Johnny, and if nothing else, she knew he wasn't evil.

"What a quack," she said to herself as she opened the door.

The room smelled heavy with lavender and something else she couldn't put her finger on. The smell filled the air, and Emily could feel herself losing her breath. Johnathan walked up to her and caught her as she began to fall to the ground.

"What are you—" Emily fell unconscious before she was able to finish her sentence.

"Quiet now. It will all be over soon."

Emily's eyes fluttered closed, and Johnathan placed her onto the bed, binding her in rope in case she awoke during the ritual.

Meanwhile, in the basement, Emily's phone began to ring. Andres picked it up and looked at it. Someone named Mel was calling her. He opened up the back, removed the battery, as well as the sim, broke the phone in half with no effort at all, and tossed the phone in the trash can beside him. Andres knew Emily would not be coming back. At least he hoped she wouldn't. He didn't want her to return. He'd hoped that he scared her enough to catch the nearest flight out of Mexico. If Emily stayed another night, Andres could not guarantee that she would be safe from his mother, siblings, and maybe even himself.

"Who was that girl Andres?" asked Andrea with interest.

"The one mother is in pursuit of, the one she told us to stay away from."

"And you have been interacting with her? You have always been the hard-headed one out of all of us," responded Andrea.

"Yeah, whatever, call me what you want. If you had seen her, you wouldn't be able to resist either."

Johnathan gathered the herbs he had mixed before Emily's arrival and smeared them over her forehead and arms. He pulled the serrated knife from under his pillow and placed it beside Emily's body.

"I call upon Gruhnekzhal, Demon of the ancients, once more grant me the power to destroy my foes, once and for all. Accept this sacrifice as payment, a sacrifice worthy of your aid."

Johnathan picked up the knife and stared back down over Emily one final time. There was a sudden hesitation. He didn't know if he wanted to go through with it anymore. Emily began to shift slightly. The drugs were starting to wear off.

"Johnathan, what are you doing?" Emily cried, attempting to move her arms only to realize that she was restrained.

Do IT! Send her soul to me... said the voice in Johnathan's head, immediately ridding him of all hesitation.

"I'm sorry, Emily, I really am," Johnathan raised the knife and slit Emily's throat in one clean motion.

Emily struggled, choking on her own blood, staring at Johnathan in disbelief. The air in the room grew thicker as she struggled to stay alive. Emily was a fighter, through and through, and she knew she didn't want to die. When she realized death was inevitable, she did the one thing that she could. Emily made direct eye contact with Johnathan, making sure he didn't miss a moment of her death. If nothing else, she wanted this image to haunt him, for the rest of his life. Remaining spiteful, even in death. Johnathan could feel his own breath hitch in his throat as Emily took the last one. Instantaneously, Johnathan felt a surge of energy racing through him. His eyes flashed red briefly before returning to their normal shade of blue. He gathered his suitcase and made his way out of the room. It was time for him to return home, back to Amelia.

Andres smelled the sweetness in the air. He knew immediately what had happened. The smell of Emily's blood was noxious. Andres couldn't fathom he'd once wanted to drain It form her veins. Andrea and Luis also smelled it, and they became alert, inhaling deep breaths, ready to find the source. Andres left the room and made his way up to 312. If there was any hope of saving Emily, he would do his best.

The elderly cleaning woman made her way to room 312. She had her cleaning supplies in hand as she knocked on the door, "Housekeeping."

No one answered the door, and the reason was evident. She could smell the blood from outside the door. Andres suddenly stood beside Her and his presence didn't startle her in the slightest.

"Lucinda, we have to get in."

"It would seem you were getting yourself acquainted with this girl?"

"Only to an extent. I was aware you didn't want us to interfere with your… work.

"We have to get inside. There's no time for chatting." Lucinda noted the concern in Andres's voice.

"There is plenty of time. She is already dead."

Andres stared blankly. He didn't know how to react to that news. He tried to save her; he wanted her to leave, get far away from this hotel. *Maybe I should have just told her the truth… there is only one option now…*

Lucinda opened the door and walked inside with her cleaning supplies, and Andres close behind her. The man was gone, and only Emily remained, tied to a bed with sheets drenched in blood. Her body was lifeless as she stared toward the wall. Lucinda could tell she was conscious during death—she looked her lover in the eyes as he murdered her.

Lucinda was filled with hate, and this only worsened it.

"Go. Gather your siblings, Andres. You know what to do."

She placed her cleaning supplies down by the bed and began to untie Emily. Andres flitted downstairs to gather Andrea and Luis. They had to clean the room. They had plenty of experience with leaving no evidence.

Lucinda lifted Emily's body, still warm, which was a good sign, and proceeded to make her way down to the basement. Emily's old life had come to an end, and her new life was only beginning.

Chapter 7
The Hunters

Amelia woke up in a car. She remembered being abducted and didn't know how long they had been driving. She had a feeling however, that it was a great distance from her house. The car was completely dark on the inside. The windows were tinted, and she could not see out of it. As a result, Amelia had no idea where she was being taken.

Amelia had a cloth covering her mouth, so she couldn't speak or cast any spells, for that matter. Amelia started kicking on the back of the van. Jared looked over at Zak as they began to slow down the car.

"I think we should keep moving. This seems like a distraction."

"What's the matter, Zacky Scared of a little witch?"

Zak rolled his eyes, and Jared parked on the side of the road.

"Stay put, Zak."

Zak nodded in agreement as Jared made his way to the back of the van and unlocked the tremendous bolt lock. The truck was completely witch-proof, and so were the hunters. They wore medallions and pendants that kept them from being hexed.

"I'm going to uncover your mouth. But I warn you. If you say anything that even sounds like a spell, it will be the last words you utter. Nod if you understand."

Amelia nodded, and Jared took off her covering.

"Aianm renodo," Amelia practically spat the words at Jared.

Jared rolled his eyes before smiling at Amelia, "Nice try." He patted Amelia's head, belittling her. "I already warned you, but as you can see, your magic has no power with us. We are hunters."

"Hunters?" Amelia shuddered; she remembered Sir Charles warning about them only days before.

"Indeed, although that is exactly what I just said. I guess this one's a little slow. Alas, you requested we stop for a reason. What is it that you want?"

"I have to use the bathroom," said Amelia.

"Ok but make it quick. We are nearing our destination," Jared said, leading Amelia over to the nearby pasture.

"I can't do anything with you standing right there like that."

"I suggest you try. I am not letting you out of my sight. If you run, I will catch you; if you hide, I will find you."

Not realizing his strength, Zak got out of the car, slamming the car door in the process, which briefly distracted Jared. As his concentration was broken, Amelia seized the opportunity and started to run into the woods.

"Great, now I have to chase her. What part of I will catch you and find you did she not understand?"

Amelia ran as fast as her feet could carry her, looking around for cover as she did so. Amelia found a particularly wide tree that she stood behind. Jared ran right past the tree at an almost inhuman speed. Amelia stayed in position for approximately three minutes before she started to move.

"Some hunter he is," said Amelia as she remained in position.

Someone grabbed Amelia from behind and tossed her over their shoulder effortlessly. It happened so quickly; she didn't have time to react.

"Correction, I'm not just some hunter. I am *thee hunter*. Jared Stone, at your service, I'd give you my business card in case of any supernatural emergencies but seeing as you are all tied up and a supernatural yourself, I don't think the timing is appropriate."

"Hilarious, so funny," responded Amelia sarcastically. "What do you want with me, anyway?"

Jared paused as he pondered the question.

"Hmm, I'm sure the same thing any man would want?"

"What?"

"I'm just messing with you, don't worry about it. You will find out in due time."

"You seem to be pretty cheery for a ruthless killer."

"I appreciate the compliment. I like to think it is part of my charm. If you're going to die anyway, I at least strive to make it pleasant," Jared smiled cunningly, making his way back to the van.

He was very fast, even while carrying Amelia on his shoulder. Jared placed Amelia back into the van and covered her mouth as she looked at him in disbelief.

"You earned it," he said as he closed the door and got back into the driver's seat.

"What happened?" asked Zak.

"Nothing important, let's get back to business."

Jared pulled up to the gate of their headquarters, where Sarah, who was on the night shift, greeted them. When she saw it was Jared, she signaled for the gate to be brought up with a swift hand gesture.

"What's the damage, Sarah?" asked Jared.

"As you can see, we had two rogues pass through, but I took care of it. We were in the middle of torching them when you arrived."

"Good, I can always count on you."

Sarah blushed and looked down at her feet.

"If you guys are finished fooling around, Jared, unlock the car. I'm out. Going to give her a hand with the rogues unless you need me."

"No worries, I got it all from here. See you later, Zak. I'll send one of the hunters to fetch you if you are needed."

Zak got out of the car, and he and Sarah walked away toward the bodies. Zak and Sarah were siblings; they were brought into the hunters very young. This was the only family they knew. The three of them trained together from a very early age. They were four and five when first brought to the hunter's headquarters. Jared, however, was born and raised there. It was not common to take in such young children, but Jared's uncle, James, thought it would be a good idea. A vampire murdered their mother, and the children were left to fend for themselves. James took sympathy on the children, and upon murdering the vampire that killed their mother, he returned to base with them.

Jared drove up to a large field where there was nothing in eyesight but a box on a wooden post. Upon inspection, it appeared to be a retina scanner.

Jared scanned his eye, and a circular door hatch covered in moss unearthed itself, revealing a tunnel. He drove through slowly, further leading them underground. The hunters had an underground fortress, which was their way of staying hidden from society.

They entered the complex basement level, where they dropped the car off and entered an elevator. To take Amelia to the ground-level dungeon for interrogation. On the way out of the elevator, they were bombarded by two people, a hunter and a poisons master—Amber and Thomas Moore, Amelia's parents. This was the first time in history that two hunters conceived a witch. Not just any witch either, the reincarnation of chief Amari's daughter, Amara.

"Is she okay?" asked Amber. Despite the circumstances, her maternal instinct was still present.

"You didn't harm her, did you?" asked Thomas with concern.

Before Jared answered, he removed Amelia's blindfold and mouth cover. She had already recognized the voices and was slightly in shock. *So, this is where they go on their "conventions,"* Amelia thought to herself. The misplaced white candle invaded Amelia's thoughts. Her parents must have found her altar. She realized that her hunter parents sold out their own flesh and blood to an organization of ruthless supernatural killers.

"Mother? Father? Why am I here? How did this happen? You never told me you were hunters!"

"We're sorry it had to be this way, sweetheart, but it was for your own good. We didn't want to involve you in any of this sooner than necessary. We planned on sending you here on your 16th birthday to initiate your

173

training as a hunter, but... that was before we found out you were a witch," responded Amelia's mother, Amber, expressing slight distaste.

"How could you not tell me, mom? And what if I didn't want to become a hunter?" Amelia was in disbelief, feeling as though she was having a horrible nightmare.

"That's enough chit chat. You'll have plenty of time for that later... Maybe, depends on how this goes," Jared turned Amelia in the direction of the dungeons.

As she walked forward, she looked back at her parents. Jared proceeded to make his way to the dungeons when he was bumped into by another hunter. Anthony regained his composure and picked up his notepad off the floor, "Oh, Jared! Just the man I wanted to see. Thomas and I have been going over the weapon characteristics sheets. I'd really like to discuss some weapon modifications we have been developing."

Anthony looked up from his paper and noticed Jared seemed to be transporting a prisoner.

"Oh, sorry, I can catch you another time. I didn't realize you were carrying cargo."

"No problem, Ant, I'll take a look at those when I wrap this up; it shouldn't take long."

Anthony was the weapons master for the hunters. He was charged with crafting, modification, and assembling weapons and their parts. He was the engineer and could repair more than just weapons. Aside from his duties at headquarters, Anthony was also a very skilled hunter. Jared never took his opinions or suggestions lightly, or anyone else for that matter.

Anthony closed his notepad and began to walk in the opposite direction.

Amelia had no idea what was about to transpire as she was untied and placed into a chair in which she was strapped in by the wrists and ankles.

"Now," said Jared. "I am going to ask you a series of questions. Answer honestly, and you will be fine. If you lie, well, I'll just let you find out for yourself. But I'd hate to be the one to break it to your parents."

Amelia swallowed hard.

"So, let's get started, shall we? Who are you?"

"Amelia Moore… but that's not what you're asking, is it? In short, I guess I am the reincarnation of Amara, an African King's daughter. Still not sure I really believe that"

"Good, good, you aren't slow, after all. Here I was thinking this was going to be hard. I might not have to use this after all," Jared said, motioning toward the baton on his hip; the top piece had two prongs on it, and Amelia could tell it was electric.

Jared paused as if contemplating something, he placed his hand to his chin, and his face lit up as if he had an idea.

"I'll be right back. Stay here," Jared smirked at his remark, knowing Amelia was in no position to move, not even an inch.

Amelia looked around frantically as Jared left, trying to find a way out. It was hopeless. If by some miracle she managed to escape the chair, there were only two points of escape. There was the door in which they entered, but it was barred, and a hunter stood guard directly outside of it. It was evident the hunters took every precaution to ensure their captives remained exactly that, captives.

Jared quickly returned with a large dictionary-style book in hand.

"This Amelia is the encyclopedia of the most powerful beings. We call it the EMPB for short. It was created long ago by a powerful witch. Every being that poses a threat to humankind is in this very book. It has been essential in our quest to eliminate these beings and their descendants. I'd like you to take a look at something."

Jared opened the encyclopedia and turned it toward Amelia. The name written in bold was—Amara Imari—with a beautifully drawn illustration of how she looked. At that moment, as Amelia stared at that picture, she realized the resemblance was undeniable. In the same room, the two of them would be considered twins, except that Amara was slightly more pigmented.

"As you can see, it is not by chance that you look exactly like Amara Imari and are a witch as well. Which brings me to my next question—what coven are you a part of?"

"Coven? I am not a part of any coven. I only recently found out that I'm a witch. Barely enough time to actively search for a coven to join."

Jared stared at Amelia, trying to read her response. He turned on his baton and brought it in front of her. The electricity flashed in front of her, and she flinched. She could smell the ozone being emitted from the charge.

"I'm telling the truth."

"Oh, I know, just teasing. This interrogation is actually very fun. I haven't enjoyed myself this much in a while. Anyway, let's resume—"

Amelia cut him off mid-sentence, "I'd like to ask you a question."

Jared raised an eyebrow at Amelia in amusement, "Is that so? I'm not sure you really understand how an interrogation works. You're pretty brave I'll give you that. Fine, I'll allow it, but don't make it a habit. Do remember, I'm not obligated to answer any of your questions."

Amelia pondered several questions before deciding on, "How did you become a hunter?"

Jared glared at Amelia, cautiously assessing whether he should answer the question.

"Well, it was a birthright, as it would have been for you as well had you not been a witch. My mother was a powerful hunter, and my father was a… well, that is a story I'd not like to get into. If I told you, I'd have to kill you."

Suddenly Jared's demeanor changed. In his last words, his voice became incredibly deeper, and his face became unforgiving. Amelia knew that he meant every word, and it sent a chill down her spine. Even with the interrogation, Jared seemed oddly friendly to Amelia. It put her somewhat at ease, and she felt as though she might not be harmed.

"May I be permitted to ask one last question?"

"Hurry it up, and this will be your last."

"What is your position in all this? Why is your leader having you interrogate me? Why you? You don't seem like the type to prefer interrogations, and you also seem pretty young. You can't be a day older than 20."

"Pretty positive that was three questions, but I suppose I'll humor you. At this time, I am gauging that you won't be much of a threat. However, if you become a nuisance, I hope you are aware that I will not hesitate to eliminate you. My position in all this is simple, I have a title to uphold, and therefore our fellow hunters look to me for guidance. I do the things that some others would not, cannot. I have to create a guideline for the hunters. Especially the youngest of them weakness is a vulnerability one that no hunter can afford to have. As for the leader requesting me specifically, quite frankly, I am the leader. As an additional answer, though, it wasn't necessarily a question. I am, in fact, 19."

"19 and the leader of the hunters? How did that transpire?" Amelia had to keep him talking, trying to exploit any weaknesses he may have.

It wasn't hard to do. Jared liked to talk, but he seemed like he was too cunning to give up pertinent information. *If by some chance he did happen to, he may just kill me to keep me silent.*

"Yes indeed, 19 and the leader of the hunters. My mother was the former leader, and when she was... murdered, the task fell to me. It's been 16 years since her death, and I feel the hunters have never been in better hands. I do what I can to ensure the safety of the hunters and all future hunters."

"I'm sorry to hear about your mother. Managing an entire group of individuals must be pretty taxing. What about your father? Could he not replace your mother in her passing?"

Jared began to ease toward Amelia. He lifted Amelia's chin so that she was gazing into his face as he looked at her with intrigue. Their brown eyes meeting each other in a deep gaze, Jared slid his baton on the inside of Amelia's inner thigh, not breaking his eye contact.

"What are you—"

There was a surge of pain. It was piercing though it was also brief. Amelia gasped in pain, realizing that she had just been electrocuted, and tried to jerk her head away from Jared's grip, but it only got tighter. He released her and returned to his spot standing in front of her.

"That will be enough of that, no more questions from you. Are you in contact with any other witches?"

How should I answer this? I have to lie, I have to protect Alex no matter what.

"No, as I said previously, I only recently found out that I was a witch myself. I wouldn't even know the first thing about contacting another witch.

"Is that so? Are you telling me the truth?"

Amelia kept her composure. There was no way she was telling him the truth.

"Yes, I haven't lied to you thus far. I am not going to start now. I have nothing to hide."

Jared watched Amelia with intent as he contemplated his thoughts.

"Your interrogation is over for now."

Jared began to walk towards the door, leaving Amelia tied up to the chair.

"Wait, you aren't going to leave me here, are you?"

Jared smiled deeply and walked out of the room, closing the door behind him.

"What am I going to do? I have to find a way out of here..."

I can't believe mother and father are hunters! But it does make a lot of sense... between the secret conventions and large sums of money stashed away, it made a lot of sense. And I was to become a hunter? That is just unreal. I have to break out of here... somehow.

The room grew slightly chilly, and the silent room caused Amelia to begin drifting off to sleep. She shook her head frantically, trying to shake the exhaustion out of herself, to no avail. It wasn't long after that Amelia was brought into a deep sleep. It came over her all too sudden, and she had no control over anything.

Chapter 8
The Final Battle

Amara tossed and turned beside Alexander as she slept. Her dreams had been becoming more nightmarish with each one. Different scenarios ran through her mind of how it would end for the three of them. It was all she could think about anymore. Johnathan would be there any day, and Amara was no longer ready to face him.

Amara sat up, awoken abruptly from her dream. Alexander was still asleep as Amara eased her way out of the bed, trying not to wake him. She made her way downstairs and proceeded to walk to her altar. Amara required guidance; the gods must hear her plea. For she feared to defeat Johnathan, she would need the gods themselves to intervene. That was the only scenario she could agree with to avoid Alexander getting hurt.

On her way to the altar, Amara heard something rustle in the foliage. It sounded small, but something was indeed following her. She smiled as she turned around, seeing nothing but darkness. Amara looked down to find a white blob of a creature, none other than Sir Charles.

"You caught me, princess. I just wanted to keep you company, seeing as you are out here all alone. Why didn't you think to wake Alex? It's dangerous out here for you, especially in your condition," Sir Charles looked up at Amara, eyeing her stomach.

"I appreciate your concern, Charlie, but I had to come alone. I need to speak to the ancestors on my own. I am in desperate need of guidance and don't need any distraction."

"Suit yourself, Amara, but I will be close by should you need me."

With that, Amara proceeded to her altar and lit the incense with a flick of her hand. During her recent training, Sir Charles had taught Amara to conjure many things, spirits, weapons, flames, energy balls. Still, she couldn't help feeling completely helpless. Despite everything, Amara hoped the three of them could all survive the ordeal unscathed. Amara took a deep breath as she sat down and concentrated.

"I call upon my ancestors. Please, hear my plea. A sign, a symbol, something to guide me," said Amara feeling defeated.

White smoke began to surround the area resonating from the Altar. A silhouette of a figure appeared above the altar.

"F-father? Is that you?"

"Oh, my Amara, how you've matured. I only wish I hadn't been taken from you so soon. I could have guided you through all of this... You will be faced with a choice that only you can make. Your intervention can turn the tide. Trust in yourself, my daughter, and know that I am always with you."

"Father! Please don't leave, not again..."

It was too late. The figure had vanished, candle blown out, and smoke dissipated all before she could finish her sentence. Amara's heart grew heavy, and her vision became foggy. She could not hold back the tears after seeing her father, so close and yet so far away. Whatever did happen, Amara found solace in the fact that her ancestors, and more specifically, her father, would always be with her. Left in the place where

Amara's father once was now a clear crystal. It sat atop the altar and began to glow a deep purple color.

Amara reached forward and grabbed it, feeling its warmth in the palm of her hand. The energy from the crystal seemed to radiate through her from her hand throughout her body. Amara clenched her fists, still holding the crystal. She didn't know what exactly the crystal was for, but she knew her father played a role in her having it. Whatever the use was, she had every intention of finding out.

Stumbling through the woods, Amara made her way back to the main house. Entering the bedroom, she found Alexander fully dressed and, on his way, out. Alexander noticed the streaks of tears running down Amara's cheeks. He pulled her in close to him as he caressed her hair. Amara buried her head in his chest, quietly sobbing.

"Don't worry, love. We are going to get through this. It's going to be alright... I promise."

"B-but how c-can you make s-such a promise?" responded Amara between sobs as her voice quivered.

She wanted to believe him, but she just felt so much doubt, so much worry, it was impossible to know what would transpire.

"I don't know. I just have a feeling. I won't let anything happen to you," Alexander said and kissed Amara's forehead.

"It's not me I'm worried about," Amara pushed through Alexander and made her way to the bed, leaving him standing by the door. "We should sleep. There is no knowing when our last day together will be. Let's make the most of it, Alexander."

Amara motioned for Alexander to come over to her, and he did so. Alexander laid in the bed beside her embracing her as they fell back asleep.

Johnathan sat in his father's office, with muddy boots sprawled across the desk. He imagined his father's reaction had he ever found him in his office like this. Johnathan had been becoming more and more malicious with each passing day. He had developed an affinity for torture; he rather enjoyed it. The screams of the slaves as they endured his agonizing torture and how they pleaded, "Please, please, master, I'm sorry, master please." It was music to Johnathan's ears. His slave population had been gradually diminishing. Not only due to his relentless sacrificing but also his extreme forms of entertainment.

At times, Johnathan found his thoughts lingering as to how Amara would feel about him if she knew what he'd been up to. Quickly overshadowing these thoughts to darker extremities. Johnathan gathered himself and headed out to the "cage," as he referred to it. It began as a means of torture but turned into a holding cell for all the slaves. It was easier for Johnathan this way—no resistance, the slaves were feeble and weak. It was interesting to see what weeks without food can do to even the strongest of the slaves.

Johnathan opened the cage door, and the cries came to a halt when he did so. They were petrified, no one wanted to be picked, and they knew what fate awaited them. When Johnathan Sharpe came to select one of them, they never came back. Johnathan looked over the many faces in the wooden chamber. Once he decided, he grabbed one of the slaves by the shoulder, closing the door behind him and walking off toward the house hastily. He led the slave toward a back room in dark silence. Candles were lit in the room in various arrangements. The slave panicked and tried to make for the door, but Johnathan's grip was too firm. Johnathan tossed the slave down roughly on the floor with a strength that was more than a normal human being could muster, immediately rendering him unconscious. Johnathan tied the slave up near his makeshift altar and readied his dagger. He began to burn incense, muttering something unintelligible to himself as he passed the smoke over the unconscious body.

"I must prevail in my endeavors, whatever they may be," muttered Johnathan as he plunged the dagger into the slave's chest, twisting it to the right once before removing it.

A blood-curdling smile spread across his face as he stood over the body. Johnathan's eyes glowed red as he felt the power surging through his body.

"Tomorrow, I will take Amara for my own, willingly or otherwise. I will stop anyone who tries to interfere," said Johnathan to himself as he made his way to his bedroom in the darkness.

Amara and Alexander set up wards in the house as well as outside. They were meant to prevent Johnathan from entering, which would give them an advantage in defeating him.

"Those are anti-witch wards typically used by hunters to prevent witches from infiltrating places. Though you're able to set them, you may not pass over them once they are set, or you may be trapped inside. You and Amara should have the advantage with your traps and Alexander's newfound abilities Johnathan is unaware of. It seems we are at a slight advantage. He will not know what to expect. Oh, and that crystal in your pocket Amara, it's a honing crystal. It aids in focusing and strengthening the mind for stronger spells. Basically, it is a magical amplification device. You should keep it near you at all times. It should be an additional aid in our fight," said Sir Charles with slight uncertainty.

"Don't worry, Sir Charles. The odds are favorable. I believe we will be victorious," responded Alexander confidently.

Alexander noticed Amara's disapproving facial expression and made his way over to her. He caressed her cheek as he looked into her large brown eyes reassuringly. She smiled back at him, tiptoeing up to him and planting a kiss on his cheek. Alexander picked her up in his arms, cradling her as he spun her around.

"Don't worry, we will be o—" Alexander stopped abruptly, noticing another change of expression in Amara's face.

"Something isn't right," Amara said, feeling a sudden surge of energy in her stomach. "Johnathan's coming."

"How can you know?" asked Alexander with concern as he placed her down on her feet.

"I don't know how I know. I just know we have to prepare." Amara placed her hand on her stomach.

"We must prepare," said Sir Charles to Alexander.

Alexander turned to Amara pulling her close as he whispered something in her ear, "Dormir."

Amara pulled away from Alexander, realizing what he had done, but it was too late. She slipped into a deep slumber, losing all of her senses. Alexander held her up in his arms for a moment. He placed her inside a nearby room. Alexander had to defeat Johnathan alone, and that was exactly what he planned to do. He kissed her deeply as she slept and returned to Sir Charles.

"A noble act Sir Alexander, but our foe will not be as courteous. Are you sure you can handle this by your lonesome?"

"To be frank, no, not at all. I can't let Amara be harmed. If I perish, so be it. I accept my fate but promise me, Charles, you will stand by her if I fail. You have to ensure she makes it out, away from him."

"You have my word Alexander, so long as I live, I shall allow no harm to come to her in your absence."

Their surroundings suddenly grew dark. It looked as if a dark cloud passed over the area, and the air became thick. Alexander could feel his palms sweating as he waited in anticipation for Johnathan to make his way to them. They had set a trap directly in front of the door to keep Johnathan in place as they faced him.

Johnathan arrived at the gate of the Francisco plantation and entered with ease. He began to walk forward and found himself stuck in place. Johnathan cracked his neck and smirked as he forced himself forward. He felt the force holding him in place and, with even more force, pushed through it with ease. Johnathan smiled as he wiped a bead of sweat from his brow.

"Too easy. I shouldn't have any trouble at all," he said aloud as he proceeded to the doorway. Johnathan opened the door and found himself staring at Alexander across the room.

Johnathan began to laugh uncontrollably, doubling over as he did so. He noticed he had walked into another of Amara's traps, but he continued to laugh.

"Is this the cavalry? What do you possibly intend to do? You are making this too easy. Don't just stand there; I'll eviscerate you. Please, for old time's sake, why not give yourself a head start?"

Johnathan stopped laughing and regained his composure as he began to attempt to break out of the trap. Johnathan concentrated his energy as he began pushing through the invisible field that restrained him.

Alexander displayed a look of disgust as he conjured a plasma ball and sent it soaring furiously toward Johnathan. It hit Jonathan in the stomach catching him off guard and sending him back inside of the trap. Johnathan looked at Alexander with disbelief

"H-how? How is this possible! Y-you're a... She... taught you?"

"You're quite the scholar I see. Obviously, I'm a warlock, and it would seem she cared enough for me to make me like her. Destroying you will be all the more satisfying—"

"S-she made you like her?" Johnathan repeated with confusion.

"Get over yourself. She never loved you, nor will she ever. Be a good lad and let me put you out of your misery for good," Alexander sent another plasma ball soaring toward Johnathan's face.

Johnathan's face grew dark, and his eyes became a deep red. He raised a hand in front of the energy ball, stopping it in its pursuit. The plasma ball remained there in midair in front of Johnathan's face. He grinned a crooked, evil smile and turned his hand in the opposite direction sending Alexander's energy ball straight back toward him at an incredible speed. Alexander was hit with his attack sending him flying into a nearby column with a loud thud. Meanwhile, Amara remained asleep in the room nearby. As she laid there, she heard a sudden voice from deep within her subconscious.

"Despierto," said the voice, which sounded exactly like Alexander.

She awoke immediately to a loud thud coming from the entry hall.

"This is the end. Ancestors give me strength."

Amara got out of the bed she'd been placed on, not realizing her crystal had slid out of her pocket. She placed her hand on her stomach and ran out of the room. She saw the battle unfolding before her eyes. She looked around frantically, finding Alexander on the floor against a column, trying to pick himself up.

Everyone turned toward Amara as she abruptly entered. Sir Charles, sensing an opportunity, lunged at Johnathan latching onto his face, biting and scratching him.

"Get Amara out of here! He's too strong."

Alexander gathered himself to his feet, a tear rolling down his face as he realized he had been defeated, and Amara was now in the face of danger. He had failed her and the children. In a frenzy, Johnathan hurled a dark plasma ball outward blindly as he tried to remove Sir Charles from his face. The black energy ball was full of dark energy, and though it was thrown blindly, it made its way straight toward Alexander.

"No! This is completely wrong," said Amara before instinctually jumping in front of Alexander to stop the impact of the energy ball.

The impact of the energy ball was a pain she'd never felt before. Amara gasped as she looked down at a gaping hole in her stomach. Alexander scrambled to his feet, gathering Amara in his arms. The room grew silent as Amara smiled up at Alexander. Alexander completely forgot he was in the middle of a battle with Johnathan; his world quickly came crashing down.

At that moment, Alexander didn't care what his fate would be; Amara was dying. Johnathan threw Sir Charles from his face and became a part of the scene unfolding before him. Johnathan conjured another energy ball to hurl at Alexander before realizing what he had done.

Kill her! Finish it, called out the demonic voice in Johnathan's head.

Johnathan's energy ball quickly fizzled out as he fell to his knees. He had struck Amara in his frenzy— Amara, the love of his life, was dying, and it was his fault. Johnathan's face turned white, disgusted. Johnathan slammed his fist to the ground in defeat.

"No, no, it wasn't supposed to happen this way. It's Alexander's fault it should have been him! He is supposed to be dying not... not Amara," Johnathan muttered to himself.

Amara smiled up at Alexander as he cradled her in his arms, sobbing uncontrollably. Amara placed a hand to his cheek tenderly.

"Don't cry, love. I'll be fine."

"Amara, why! Why did you do it! It was meant to hit me."

Amara wiped a tear from his face. She could feel the life slipping away from her. Smiling still, she turned to meet eyes with Sir Charles and then to Johnathan, who looked to be in even more distress.

"Amara, I—" said Johnathan as he looked away, not able to meet her gaze.

"I call upon the goddess, you who granted me the power I have today. Accept this final sacrifice and hear my final request. I must be wiped clean of Johnathan and Alexander's memory. They will live their lives without knowledge of me... They will be cursed with temporary immortality. Every 15 years, their memory will be completely wiped clean, and they will continue to start life anew. Moving from place to place experiencing different lives until the day I am reincarnated," Amara coughed, and a streak of blood was left on her palm.

"Amara, what are you—"

Amara cut Alexander off, continuing to speak her request, "On the day I am reincarnated, your memories will slowly begin to return. In which we can all be together once more."

Sir Charles met Amara's gaze. The sadness on his face was apparent.

"Charles, I ask you to please not intervene. Keep close to Alexander but let him remember me on his own. Let us hope we get it right in the next life."

Sir Charles nodded in agreement with Amara's final request. Time seemed to slow around them as Amara took her final breath in Alexander's arms.

Amara's body turned to ash, and Johnathan stood up with uncertainty about how he wound up in Alexander's house. Johnathan walked out and made his way back to his plantation.

Alexander stood up, looking around confused. He noticed Sir Charles and smiled.

"I wonder how you got in here," said Alexander as he noticed a scattered pile of ash on the floor.

Alexander retreated to the kitchen and returned with a broom as he started to sweep away Amara's ashes. Sir Charles grimaced and walked away as a feeling of profound depression came over him.

Chapter 9
The Escape

Amelia woke up abruptly, still strapped in the seat, at the hunter's headquarters. Tears streamed down her face as the events of Amara's death replayed in her mind. Whether it be by mistake or otherwise, Johnathan was the direct cause of her death. Amelia was now aware of everything that had happened to her past self. Despite this, she felt unchanged; she still felt like herself, like, Amelia. She thought that somehow realizing Amara's fate would create some change in her, but it didn't.

She had to get out of there. No one would come to her rescue. She was on her own. Realizing defeat, the only thoughts that filled Amelia's mind were about Emily. Amelia knew she was to be returning soon if she hadn't already. *She probably won't even realize I'm gone. She's probably so worn out from her trip she went home immediately and is sound asleep.*

Johnathan made his way back into his house from his vacation in Mexico. He placed his suitcase against the wall and went to his bedroom for a shower. It was 5 a.m., but Johnathan had an insatiable urge to see Amelia. He couldn't see her just yet; he had to do something first. A memory spell for the town to forget Emily's existence. That way, he'd be getting off scot-free; if no one remembered her, no one would realize she was missing.

Johnathan said the spell aloud before burning it with the flame of a black candle he ignited with the force of his mind alone. He left immediately after the spell was completed, he was headed toward Amelia's house, and he had to see her. Part of the reason was to see if his spell had been successful.

Johnathan knocked on Amelia's door to find it was completely unlocked. He walked in cautiously, taking in all the surroundings as he did so. Johnathan proceeded upstairs to Amelia's bedroom, which was also open. She was not inside, and her parents did not seem to be home either. He made his way downstairs, looking around for any clues. Aside from the door not being locked, there were no signs of struggle, no evidence of anything being out of place.

Johnathan had to find Amelia, which left him only one option, Alex. Johnathan grew disgusted on his way to Alexander's house. He had a feeling Amelia was over his house, although he hoped it not to be the case. Johnathan knocked on the door angrily with much more force than necessary. Alexander opened the door too abruptly as if he were anticipating someone's arrival. He grimaced as he opened the door to come face to face with Johnathan.

"Where's Amelia? I need to speak to her. It's urgent." As Johnathan asked, he noticed a sadness come over Alex, and he knew in an instant Amelia was not there.

"She was taken... by hunters."

"And you're still here! How pathetic," Johnathan spat on the pavement beside him with disgust. "You are pathetic. I don't know what she sees in you."

Alex, feeling defeated, took the insult without protest, "There's nothing I can do... magic doesn't work on them... I have no idea where she is."

Johnathan rolled his eyes and walked away. He was going to find Amelia and bring her back; there was no room for failure. Johnathan channeled the demon inside of him and spoke aloud, "Find Amelia," as his eyes glowed red and he vanished into the night.

Johnathan came up to a large iron gate where a woman was standing on the opposite side, wielding a large gun. She was accompanied by a male equally intimidating with a larger gun.

"State your business," said Sarah bitterly.

Johnathan could sense Amelia's presence, he knew she was inside, somewhere, and he had no intention of leaving without her. Johnathan's eyes glowed red, and Sarah noticed as she readied herself to fire. She gave Zak an all too familiar look, and they both began to fire. Johnathan waved his hand in the air stopping the bullets and the hunters in place. He walked up closer to the gates, and they flung open, allowing him to enter. The bullets fell to the ground, and time resumed. Sarah and Zak simultaneously took out their daggers. Before they could throw them, Johnathan again raised his hand and sent Sarah and Zak flying in opposite directions. They both collided with nearby trees with a great force, rendering them unconscious as Johnathan proceeded through the complex unscathed. Arriving at a secret door covered in moss, Johnathan tore it off and sent flying with a single hand gesture.

Alarms flashed in the hunter's underground facility. "Warning: Security Breach" kept playing repeatedly. Amelia could hear it playing back over and over again on the loudspeaker.

"This may be my only opportunity for escape," said Amelia aloud as she looked around in anticipation.

As Johnathan walked through the tunnel, large metal grids came down from the ceiling in an attempt to seal him out. Johnathan smirked as he brought all the grids down with two hand gestures. He clenched his fist, and every barrier was brought down. Johnathan made his way to the main hall, where approximately 100 hunters all stood with guns ready.

"Now!" yelled Jared to the hunters as they unleashed an array of bullets toward Johnathan.

Smiling, he placed his hand in the air halting the bullets, sending the hunters in midair, and bringing each one down with a simultaneous thud. Johnathan walked past one of the hunters on his way towards the dungeons. He was not unconscious like the others. Johnathan sensed him to be stronger than the rest. Must be the leader, but something was different about this one; there was no way he shouldn't be unconscious.

"What are you?" muttered the leader as Johnathan walked past him.

Johnathan made his way to Amelia's cell. He was being drawn to it like a moth to a flame. In stating his intent clearly, Amelia became like a beacon in his mind. It was like he had been there before, except he hadn't. For some reason, Johnathan knew every room of the facility and knew exactly where Amelia would be. The door flung open suddenly, and the baffled, slightly scared Amelia looked toward the doorway to find Johnathan standing at the threshold. He looked at her with deep concern.

"H-how did you get to me?" Amelia stared at Johnathan in amazement. "I mean, you were able to get through the anti-witch wards and everything? Their defenses? Johnathan, how is this possible?"

"Shhh, don't ruin the moment. The point is, I'm here, and Alexander is not. Do you think I would let you remain in the clutches of these filthy hunters? Amelia, you must not know me at all," Johnathan smiled, snapping his fingers, and Amelia was unbound completely. "When I got back from my vacation, I came to see you. When I found that you weren't home, I confronted Alex and found out you were taken."

"Vacation? Oh... Was it nice? Did you have fun?"

"Not the best time to be discussing this but, I thought you'd know already. With Emily's big mouth, I thought you'd have been filled in already."

"Who?" Amelia stared at him confused, and Johnathan smiled mischievously as he reached down in the chair and lifted Amelia into his arms.

"Nothing, forget I mentioned it."

"Johnathan, you don't have to carry me. I can walk perfectly fine."

Johnathan ignored Amelia as he proceeded to exit the facility. The hunters began to scuffle frantically, ready to initiate another attack.

"Let them go," said Jared to his hunters. "That isn't any ordinary witch. We need to regroup and fortify this facility. With all the damage tonight, we are vulnerable. There will come another time to take action, but now is not that time."

Amelia looked around, noticing several unconscious hunters sprawled out on the floor.

"Johnathan, did you do all of this?"

Johnathan didn't respond. He only smiled as he continued to walk out. Johnathan made his way out of the large gate he entered through when Amelia realized her arm was suddenly becoming wet. A strong smell of iron wafted through the air almost overwhelmingly.

"Johnathan, you're bleeding."

He didn't seem to be phased by her observation. The world around them began to become warped and as Johnathan walked through what seemed to be some type of portal. They were back on their block. *How did we get here so quickly?* Amelia didn't know what Johnathan was doing, but she couldn't complain.

Amelia found herself staring up at Johnathan. Until now, she never noticed how attractive he really was. Johnathan, still wordless, brought Amelia inside of his house, and upon entering, he stumbled and fell onto the ground, Amelia still in his arms. He fell backward, making sure not to hurt Amelia as his legs gave out. Amelia knew immediately he had lost too much blood.

Her pajama top was stained crimson. Amelia panicked, "Johnathan, stay with me, ok? I'm going to patch you right up, don't worry!"

Amelia scurried off, looking for the bathroom. Finding it, she quickly rummaged through the medicine cabinet, searching for peroxide, pliers, and gauze. She gathered all the components and ran back into the entryway to tend Johnathan's wound. Amelia ripped off Johnathan's shirt and pulled his arm toward her. The gash in his arm was deep, but there was no bullet. It shot straight through him. Amelia doused his wound with peroxide, and he winced.

"Good to know you are still with me."

Amelia then wiped the wound down and wrapped it up with the gauze.

"I'll go back and find some pain killers."

Johnathan grabbed Amelia by the waist before she got up and pulled her on top of him, "No, stay here with me. I don't need any painkillers. I'll be fine."

He stared up at Amelia's face. She was even more beautiful than he remembered her before going on vacation. Johnathan reached up and placed a stray strand of Amelia's hair behind her ear. Amelia felt her cheeks grown warm. She could tell she was blushing. Stricken with embarrassment, she got up abruptly and ran towards the bathroom.

"Painkillers, painkillers, got to find painkillers!" Amelia realized she was yelling but flustered, and she couldn't control herself. "Get it together, Amelia! Oh, ibuprofen found it!"

She ran the cold water and splashed it on her face before returning to Johnathan. He was gone. All the remained was a small puddle of blood on the ground where she left him.

"Johnathan!" Amelia called out as she began searching for him. "Johnathan, where are you?"

Amelia opened the door to his bedroom and found him lying in bed. He had removed the rest of his clothing and tossed it all on the floor at the foot of the bed. Amelia walked in with a glass of water and the painkillers in hand. Almost dropping them as she trembled walking toward him. She was petrified especially considering her and Johnathan's history… or better yet, Amara and Johnathan's history. Johnathan sensed her uneasiness as she was now standing in front of him with the medicine and a glass of water in hand, speechless.

"What's the matter? You and Alex never?"

Amelia didn't answer, only looking away with embarrassment. Johnathan was taken aback; he was sure Alex had already seized the opportunity. He smiled delightedly and grabbed Amelia's arm. Pulling her on top of him, she dropped the glass on the floor by accident.

"I'm sorry, Johnathan, I'm so clumsy."

"Don't worry about it," Johnathan flipped Amelia over onto the bed, bringing himself over her.

He stared at her for a few moments, wanting to savor the experience. He had dreamed of being with Amelia so many times it felt unreal, more so he never expected her to be a virgin. Johnathan leaned down and kissed Amelia's neck biting her ear gently as he did so.

"Johnathan, I'm... I've never..."

Johnathan smiled as he unfastened Amelia's pajama top. Blushing once again, she grabbed his hands pleadingly, "Johnathan I— Alex."

Johnathan rolled his eyes in the darkness.

"Where was your precious Alex when you were abducted? I don't recall Alex being the one who rescued you," responded Johnathan coldly.

"You're right..." Amelia thought about it and grew angered.

Johnathan risked his life for her, injuring himself in the process. Amelia looked up at Johnathan, caressing his cheek with her hand. He grabbed her hand with his and kissed it.

"Let's not worry about Alex, at least not tonight," Johnathan resumed kissing Amelia's neck, making his way down her body.

He kissed her stomach as he began to unfasten her bra. Amelia felt butterflies flying around in her stomach. Johnathan caressed her chest as Amelia looked away, not able to look at him in embarrassment.

"Don't be embarrassed. You're beautiful, Amelia," Johnathan grasped Amelia's chin and turned her toward him.

He kissed her passionately. Amelia kissed him back, getting lost in the moment Johnathan slid off Amelia's panties slowly as he kissed her.

"We can stop if you want to," said Johnathan to Amelia.

He wanted to reassure her, though he had no intention of stopping. He'd longed for this moment for too long.

"No… we don't have to," she leaned up and kissed him.

He returned the kiss with a deeper, more passionate one. Johnathan pressed his lips against Amelia's as their bodies became one.

Amelia woke up that morning. Johnathan was sound asleep, so she nudged him until he woke up.

"Good morning. If we plan on going to school, I have to get out of here, and you have to get dressed. My toothbrush and uniform are at my house. I have to go."

"You don't have to go anywhere," Johnathan stared at Amelia, mesmerized.

The sunlight shone in, lighting up her already beautiful face. Amelia was a vision, to think all he had to do to win her over was commit a valiant act. Amelia blushed again, turning away from him once more.

"I have to. I'll see you in school," Amelia picked up her clothes and began to get dressed.

Her shirt, still covered in blood, was all she had to wear. It was early enough that she wasn't worried about getting spotted by anyone. Amelia ran home, trying to get into her house as quickly as possible. She did not want to bump into Alex, especially after what happened between her and Johnathan. Sure enough, as she came up to her stairway, Alex made his way out of the house. He looked like he hadn't slept in a while. Seeing him looking so distressed made her feel horrible. Though he didn't save her, she could tell he'd been beating himself up about it. Alex looked at her with relief, and then his vision shifted toward her shirt.

"Are you bleeding?" Alex asked with concern.

"I-it's not mine," she responded, looking away from him.

"It's Johnathan's... and I take it that's where you're coming from as well? You know what, I don't even want to know. I'm glad you're okay, Amelia Moore," Alex began to walk away back toward his house.

"Alex, I—" Amelia tried to form a sentence, but she got choked up.

She knew there was nothing she could say, even if she could find the words to speak. Alex didn't look back, only continued into his house. Alex closed the door behind him and leaned against it, unable to move. Amelia made her way inside, closing the door behind her. She leaned against it and began sobbing into her hands.

"W-what's wrong with me? Johnathan's evil... how could I? Especially after finding out Amara's fate."

Amelia gathered herself and made her way upstairs to her bedroom. It felt as if all the energy had been drained from her body. Amelia laid down in her bed, not bothering to change out of her soiled clothes. She felt as stiff as a bag of cement and couldn't imagine going to school in her current state. Amelia lay there in bed crying, and eventually, she fell asleep.

She woke up around 5 o'clock to the sound of her doorbell. Amelia made her way downstairs, looking out the window to find Alex standing at her door.

"I know I kind of just ignored you earlier, but when you didn't show up to sch—"

Amelia kissed Alex abruptly, stopping him mid-sentence as she pulled him inside her house by the arm, closing the door behind him.

"Alex, let me explain I—"

Alexander kissed her back passionately, also stopping her from speaking.

"Stop; I don't need any explanations. I take full responsibility for whatever transpired between you two. I should have been there for you. I should have been the one to save you, not Johnathan..."

"Alex, how can you say something like that? Sleeping with him was my choice."

Alex grimaced hearing her say she slept with him aloud, "No, Amelia, it's my fault. I should have been there, magic or no magic. I should have done something... anything. You were in a vulnerable state, and he took advantage of that. If anything, I feel like bashing his skull in. Amelia, you didn't deserve how I treated you this morning... I—"

Amelia hugged him tightly, tears streaming down her cheeks. "Alex, I'm sorry."

"Don't be. Everything will be okay. I just... I need some time."

"Alex, wait, Alex!" Amelia yelled after him as he walked out the door back to his house.

This time, he turned around as she called him instead of completely ignoring her as he did earlier.

"Take care of yourself, love," Alex winked at her and left.

Amelia slumped to the floor, not knowing how to react to the situation she was just faced with. He was trying to mask it, but Amelia could tell Alex was greatly hurt by her actions. *Does he really love me? Alex? Johnathan? Or are they in love with a memory of someone I am reminiscent of? Someone that is no longer living... are they in love with me or... Amara?*

Amelia got up, regaining her composure. She had to know the truth, and she planned on confronting both of them. Amelia made her way to Alex's house and knocked on the door twice. On the third time, he opened the door, not allowing her to complete her series of knocks.

"Alex, I— we need to talk about something."

"Sure, what's on your mind?"

"Alex, how do you feel about me?"

"What do you mean?"

"Alex, how do you feel about me? Not Amara, me Amelia. I'm not her, and she isn't me."

"Well, I feel the same in certain things and different in others. Amelia, I know you aren't Amara. The resemblance is uncanny, but when you are as close to her as I was, the difference is obvious. I find myself drawn to you as I was with Amara. Amelia, you have to understand I am a bit hurt by your relationship with Johnathan. I have a deep hatred of him, and though I'm not sure why exactly, I know he's bad news."

"I-I know why. I think I can... show you," Amelia took Alex's head in her hands and concentrated on the memory of the battle between the three of them.

Alex's eyes went blank as he stared off into nowhere. Tears started to stream down his face as he relived Amara's final moments. He shook away from Amelia, "How long have you known this? The twins... Johnathan murdered Amara... how long did you know!"

"I-I only found out when I was with the hunters it came to me suddenly."

"So you knew what he did... before you slept with him?" Alexander spat the words at her with disgust. "Get out," said Alexander coldly.

"Alex, I—"

"Now!"

Amelia hastily ran out of his house with tears streaming down her face once more. Crying seemed to be the highlight of her day. Amelia ran into her house, slamming the door behind her. She headed to the kitchen and started to do the only things she knew could take her mind off everything. Amelia rummaged through the refrigerator, looking for ingredients to put a meal together. With tears still streaming down her face, she began to make her rendition of Chicken Alfredo. By the time she was finished, she had wound up making dessert as well. Cheesecake with a homemade strawberry sauce that she drizzled over the top. Amelia couldn't help but smile at the sight; it looked like something out of a cookbook.

The doorbell rang suddenly. She hadn't invited anyone over and ran to the door expecting to find Alex. Standing at her doorstep was none other than Johnathan, seemingly there to make more trouble than he'd already caused. Amelia couldn't help but smile as she met his gaze, she didn't want to be alone for the night, and Johnathan seemed to show up lately when she was most in need. Amelia noticed he was holding something behind his back. Although she couldn't see it, she could smell a faint pleasant scent. Jonathan removed his hand from behind his back and displayed a beautiful bouquet.

"You look beautiful tonight," said Johnathan as he stared at Amelia.

She blushed reflexively, embarrassed at his comment. She was dressed modestly in a T-shirt and a pair of ripped jeans. Still, with words alone, Johnathan made her feel like she was wearing a sequined gown with ribbons in her hair. She took the flowers and stepped aside, beckoning him to enter. Johnathan took a deep breathtaking in the air of the recently cooked dinner.

"You must have known I was coming, and Chicken Alfredo, my favorite."

Amelia's face lit up. She hadn't informed him of the meal she'd cooked, especially of its contents. Her face quickly returned to normal as she realized that despite everything, Johnathan knowing what she cooked without her telling him was the least bit surprising.

"I'm glad it's your favorite," said Amelia with a smile. "It's the least I can do considering you saved me yesterday… I don't know what I would have done without y—"

Johnathan pulled Amelia in for an embrace. Holding her tightly in his arms, she returned the hug with a smile, "Yesterday will never happen again. If I can help it, no one will hurt you ever again."

Amelia pulled away from Johnathan, "I'm going to go get dinner set, have a seat at the table, and we'll get started."

Johnathan sat down, and Amelia retreated off to the kitchen. Amelia began to talk to herself as she made the plates.

"Oh god, what am I doing? Do I really have feelings for Johnathan? Despite what he did… I"
Amelia stared down at the plate as if looking for affirmation. She took a deep breath and turned out of the kitchen with two plates in hand. She placed one of the plates down as she sat down across from him. Johnathan noticed Amelia was smiling while eating, and he met her gaze from time to time as he caught her looking at him. Johnathan smiled as he stared at her in response, "It seems you are pretty happy that I'm here If I'm reading that correctly."

Amelia smiled, "Johnathan… do you know how Amara died?"

Johnathan hesitated as he pondered her question. Briefly, Amara's death replayed in his head.

"Yeah, I'm aware of how she died. Why do you ask?" Johnathan's face was disgruntled, and he seemed to be uneasy by the question.

"Johnathan, I don't blame you for it," Amelia gasped, unwilling to believe what she had just uttered.

"Y-you don't think it was my fault?" he asked in disbelief.

"No, I mean, it wasn't intentional, and I believe in second chances."

Johnathan was taken aback by Amelia's response, stunned by her forgiving nature.

"Amelia I—"

He hadn't realized Amelia was standing over him now, she had gotten up from her seat, and she placed her hand on his and held it tightly.

"I understand how her death must be making you feel, but Johnathan, I am here for you... whatever you need. I want you to understand that you can confide in me, and I'll always be here to talk to."

Johnathan couldn't find words to respond to Amelia. He couldn't believe how she was taking this; he swallowed hard, imagining how she would feel if she knew what he'd done to Emily. Johnathan closed his eyes, briefly taking everything in.

"Hey, it's time for dessert. I hope you like cheesecake," said Amelia as she trailed off toward the kitchen.

Johnathan could sense a presence at the door. He got up to look out the window to see who it was. It was Alexander, his hand in the position to knock. Johnathan opened the door and smiled at him.

"What are you doing here?"

Before Johnathan could answer, an energy ball sent Johnathan flying backward into Amelia's stairway. Johnathan laughed as he gathered himself, "Jealous, are we?"

"You wouldn't know the half of it," Alex spat the words at him as he conjured another energy ball. Just as he began to throw it, Amelia ran out into the dining room, hearing the commotion.

"Stop!" Amelia screamed at the top of her lungs, tossing her hands in a downward motion both Alex and Johnathan's energy balls immediately fizzled out. They both stared at Amelia in confusion towards her ability to put out their energy balls with no effort.

"Amelia, how could you be entertaining the likes of him? After everything..."

Amelia turned toward Johnathan's direction ignoring Alex's question, "Johnathan... I need you to leave, please. I need to talk to Alexander, alone."

"Fine, suit yourself, love. I'll see you later. I had a wonderful time," Johnathan pulled Amelia up to himself and began to kiss her.

She turned away in embarrassment, and Johnathan let her go. Johnathan turned to leave, smiling at Alex as he passed him out the door. Alex slammed the door behind him, hoping it hit him on the way out.

"Alex, why are you here? I don't understand you, and I don't understand any of it. You say you want me out of your house, and then you show up here—"

Alex pulled Amelia in for a passionate kiss, "Amelia, I'm sorry. I just can't be without you, not even for a second. I think I'm in love with you, Amelia Moore. Not Amara, a distant memory, you, only you, Amelia. I just... I can't lose you the same way I lost Amara, and Johnathan has been becoming an influence on you as of late. Amelia, I'm horrified of the outcome."

Amelia hugged Alex, "Alexander, you have nothing to worry about. Johnathan would never hurt me, I'm sure of it. He's changed; he isn't the same Johnathan from the past."

"I'd like to believe that, but he also professed to be in love with Amara. Not seeming to be capable of hurting her either, accept he murdered her. You have to understand, Amelia. I don't know what I'd do if I lost you. I'd kill him... and this time, a memory spell wouldn't stop me. I'd finish him once and for all."

"Alex, I'll be fine. Don't worry about me so much."

"I can't help it, Amelia. I... love you."

Alex ran his fingers through Amelia's hair as she laid against his chest. Amelia smiled as she stood there in the warmth of his embrace.

"So... you made him dinner?" asked Alexander with curiosity.

"Why, are you jealous?"

"It's not obvious?" asked Alex as he swooped Amelia into his arms.

"Well, I was stress cooking, actually. He just happened to show up... I-I was hoping it would be you."

Alexander kissed Amelia's forehead as he proceeded to take her up the stairs to her bedroom. He placed Amelia down on her bed and sat next to her.

"Amelia, I have to ask you something both Charles and I have been curious about. What did the hunters do to you?" asked Alex expressing deep concern in his voice.

"Well, not much of anything really. But I did get electrocuted."

"What? Are you okay?"

"No, I'm fine. Mostly I was just asked a series of questions, am I a part of a coven? Do I know any other witches? Stuff like that. I answered no to pretty much everything but when Johnathan stormed in, it kind of exposed my lie."

"What happened in there?"

"Johnathan pretty much trashed the hunter's underground facility. He breezed through there with no effort whatsoever. He took down at least 100 hunters. I don't know how and left pretty much unscathed. He also wasn't affected by the wards... If he hadn't been there to rescue me, it actually would have been pretty scary."

"I'm sorry I couldn't do anything Amelia, you don't know how it was eating at me inside."

"I understand, Alex. Honestly, I wouldn't have wanted to put you in danger. There's something else, though. Their leader, Jared, could be a potential threat in the future. I couldn't get a great read on him, but he is harboring many secrets... I feel like he would be a more than worthy foe if it comes to that."

Amelia almost forgot to mention her parents, "And my parents... mom and dad are..."

"Hunters."

"Yeah, and I don't know what that means for the future. Would they be able to murder me, their daughter, if given the order? I'd like to believe they wouldn't be capable, but... how well do I know my parents? I didn't even know they were hunters..."

"Don't beat yourself up about it, Amelia. There really wasn't any way for you to know. If they come for you, just know we will be ready. I hate to admit it, but I don't think they'd stand a chance against Johnathan. If nothing else, I can see that he will stop at nothing to protect you, and with his... abilities, he would seem like someone the hunters wouldn't want to make an enemy out of."

Alex didn't like saying it out loud, but it was evident they would need Johnathan's aid if the hunters decided to return for Amelia.

"Well, it's getting pretty late, and you have school in the morning. No more ditching for you. It seems like I'll have to be your personal escort just to make sure."

"Oh, is that so?"

"Indeed, missy," said Alex as he waved his finger at her bending down to kiss her on the forehead as he began to walk off. "I'll let myself out."

"Alex."

He turned around once more

"I love you too."

Alexander smiled as he turned and walked out of the room, closing the door behind him and returning to his house.

Chapter 10
Can We Dance?

Amelia stared at one of the fliers posted throughout the school. There was to be a school dance held in their gym. They had annual dances at their school taking place at various times. This happened to be the fall dance and Amelia had completely forgotten about it. Who could blame her with all that had been going on in her life? She couldn't believe that at one point she thought her life was boring.

Even if she wanted to go, Amelia had nothing to wear. No one had asked her yet, and she knew it would be between Alex and Johnathan, but she didn't know who she'd go with. Amelia felt she owed it to Alex after what she'd put him through recently. In any case, if Amelia took any more time to stare at the flier, she would miss her class.

Making her way into the classroom, Amelia sat in her usual seat. Johnathan was eyeing her as she sat down. He wrote a message down on a piece of paper in his notebook. Amelia opened up her textbook, and in the center of the page, she saw a note in Johnathan's handwriting, *Since we both enjoy chemistry, won't you come to the dance with me? Yes_____ of course Johnathan you make my heart melt.   NO_____ I am already going to go with Alex. I feel sorry for him and do not want to hurt his feelings.*

Answer quickly. You are running out of time, Amelia.

Amelia smiled as she read Johnathan's note. She decided she wouldn't pick either of his choices. *Sorry, Johnny, I need time to consider who I am going to the dance with. If I go at all, 10 points for your cheesy note, though. My heart is definitely melting.*

Amelia placed the note back into her textbook. As she closed her book, Johnathan opened his. She watched as he read it and looked over her response. Johnathan smiled contently and placed the note in his pocket. The two of them returned their focus to the chemistry lesson.

After school, Amelia stood at her locker, loading her bag with the books she needed to do homework. Amelia had been working diligently to improve her grades. She closed her locker to reveal Misty standing beside her on her right side. Amelia jumped slightly, not expecting anyone to be behind her locker.

"Oh, I didn't see you there. You scared me."

"Sorry... it's just that I... I need someone to shop with for the dance. The girls seem to all have it together, but you know I've never really shopped by myself. What I'm asking is, if you wouldn't mind coming with me?"

Amelia smiled warmly. She was enjoying the change of character in Misty.

"Sure, I'd be delighted to join you, but I have to make a quick stop at home first. That is if you don't mind waiting a couple of minutes."

"No, of course not, ready to go?"

The two of them began their walk to Amelia's house. As she passed by 741 spring drive, she came to a sudden halt. Amelia didn't know why she'd stopped in front of the house, but she felt a void like something was missing. It felt like a large part of her had disappeared, and for some reason, she felt it was because of that house.

"Hey, Amelia, are you alright? We should get going."

"Oh, sorry, I don't know what came over me just now."

Misty and Amelia made their way into her house.

"I'll be five minutes. Just make yourself at home. There are drinks in the fridge."

Amelia quickly changed out of her school clothes. It dawned on her that Misty didn't have a change of clothes. The two of them were practically the same size, except Misty was a bit tomboyish. Ironic because she was a cheerleader, which stereotypically would make her a girly girl.

"Do you want to change clothes up here, Misty? I can lend you something in my closet."

"Ah, thanks. I'd appreciate that."

Misty could be heard coming up the stair as Amelia slid her altar back under the bed out of sight.

"So, I have a lot for you to choose from. Just take a look inside."

"Do you, I mean, would you mind helping me pick something out? I don't really have a lot of experience in this department."

"Sure thing… hmm, you should try this pink top and these ripped blue jeans. Something tells me pink is your color, and I have these earrings that would match perfectly," Amelia said, handing Misty the items.

Soon after, Amelia left the room to give her some privacy. Misty walked out of the room so Amelia could give her the once-over.

"Wow, Misty, you look better in that outfit than I did."

Misty blushed as she viewed herself in Amelia's full body mirror, "Are you sure it's okay?"

"Definitely. Hey, give me a second. I'll meet you downstairs."

Amelia rummaged through her drawer, pulling out the lump of money her parents left her.

"How much do I need?" she asked herself as she decided somewhere around seven hundred dollars would suffice.

Amelia hadn't been left that much money ever. Though after what her parents put her through, she felt she'd earned it. The two of them drove about 20 miles into a town called Cedar Grove. Misty recommended that it was a great area to shop, especially at a small cozy boutique.

"Hi! Welcome to The Red Dress. Can I help you two with anything?" responded a woman whose nametag read, Delilah.

"Well, Delilah, we are looking for two dresses for a school dance," said Amelia as she gave the display racks a once over.

"Sure, I can assist with that. It would be my pleasure!"

Misty and Amelia exchanged glances as they held in laughter. Something was very off about Delilah. She was unusually friendly, but that wasn't quite it.

Delilah sifted through the clothing racks with Misty and Amelia close behind. Every so often, glancing at the two of them in an attempt to find the perfect dress.

"Hmm, I think the color pink would suit you very well, Misty."

Amelia nudged Misty's shoulder, reminding her of their previous conversation. Misty disregarded Amelia as she was made aware of something even odder

"Hey, Delilah, was it? I never told you my name was Misty."

Delilah seemed to stop moving completely as she searched for the words to respond.

"Oh, I'm so sorry, how rude of me. It's just that you look like a Misty. Yes, that's what it is."

Amelia turned to whisper in Misty's ear, "The sooner we find our dresses, the sooner we can get out of this creepy place."

"You're telling me."

"Oh goody, here it is, a beautiful pink dress and this nice black number. The sequins on the gown will really do well to bring out your eyes," Delilah handed Amelia the black sequined dress with a side slit and Misty the pink dress with an open back and highlights of glitter throughout the design.

"Wow, this is really... pretty," said Misty with concern as she looked to Amelia for reassurance.

"Oh, come on, Misty, just try the thing on," Amelia shoved Misty gently into the changing room as Amelia went into the one beside it.

The dress slipped onto Amelia easily as she admired herself in the full body mirror. She stepped out to show Misty how it looked, only to find her still occupied in the changing room.

"Misty? Is everything alright?"

"Yeah, give me a second."

Amelia waited in anticipation for the two of them to critique each other's dresses. Misty stepped out of the changing room, the dress fitting her perfectly. The glitter did well to bring out elements of her face. It was perfection, and the dress looked like it was made especially for her.

"Wow, Misty, the dress looks really good. I think it's a definite buy."

"Do you really? I mean, do you think he will notice me?" Asked Misty as she looked away, blushing.

"Oh my god, Misty, are you seriously crushing on someone? I always thought you were…"

"Gay? Yeah, I know… everyone seems to think that… but no, I like men, at least I think I do."

"Sorry, well you have to tell me who it is, now I'm dying to know."

"At first, I thought it was George."

"Samantha's boyfriend?"

"Yeah, there's just something about him, you know?"

"You do realize they are totally still together, right?"

"I know, but sometimes I catch him staring at me, and that has to mean something. Recently though, I found myself falling for our team's football Captain."

Amelia swallowed hard, "You mean Johnathan Sharpe?"

"Yeah, of course, we only have one football captain."

"You know he's totally taken. I don't think he'd be interested. Besides, I don't think you are his type, anyway."

"Oh yeah? Who gave you the authority to dictate whether he'd be interested or not? As far as I know, he's completely single. You know Amelia, I thought you were cool, but you're a real bitch. Oh, and by the way, your jealousy is showing."

Misty stormed past Amelia, nearly knocking her down as she brushed her aside. *Oh god, no... am I developing feelings for Johnathan? Am I really... jealous?* Amelia ran after Misty at the checkout counter.

"Misty, I'm really sorry. I don't know what came over me."

Misty shrugged her shoulders as she pulled out her wallet to pay for the dress. Delilah stared at the two of them as if deeply involved in their conversation. The woman seemed to be hanging on to their every word.

"You know, you're probably right. Why would anyone be interested in me? I'm Misty, the mean girl... I guess it's my fault. I am a bit of a bully after all."

Misty paid for the dress, and her stomach began to growl. Amelia smiled as she heard the noise.

"Hey, tell you what, let's get these dresses paid for, and I'll make it up to you. A while back, I spotted a seafood restaurant, The Golden Prawn. If you are allergic or something, let me know."

Misty opened her wallet and looked inside. She only had enough to pay for the dress but not for any extras. "Don't worry; it's my treat," Misty smiled as the two of them finished up in the dress shop and made their way to the restaurant.

On the way back to Crimson Springs, Amelia dropped Misty off at her house. She was happy with the way the day with Misty had turned out. Amelia decided she would stop by Johnathan's house for a favor before going home. Amelia parked the car in Johnathan's garage, making her way to his doorstep. Before she could ring the bell, he'd already opened the door.

"You know, I will never get used to that."

"To what do I owe this pleasure?" asked Johnathan with a smile, stepping aside to let Amelia into his home.

"I don't want to keep you too long. It's just that I need a favor."

"Amelia, you know all you have to do is ask. Anything you need, I will gladly do," Johnathan eased in closer to Amelia.

She noticed and stopped him by placing a hand on his chest, "Johnathan, I want you to take Misty to the dance. I recently found out she has something of a crush on you. It would make me happy if—"

Johnathan pulled Amelia in close, kissing her passionately, abruptly. Pulling away from him, she returned to the conversation.

"Johnathan... please—"

He placed a finger over her lips, "Okay, I'll do it. I want you to know I'd want nothing else in this world than to be your date. I will only do this because you asked it of me."

Amelia embraced Johnathan, "Please show her a good time. Johnathan, I know there's good in you. Here's your chance to prove me right."

Johnathan returned Amelia's hug briefly as he watched her return to her car. She glanced at Johnathan once more before she pulled out of his driveway and made her way home.

"What am I getting myself into?" Amelia asked herself as she made her way into the house.

She was greeted at the doorstep by three faces she wished she never had to see ever again. Her parents and Jared who seemed to be making himself at home at their kitchen island.

"Oh god, what did I do to deserve this? Leave me alone I don't want to talk to you, any of you."

Thomas Moore grasped Amelia's arm she attempted to run past them.

"Let me go!" screamed Amelia sending Thomas into the wall with great force.

"I- I didn't mean to..." said Amelia as she seized the opportunity to retreat to her bedroom.

"I'm sorry, Amber," said Thomas.

"It's alright, sweetheart. She needs time."

"Time is a luxury we can't afford," responded Jared as he got up from his seat and made his way upstairs after Amelia.

He knocked on the door to her bedroom impatiently.

"Go away, unless you're looking for round two. I have plenty more energy where that came from."

"One, I am not your father, two, I am not easily spelled, and three—" Jared opened the door breaking the doorknob as he exerted much more force than necessary.

Amelia picked up the nearest item she could find and launched it at him. Realizing too late, she had thrown her diary straight at him. Jared caught the book with little effort and opened it quickly, skimming through it.

"Johnathan, Alex, blah blah oh... Jared? This should be interesting. I wonder what you think about me," Jared began to read through her entry about him as Amelia's face grew red with embarrassment

"Give it back!" yelled Amelia as Jared continued to read, completely ignoring her.

A mischievous grin spread across his lips. Jared had been so involved in the entry he didn't realize Amelia launched a fireball straight toward him. Reflexively Jared blocked the fireball by holding up the diary, which was instantly set ablaze. Amelia's diary was thoroughly charred in seconds burnt to a crisp, and the ashes fell from Jared's hands. Unbeknownst to her, Jared had already read through the entire entry.

"Well, it seems you painted me with a pretty colorful description. Don't worry, your secret is safe with me," Jared winked at Amelia, Disgustedly, she threw the lamp on her nightstand straight at him.

This time Jared didn't block. The porcelain lamp shattered into pieces against his face, but it didn't leave as much as a scratch on Jared.

"What the hell are you?" Jared smiled once more.

"Now, Amelia, don't you remember our time in the dungeons. If I told you, I'd have to kill you, and I don't think either of us wants that. Now enough childish games, there is a reason your parents returned. More importantly, there is a reason I am here in particular. Your demon witch friend has to die, and I intend to kill him. You should know, I took the liberty of having myself enrolled in your high school."

"Aren't you like 30? How did you manage that?" Jared rolled his eyes, recalling that Amelia knew his age exactly.

"You'd be amazed what a couple of potions can do. You're looking at Crimson High's newest Jaguar. Not exactly my spirit animal, but it will have to do. You should also know, your parents agreed to put me up in the spare room for as long as the duty requires. Just think of me as your new annoying older brother. Going back to your diary entry, that might be a little hard for you."

Amelia seemed to turn pale after Jared's comment. He began to walk to the door smiling, obviously pleased with himself.

"Oh, and Amelia, don't even think about telling anyone about me. There will be consequences. Oh, and you should have this doorknob checked out. I think it's broken."

Jared walked out, closing the door behind him.

"As if my life wasn't crazy enough," Amelia tugged on her hair and fell backward in her bed with a thud.

About an hour later, Jared returned upstairs with two plates of food in his hand.

"Here, Amber says this is for you."

"Tell Amber I wasn't hungry," responded Amelia as she turned away from him.

"Suit yourself," said Jared turning to leave as he finished eating both plates at an inhuman pace.

Jared took a deep inhale as he looked back in Amelia's direction.

"Someone is at the door. You better get that it's for you. This town seems to be crawling with witches. I guess honesty isn't one of your better qualities. I guess it's my fault as well, time to buckle down on my interrogations, I see."

The doorbell rang, and Amelia ran past Jared, nearly knocking him sideways. She wanted to get to the door before anyone else had the chance to. Her house was currently crawling with hunters. Then there was Jared, and Amelia had no idea what he was. Alex stood at the door anxiously, he was excited to show Amelia what he'd done. Amelia opened the door seemingly as anxious as he was

"Hey Amelia, come with me. I want to show you something,"

"Right about now, I'd go anywhere with you, Alex. My parents are back home. Long story that I care not to tell."

"Then please, let me take you away from all this tonight. At least for a couple of hours," Alex extended his arm, and Amelia linked hers with his.

The night was beautiful. All the stars could be seen in the sky, seeming to light their path. They made their way to a nearby park in which Alex instructed Amelia to sit down on a nearby bench.

"Watch this beautiful," Alex stood on the bench next to her, muttering something into his hand as he conjured an energy ball.

Alex threw the energy ball into the sky with great force. It caused an explosion that became a bright blue fireworks display. Amelia looked up to read the message the fireworks left behind. It read, "Will you go to the dance with me?" Amelia smiled as she looked up at Alex.

"Of course I will, Alex. That was amazing."

Alex pretended to wipe a bead of sweat from his brow, "Oh, that's a relief. I wasn't sure if you'd say yes."

"Why would you think that, Alex?"

He slumped down on the bench beside her.

"Well, with the recent competition, I thought it might be a little harder. I thought maybe…"

"Maybe what? That I'd be going with Johnathan? Well, I'm not, and I'm tired of everyone trying to ship us. I mean, I like Johnathan, I do but—"

Amelia leaned toward Alex kissing him deeply.

"I'm sorry, Alex, for the way you've been feeling; it's my fault entirely. Johnathan and I should never have…"

Alex placed his arm over Amelia's shoulder, pulling her in closer to him, "What's done is done, water under the bridge. Let's just enjoy the rest of tonight together. While we can."

Alex and Amelia spent the rest of the night gazing at the stars together.

The following day Amelia got ready for school. She made her way downstairs to make herself breakfast, only to come face to face with her mother, who had cooked breakfast and was setting plates. When she saw her, Amelia immediately began to turn away.

"Amelia, please hear me out."

"What could you possibly have to say to me?"

"I'm sorry for starters."

Amelia's face softened as she heard her mother's words. She knew her mother was sincerely apologetic.

"How could you not tell me you were hunters? How could you allow them to capture me?"

"All I can say is your father, and I are sorry. We had no other choice. Once your name appeared in the encyclopedia, we were given one option, kill you. The circumstances of your birth were not important to the hunters. You are our biological daughter, your father, and I couldn't just sign your death warrant. Amelia, I know sometimes we are distant, but we love you very much. We always have loved you and always will."

"So, why wasn't I killed?"

"Your father and I have a decent standing with the hunters. We pleaded with Jared to spare you if you could be proven not to harbor malicious intent. He agreed, with the stipulation, that he would be the one to interrogate you. If he found you to be dangerous, he would kill you without hesitation. That was all we had. You can't understand how happy we are that he spared you."

"He didn't spare me, though. If you've already forgotten, I was rescued."

Before Amber could respond, Jared was already upon them, digging through the refrigerator.

"Make no mistake Amelia," said Jared with food stuffed in his mouth. "The moment I walked out of that interrogation room, you'd been spared. Had I intended to kill you, you would have been dead. It is seldom I leave an interrogation with the prisoner alive. You should consider yourself lucky, I believe a thank you is in order?" Said Jared as he probed the room for a response. "Nothing? Hey, you got any jelly? I mean, this toast is a little dry."

"You're a pig," said Amelia as she grabbed her bag and walked toward the door.

Jared quickly gathered his things and scurried after her, "Hey, wait up. I'll walk you to school."

"No, thank you, I'm fine," Amelia quickened her step, trying to get away from him to no avail. With a bag and a handful of food, Jared still seemed to be faster than her.

"Oh, I must insist. We are going the same direction after all."

With an eye roll, Amelia began to walk ahead of him. She quickly wrote up a text message, telling Alex not to walk with her this morning.

"Who are you texting? Is it your boyfriend from last night? Don't tell me, Alex? Yeah, that was his name. I remember from your diary."

"Our relationship isn't any of your business."

"So he isn't your boyfriend, got it."

Amelia didn't respond as the two of them arrived at the school doors. Jared opened the door and stood to the side, "After you."

Amelia walked forward with Jared beside her. Amelia noticed faces agape as she walked through the halls with Jared. Everyone seemed to be in awe as the two walked together. Amelia stopped in front of her locker. Misty was already standing there waiting for her. She was equally mesmerized as she stared up at the tall, handsome figure beside Amelia. Misty whispered in Amelia's ear, "Who's your friend? And is he... single?"

Jared chuckled as he heard every word.

"Trust me, Misty, he has baggage." Said Amelia loud enough for Jared to hear her. Jared only smirked in response. Amelia's effort to villainize him only amused him more.

"Well, Amelia, I will see you in class. I'm going to find my locker. Nice to meet you... Misty," Jared smiled, and Misty slumped back into the locker as if she was becoming a part of them.

Amelia stood there shaking her head as she pulled out her chemistry textbooks. It then dawned on her that it was a class she shared with Johnathan.

"Oh god..."

"I know, right? He has to be some type of god."

"Misty, pull it together. You are going to be late for your first period."

"I almost forgot, Amelia! Johnathan asked me to the dance. I know you had something to do with it, but I'm grateful. Anything you need, just let me know. I am forever indebted to you."

The two of them busted into a fit of laughter.

"Alright, Delilah."

"Geeze, don't remind me, what was up with that chick, anyway? It seemed like she was trying a bit too hard. The way she hung on to our every word was pretty weird."

"Come on, or we'll be late."

"Alright, Amelia, see you at lunch."

Amelia made her way into the chemistry class. Jared was already inside, sitting in the seat beside her, barely fitting in the desk. He waved at her as she walked in as if his presence wasn't embarrassing enough.

"Oh boy... this is going to be a long day," she mumbled to herself as she took her seat beside him.

Jared looked in Johnathan's direction making direct eye contact with him. Johnathan was taken aback slightly by the leader of the hunters' presence. Jared was very intimidating, and Johnathan still wondered why he hadn't been rendered unconscious like the others. Throughout the rest of class, the two of them continued to glare at each other.

At lunchtime, Misty sat down with Amelia, who was by herself, not wanting to deal with the drama of Jared and Johnathan.

"So, Amelia, how did you meet your new friend? You know, the guy from earlier. I hear his name is Jared."

"It really is a long story, Misty, and you wouldn't believe me if I told you. Speak of the devil."

Jared casually sat beside the two of them at the lunch table.

"Well, don't mind me," said Jared turning to smile at Misty.

Misty suddenly lost her will to speak, forgetting how to form words. She got up from her seat abruptly and walked off from the scene.

"What's gotten into her? Is everyone in this school that strange?"

"No, I think it's just you."

Johnathan walked up to the table and attempted to sit by Amelia. Jared let a growl slip out.

"Did you just growl at me?"

The two of them stared at Jared with eyebrows raised.

"Johnathan, I think you should take a breather. I'll talk to you another time.

"Run along," said Jared as he demonstrated his fingers walking away.

Rolling her eyes, Amelia got up from the table, emptied her tray, and began to walk away, leaving Jared behind.

"What did I say?" Jared asked himself as he shrugged and continued to eat his lunch.

After school, Amelia rushed home as quickly as she could. It was the night of the school dance, and Amelia wanted time to make sure she was in order. After she showered, she got dressed and put on a few accessories. Amelia looked herself over in her full body mirror several times. Amber knocked on the door as Amelia finished, "Hey sweetheart, I wanted to know if you needed any help getting ready."

"Actually... mom, would you mind doing my hair?"

"I'd love to."

Amber sat Amelia down in her vanity chair and turned on the curling iron.

"This is nice, mom; I can't remember the last time we did something like this together. In fact, I can't remember the last time we did anything together."

"I know, and it's my fault entirely. Work is very taxing, and your father and I never really had the time to be parents. We have time now to make up for that. I hope we can become close again like we once were. There, all done," Amber said and turned Amelia's chair around to the mirror so she could see herself.

"Wow, mom, you really outdid yourself. You're a pretty good hairstylist for a hunter."

The two of them laughed as Amber pulled something out of her pocket. She placed a silver diamond-encrusted leaf-shaped hair, Barrett, inside of Amelia's hair. It accented the silver sequins in her dress perfectly.

"Your father bought that for me the day I gave birth to you. I've never had the chance to wear it with work and everything. It looks great on you, and I think you should wear it."

"Thanks, mom. It's beautiful," she said, noting how the accessory sparkled brightly in the lighting of her room.

"Well, I should get ready to go. Alex should be here any moment."

"Oh, he showed up a little while ago. I think he's downstairs with your father."

"Great," Amelia grabbed her purse off the vanity and made her way downstairs.

Alex looked up as Amelia made her way down the stairs. He felt like the room stopped, and he was watching her in slow motion. Thomas pulled out a camera taking the opportunity to get a couple of photos of his daughter.

"You look beautiful," said Thomas as he snapped several pictures.

Amelia was blushing, "Dad, please stop. You are embarrassing me."

"I want her back home no later than 12, you know what, let's make that 11 for you."

"Yes sir, I won't have it any other way." Amelia rolled her eyes, making sure her father could see.

"Shall we be off?" Amelia linked arms with Alex, and the two of them made their way to the school.

The room seemed to stop as Amelia entered. Johnathan immediately ceased dancing with Misty as he viewed Amelia in the entryway. Jared, already present at the dance, spit out his punch as he looked up at Amelia from across the room. Amelia stood there embarrassed as all eyes seemed to be on her. The recent attention she'd been getting made her slightly uncomfortable. Alex, sensing the tension, walked Amelia away from the onlookers, "How about I go get us something to drink?"

"Yeah, Alex, that'd be cool."

Jared sat alone toward the center of the room, sipping a cup of punch. Amelia could visibly see he was bored out of his mind. She made her way over to him as Alex seemed to be lost getting punch.

"Hey, Jared, why don't you find yourself a date and take advantage of the high school setting."

"Nah, isn't really my scene. By the way, you look nice... for a witch," said Jared with a smile returning to his cup of punch.

"Ha, thanks for the... compliment? You don't look too bad yourself... for a hunter."

Jared chuckled as Amelia walked off to return to Alex, who held two cups in his hand.

"Hey, Amelia, I meant to ask you, who's your new friend?"

Amelia probed around in her mind for an appropriate response, "Oh, he's a cousin of mine, on my mother's side. He's been staying with us a couple of days now. He kind of just showed up unannounced."

Amelia returned her gaze over to Jared, who seemed to be smiling back at Amelia. It was as if he'd been listening to her every word. *That's impossible; with the loud music, I can barely hear myself.*

"Oh, well, I guess that makes sense. Well, in any case, let's dance," Alex dragged Amelia unwillingly onto the dance floor; dancing wasn't one of her talents. Suddenly, a feeling came over Amelia, something she couldn't describe.

"Hey, I'll be right back Alex, wait for me?"

"Of course."

Something was compelling Amelia to leave the dance. Amelia walked away from the school aimlessly; she had no idea where her legs were taking her.

Jared got up from his seat, wondering why Amelia's boyfriends didn't seem interested in following her. Jared had a strange feeling that something horrible was about to happen. He followed Amelia, watching as she walked blocks away from the school, seemingly heading back home. She reached house 741 on Spring Drive. Jared leaned against a tree as Amelia seemed to look back in his direction. She slipped into the house, away from Jared's view.

Jared smirked, "Here I was thinking this night wasn't going to be interesting." Jared could smell something in the air, it smelled of death. Whatever it was, he was ready to face it head on.

Chapter 11
Death Becomes You

Emily sat up, gasping for breath.

"You're finally awake, amor," said Andres.

Everything was so foggy. Emily looked around frantically, finding she was surrounded by several people, seemingly standing over her and watching her with intrigue.

Emily laid on a table, her arms and legs strapped down to it. Emily felt her throat unusually dry. It felt like she had downed hard liquor. A searing pain burned her vocal cords as she attempted to form words. Her stomach was also in excruciating pain as she stared at the ceiling contemplating how she could get something to eat.

"W-where... Where am I?" she coughed between words. "What have you done to me? Please... I'm too young to... die"

The word die lingered in Emily's mind as she suddenly got a flash of memory. It caused a great stinging sensation near her temples. It was as if her mind was straining to re-experience the event. She was in a hotel room, strapped down as she was now, with great pain in her neck. Johnathan had slit her throat. She remembered it clearly.

"What? Am I in hell?"

Andres chuckled briefly, exchanging a glance at Lucinda, who smiled back at him.

"No, dear child. You are here in the same hotel you checked in. You never left."

Emily's head raced as a searing headache came on abruptly.

"What's wrong with me? Can I have a... glass of water? Or something to eat? Please, if I'm going to be murdered, please do it now, before I die of hunger."

Everyone looked around at each other, exchanging glances as Lucinda finally decided to respond, "On the contrary, dear Emily, you are already dead."

Emily lost her will to speak as the room began to spin around her. The surrounding voices grew quiet, distant as she faded in and out of consciousness.

"She needs blood," said Andres as he gestured for Luis to hand him a blood bag from the refrigerator in the corner of the room.

Luis handed him the blood bag, and Andres punctured it and brought it toward Emily's mouth. Her eyes opened suddenly. The grey hue was glowing a yellowish color as she inhaled the aroma of the liquid. It smelled heavenly to her. She didn't know what she was drinking, but almost instinctually, she scarfed it down in seconds. The feeling in her throat subsided the moment she began to ingest the fluid. Her headache was seemingly dissipating as well. Emily felt great energy surging through her. Andres unfastened her restraints, and she sat up robotically.

"T-that was delicious... what was that?"

"Blood," responded a familiar female voice in the room. It was the female that was in the basement with Andres earlier that day.

"You gave me... Blood?" Emily felt the urge to vomit doubling over as she made a choking noise, but nothing came up. "I can't vomit? What the hell is wrong with me! What did you do to me?" Emily felt like she should be crying, except she felt no tears streaming down her face.

She placed her hand over her neck, feeling a slight pain which made her gasp as she did so. Emily dropped down from the table in search of a mirror. Instead, she stood in front of the refrigerator staring at her reflection in the silver chrome paint it was covered in. Emily stared in shock as she examined the person before her. There, plain as day, was a long gash across Emily's neck. The scar was almost completely healed aside from the pain she felt when she touched it.

Emily stared at herself, finding the scar wasn't the highlight of her affliction. Her eyes, a beautiful bright grey color, were not her eyes. They were Andres's eyes, and as she looked around, viewing the faces in the room, they all shared the same grey hue. Emily realized only now, the eyes she once thought to be beautiful looked like death. The pale grey color as if stripped of all life. Her skin was also abnormally pale, like a porcelain doll in appearance. Everyone seemed to be suffering from the same affliction as Emily, except for the elderly cleaning woman. Her eyes were a deep dark brown with speckles of a lighter brown throughout her iris. Her skin was a beautiful warm brown color, not chalky at all.

Even the others in the room didn't seem as pale as Emily. She placed her hand to her face tracing over her cheeks. She took a deep inhale and realized in an instant something was different about her. She could smell the blood in the refrigerator, she could hear the beating of Lucinda's heart, the shuffling of feet from the outside patio. Interestingly, she seemed to be able to smell mold in room 304. It was as if Emily could pinpoint what was going on in the immediate area. Everything now seemed much more vivid she was experiencing the world with a new understanding. Her senses were heightened. She could smell better, see better, hear more clearly, and felt more agile.

"What did you do to me?" asked Emily

"We did what we had to, Emily. Lucinda couldn't let you die. We tried to warn you. I—"

Lucinda glared at Andres angrily, stopping him from finishing his sentence.

"Emily, I am Lucinda. In the future, hopefully, you can refer to me as mother... Your boyfriend, the demon warlock, murdered you in cold blood. Bringing us all together today. You see, there was only one way to save you, and that was by making you like my other children, Andres, Andrea, and Luis. It was the only way you have cheated death, Emily. You are reborn. Now, you are a vampire."

Emily doubled over with laughter, "Lady, you're crazy. Do you really think I'm going to believe that I am a vampire? Where is the hidden camera? This is a pretty elaborate prank. A vampire? Like Dracula? Fangs? And turning into a bat, are you serious? Did Johnathan put you all up to this? Baby, you can come out now you got me, good one."

Emily couldn't control her laughter. As she looked around, everyone's faces were stern. They did not find any humor in Lucinda's explanation.

"You guys are a bunch of loonies. I'm getting the hell out of here."

Emily made her way toward the door, and Andres grabbed her arm as she tried to exit. A sudden searing pain raced through her as she began to remember something. It was nighttime in her memory. Andres lifted her dress and bit her on her inner thigh, blood running down from two small puncture wounds. Suddenly, she remembered being in the basement. She flashed her phone's flashlight in Andres' face, revealing a toothy smile that displayed two sharp canines. The final memory replayed in her head—Johnathan apologizing and then slitting her throat as she laid in bed bleeding out.

"Oh my god…" said Emily as she lost her balance and fell backward.

She looked up when she hadn't hit the floor to find herself being held up by Andres.

"Stop being so dramatic. You might look similar, but you are nothing like Cassandra," said the young female bitterly.

Lucinda gave her a look of disgust and swatted her on the ear.

"Hold your tongue before I cut it out, Andrea."

"Couldn't you have just let me die?"

"No, I make it my business to save whomever I can. Any existence is better than not having one at all," responded Lucinda with a weak smile.

"What are you? You don't seem like us. Your eyes aren't… grey. "

"Well, that's because I am not like any of you. I am a witch."

"You referred to Johnathan earlier as… the demon witch? So… he's like you?"

"No, not in the slightest. You see, he is possessed, under control by an evil entity. I've seen cases like your boyfriend before. It's the result of human sacrifice. It's a wonder why he has not been captured by the hunters yet. They usually hunt and kill demon witches with much haste. If it's any consolation, he has been corrupted by that which dwells inside of him."

"Hunt and kill?"

As Lucinda opened her mouth to speak, Andrea intercepted, "How can you be so naïve? He just murdered you, for crying out loud! How could you possibly be concerned about his wellbeing?"

"I-I don't know, he was my boyfriend, but I suppose you're right... Our relationship was falling apart... we had problems even before coming here, but I would have never imagined him being my undoing. He actually murdered me... Johnathan killed me and is probably back in town enjoying his life. That reminds me! Andres, I think I dropped my phone earlier..."

"You did, but it was disposed of."

"That was a 1000 dollar phone!"

Andres shrugged, "Money isn't really a priority for us. We make do with what we have."

"Well, I'm going to need a phone. I'm also going to need to get back to my life. I mean, I guess thanks for saving my life? But I have to get back to Crimson Springs."

"You'll be back soon enough. You have a task to complete."

Emily looked at Lucinda with confusion, wondering why the woman thought she could dictate when Emily could leave.

Andres sat Emily down in a nearby chair and began to speak to her, "Emily, I know this is a lot for you to take in but, you don't have a choice in this. You are the same as all of us, a... vampire, and you won't survive on your own, especially not in the early stages. We didn't resurrect you just so that you can die again, or worse, get yourself captured by hunters. You need to know, we are all bound to Lucinda. As our creator, she can also be our undoing. The fact is, whether willingly or not. You will obey Lucinda or face certain death. It is a fate in which we all share. You will come to accept it in time. We do what we must to survive."

Andres looked away from Emily as if embarrassed by his circumstances.

"So... what you're saying is that we're basically... slaves? To a Mexican maid? This seems to be getting worse and worse."

Lucinda rolled her eyes at Emily's statement; she was very blunt. A trait that Cassandra never possessed. Emily slumped back in her chair. She realized that whatever was to come, she had no say in it. Her life was no longer her own, and frankly, she was not prepared to face sudden death. Emily could feel an urge deep within her being, which she had to survive. She'd already died once, and Emily didn't want to experience that again.

"Well, with everything that's been unloaded on me... can I at least step out for some air?"

Lucinda looked at Emily curiously before answering, "Sure, but Andres is going with you. Andres, keep an eye on her. You know the rules; make sure she abides by them."

"Fine," Emily got up and made her way to the exit door. "You coming?" she turned to look at Andres.

Andres got up and approached Emily, following her as she headed out of the hotel in the night. Emily stood in front of the hotel, inhaling a deep breath and exhaling. Though the breathing seemed forced, she still had a few human tendencies. Her mind was racing as to what her new life had in store for her.

"How are you feeling?" asked Andres as he placed his hand on her shoulder, his accent still as thick as she remembered it to be.

"Honestly? I want to blow this joint, but to risk sudden death? It's just, I'm so overwhelmed, you know? How is this all possible? I feel like I've been blindfolded my entire life, and now I have it forcefully removed. I don't know; I'm just rambling on, I guess."

Andres smiled at Emily, "Don't be so hard on yourself. There is a reason you didn't have any prior knowledge of this stuff. Supernatural beings try to keep themselves hidden. The fact that you weren't aware is actually a good thing. Besides, a human would not want to be involved in any of this drama."

"I guess you are right. I probably wouldn't have believed it, anyway. In my former life."

Andres turned toward Emily placing a reassuring hand on her shoulder, "Well, would you like to know how I turned?"

"If you're willing, sure. Probably not as bad as me, though, murdered by my own boyfriend while on vacation," Emily shuddered at the thought, and Andres grimaced as he began to tell his story.

"I was a street kid, me and my sister Andrea. You see, our parents were murdered in a drug ring, some problems with missing money. Without any parents, I wound up doing the only thing I could to make sure Andrea was fed and clothed. I returned to the same dealers who murdered my parents, praying they could use me for something. My prayers were answered, and I found myself selling. Though not the best salesman, I did what I had to. I started using, and soon after I started, Andrea followed... I was supposed to be her older brother, her protector, and mentor, but instead, I corrupted her. She developed an addiction... she would steal drugs I was supposed to be selling to get a fix. I couldn't exactly hide them from her we slept in the same gutters. I knew what she had been doing, but I never confronted her about it. I was to blame for creating her habit. I went back to the distributor and told him I was robbed of my supply. In anger, he beat me to a pulp, but I just stood there and took it. I wasn't going to bite the hand that kept us fed. I returned to Andrea, bludgeoned and bloody, lying to her about what caused it. She believed me and continued to feed her addiction. Eventually, the dealers got tired of me coming up short and decided to deal with me. One night, as Andrea and I slept in an abandoned house, the distributor and a few of his men showed up. They murdered Andrea first, making me watch in anguish as I was restrained. I was devastated, and after that, I wished for nothing more than death. Andrea's cries echoing in my head... until they ceased, and the world went black around me. I woke up days later in confusion. Greeted by Lucinda and Andrea, who woke up before I did. She looked absolutely radiant in her new skin and grey eyes. She seemed happier, like this had always been what she wanted. Deep down, though, I realized we traded one form of servitude for the next. We have been in Lucinda's service ever since."

"What happened to the people that murdered you? After you turned, did you?"

"Of course, it was Andrea's first kill as a newly turned... vampire. The two of us tracked the distributor to his family home. Andrea made him watch as his family was slaughtered mercilessly one by one. I watched in horror as she became the monster that Lucinda wanted her to be. It took me a bit longer to... adapt to my new life."

"Andrea seems ruthless. With her stature, she doesn't seem very intimidating. But wow... I can't imagine how you must have felt. Seeing your little sister become something like that."

Andres cringed as Emily put her hands over her mouth, realizing what she had said.

"I'm so sorry. I mean, not really; it was the truth. What I mean to say is that I didn't intend to say that aloud. Did I?"

Andres' face was taken over by a look of what seemed like understanding, "It's ok, Emily, that was to be expected. You are newly-turned, and it will take time for you to gain control of your thoughts and emotions. All of your human abilities will need to be re-learned. Control, emotion, love, those will return to you in time. As a vampire, other human traits are heightened. Hunger, lust, anger, and indifference. Over time, you will have to relearn your personality."

Emily leaned back against the wall taking in all that Andres had said. "That has to suck, I guess, being emotionless?"

"Not really. At first, it makes killing a lot easier. When you lack human emotion, everything is instinctual. We are predators, driven by the need to survive."

"But, are you emotionless? When we met... you seemed really nice, caring even. Or was that some type of illusion?"

"Well, it's harder for me to connect with human emotion. Another vampire would see my behavior as a normal means of luring prey."

Emily swallowed hard, recalling the night the two of them met, "I was prey to you?"

"Yes... and no. Emily, there was something about you that drew me in..."

"So, you guys aren't actually all Lucinda's children?" Emily decided to change the subject. "That would explain why aside from you and Andrea, none of you share a resemblance."

"No, she's kind of like a twisted adopted mother. Lucinda is barren. She never conceived any children of her own, so I feel like, in a way, we fill the void. She isn't all bad, you know. She cares deeply for all of us. In time she will care for you as well, especially because you look so similar to..." Andres found himself staring oddly at Emily, quickly retracting as she began to speak.

"How long have you.... Been a vampire?"

It was hard for Emily to say the word vampire out loud; she still couldn't bring herself to believe it entirely.

"Andrea and I have been vampires for about ten years, Luis 3, and Cassandra before you 15. She was

245

Lucinda's first vampire, and they were very close. She was like you, a tourist, and actually, she resembles you as well. She was robbed and raped by a gang of thugs while on vacation. They left her to die in the streets of Mexico, but she was discovered by Lucinda, who brought her home and prepared to preserve her life. She was still alive when Lucinda brought her in. Cassandra died while Lucinda tried to figure out how to heal her. Causing her to try something more... dark, a magic forbidden by Lucinda's mother, a powerful witch, and a healer. That night, Lucinda's first vampire was born, and she and Cassandra were thick as thieves."

"Were? What happened to her?"

"Cassandra never learned how to control her hunger... it was insatiable. With no regard for human life, she became a bit crazed. As a result, she stopped disposing of the bodies she didn't eat. Killing became a necessity for her, and she created a trail that led hunters straight to her. They planned on using her to get to Lucinda, who has been hiding from the hunters for 30 years. Lucinda did the only thing she could to protect all of us and, more importantly, herself from the hunters. She eliminated Cassandra, sudden death before Cassandra was able to spill any pertinent information regarding our whereabouts. Lucinda considered Cassandra to be her daughter, they were extremely close, and she murdered her for self-preservation. I think part of the reason Lucinda turned you was because you resemble her. I like you, Emily, but you and Lucinda aren't bonded. If she could kill Cassandra without hesitation, imagine what she could do to you. I hope you can give us a chance. You might actually prefer this life."

Andres patted Emily's head gently and motioned toward the door.

"We should return. I'm curious to find out what this supposed task of Lucinda's is. It's customary for extensive training before she sends you right into the field."

"Do you think me incapable of taking care of myself? You'd be surprised what I have tucked away."

Emily rolled her eyes as she followed Andres back down to the basement.

"Maybe you can show me one day," responded Andres as he smirked in the darkness.

They entered the basement cleaning supply room to find only Lucinda sitting patiently inside. The light flickered in the room as if it could blow out at any moment.

"Where are Luis and Andy?" asked Andres.

"They stepped out for a... bite," Emily shuddered, imagining them sinking their fangs into an actual person.

"So, Emily, I take it you are ready to hear your assignment?"

"I am."

"Well, your first task should be fairly enjoyable. Let's call it revenge, but the act itself will benefit us all. I want you to travel back to Crimson Springs and kill your boyfriend," Lucinda smiled cunningly as she imagined the demon warlock's reaction as Emily plunged a dagger into his heart. She imagined his astonishment to be greeted by someone he thought to be deceased, by his own hand none the less.

"Y-you want me to kill Johnathan?"

"Yes, but that isn't your only task. There is another I need you to eliminate. I've been getting a reading on another young witch that also resides in Crimson Springs. I want her to be dealt with as well. She is the reincarnation of an extremely powerful witch— Amara Imari, who was next in line to be the head pf the witch's council's … I should be head of the council… my power is more than many, and I possess great knowledge. If they find out Amara has been reincarnated, they will seek her as their leader. She is but a child and would be the doom of us all. I am entrusting you to take care of her, but you will need some training before sending you out into the field."

"What kind of training?"

"You might be stronger and faster than most, but you also need some basic combat training. I shall have Andres teach you what he can, for we don't have infinite time. Tomorrow you will begin your sparring with the others. I'm sure they will have their work cut out for them, small, rich, blanquita?"

Emily rolled her eyes again at the blatant insult.

"If it's combat training you are teaching, you should know I'm a second-degree black belt. I am more than capable of taking care of myself without training. If you ask me, maybe I should be the one getting your 'children' combat ready."

Lucinda was taken aback. Emily didn't look like the type to have any skills unless it involved a credit card and a mall.

"Well, I see you are full of surprises. Nevertheless, you will spar with them tomorrow and test your skills and new abilities. You may prove to be more promising than I initially anticipated. I take it your task will be carried out to the letter. Remember the fate that awaits you if you disobey."

"Yeah, got it. Kill two witches, or I face certain death. Johnathan, I guess, will be pretty easy... but this other witch? Can I at least know her name?"

"Her name is Amelia Moore. That is all I was able to grasp from my insight. How to find her, you'll have to figure that out on your own."

Emily might've felt her heart stop if it had been beating prior to that point.

"I have to kill Amelia Moore?"

"What's the matter? Do you know her?" asked Andres with concern.

"Yeah... she's my b-best friend."

Andres' facial expression showed his distaste for Lucinda's plan, "She's still new to this Lucinda, why not send Andrea Luis and me alone to complete this?"

Emily placed her hand on Andres' shoulder, "It's fine, Andres. I appreciate the concern. Honestly, I don't know how I will manage, but it's something I must do if I intend to live myself. Amelia will... she'll understand. I wouldn't wish her the same fate if the shoe was on the other foot. She's strong, she always has been, and I'm actually quite envious. If I know anything at all about Amelia, she is determined, and emotions won't get in the way of either of us getting things done... I loved her like a sister, but familial ties are cut when one's life is on the line."

Emily couldn't bring herself even to imagine murdering Amelia. Amelia had been her best friend since they were children, more than a best friend, they were sisters. Emily had always thought she could never do anything to harm her. However, after her conversation with Andres, she knew not to express opposition. If she were to get defensive, Lucinda may dispose of her right there. At least this way, Emily would have the chance to warn her friend and potentially change the outcome.

Lucinda stared at Emily, trying to read her, but it was impossible, especially with her current attributes. Emily just stared off blankly into space, not displaying any visible emotion. It took more effort for a vampire to regain their emotion after relinquishing their human life. Some decided against it entirely, opting for an emotionless life. Those vampires usually stayed hidden somewhere underground, only surfacing to feed.

Emily, being recently turned, understood how she should be feeling. However, the need to survive seemed to overpower everything else. Lucinda knew that emotions were absent, but even still, she probed Emily for any indication of hesitation. Lucinda was selfish, she had to be, and it had kept her alive this long. She understood the conflict Emily would go through, having revealed Amelia is her best friend, yet she did not care in the slightest. Emily would carry out her task or die trying whether Lucinda killed her or otherwise.

"I'm glad you don't seem to have any trouble adjusting to your new life."

Emily had only just taken notice, Lucinda's accent was completely gone she had spoken completely different from when they initially met. "Your English is impeccable. I can't detect your accent anymore. Why is that?"

"I've found that you get more out of life when people believe you can't understand them. Let's say it's a good tool to judge one's character. You'd be surprised what some tourists say under their breath. Those tourists don't seem to live long enough to regret their actions," Lucinda smiled at Andres evilly, but he didn't seem to be enthused. "At any rate, I best head off to bed. You four will have plenty to do in the morning. Unless you'd rather start tonight, Andres?" Lucinda glanced at him briefly, awaiting a response.

When he didn't respond, she walked out of the room, leaving Emily and Andres alone.

"What did she mean by that?"

"She's talking about sparring. I wouldn't throw you into that right now."

"No, I actually want to. How about we see if you can keep up, Andres?"

Andres laughed mischievously and made his way to the door gesturing for Emily to follow him.

Andres led Emily to a dimly lit ballroom. Andrea and Luis were already inside fighting each other. Emily watched as they gracefully flitted around the room, anticipating each other's movements and evading contact. Andrea was ferocious. Emily could see Luis beginning to struggle to avoid her punches. Either he was slowing down, or she was just too fast. Andrea was small and squirrely. Her petite frame seemed to pose as an advantage against Luis's tall, muscular build. Finally, Andrea seemed to be getting the better of him, finishing off with a hard punch to the jaw. Luis stumbled backward, still maintaining his form. An obvious frustration came over him as he suddenly picked Andrea up and slammed her backward over his leg. There was a loud bone shattering sound that echoed the ballroom. It sounded as if Andrea's spine had been shattered.

"No! What are you doing!? Stop!" protested Emily as she watched in horror, but her words came too late.

Andrea had already hit the ground with a thud. Her lifeless body laid on the floor in a distorted shape. Andres and Luis seemed to be unbothered as she laid there dead, on the ground. Emily ran to her faster than she could ever muster in her human body, kneeling to the floor beside her and shaking her violently.

"Please don't die!" Emily had never been in a position like this before.

She didn't know what to do to help Andrea as she held her lifeless body. Andres and Luis just stared at Emily's obvious struggle to resuscitate Andrea.

"What are you two just standing there?" Emily shook her once more, and at that moment, Andrea opened up one of her eyes, glaring at Emily.

Andrea, Luis, and Andres burst into a fit of laughter. Andres and Luis were unable to contain their laughter as they were greatly entertained by the scene unfolding in front of them. Andrea joined in the laughter as well, and Emily, seemingly unamused, removed her arms, dropping Andrea back onto the floor.

"That wasn't funny at all. I thought you were seriously... "

"Dead? Relax, Emily. We are vampires, after all. What kind of immortal beings would we be if we died from a simple body slam? By the way, Luis, you are slacking. You nearly didn't crack my spine at all this time," she said, giving Luis a look of dissatisfaction as he turned to exit the room.

"What's his problem?" asked Emily.

"You'll have to excuse him. Since Cassandra's death, he hasn't been very talkative, but this is the first time I've heard him laugh in what seems like ages. I don't know, newbie. Maybe you have some use after all."

Andrea got up from the floor, winking at Andres as she passed him, "You two kids have fun." Her last words before she exited the ballroom following Luis.

"I guess I'll have to pay you all back for that tasteless prank you just pulled."

"I guess that means you're ready to start—"

Before Andres could finish his sentence, Emily was already in her fighting stance. She stared at Andres intently, sizing him up as she contemplated her first blow. Andres threw out a punch toward her abdomen before she could strike, he was fast, but Emily anticipated it and blocked him. Andres continued to strike one after the other his fighting looked like it was choreographed, and Emily was able to anticipate his every move. Andres caught on to her techniques. He knew she was anticipating his movements and decided to change up his routine. Emily reached forward swiftly, her hand connecting with his jaw, staggering, Andres stepped backward as he lost his balance and fell onto his back.

"Are you alright?" Emily stood over Andres as he laid on the ground, surprised Emily had bested him.

Suddenly Emily found herself falling backward onto the ballroom floor. Andres had swept her legs from under her as she stood over him. Emily stared at the ceiling in disbelief.

"Wow, I should have seen that one coming."

Andres got on his feet and stood over Emily extending an arm to help her up off the ground as he smiled down at her. Emily reached for Andres' hand, and instead of allowing him to help her up, she pulled him downward, and he landed on top of her. Taking care not to exert all of his weight on her as he fell.

Andres and Emily stared at each other briefly before Andres broke the silence, "You weren't lying. You are pretty good, and I don't think you need to train further. We can leave tomorrow if you want to…"

As Andres spoke, he realized the severity of what he said as Emily turned away from him.

"I'm sorry," said Andres as he picked himself up off the ground, reaching down once more and picking Emily up as well.

"It isn't your fault. I just don't understand why I have to kill Amelia, you know? And she's a witch… I can't believe she hadn't told me… and Johnathan… I just feel so overwhelmed right now with all of this. I mean, just two days ago, I was a straight-A student who had everything. A perfect boyfriend, best friend, loving parents—"

"Well, about that, you were in… transition for more than a few days. In fact, you were turned last Sunday. It's Monday of the following week. Usually, after the spell is done, you become conscious in 1-3 days. Your transformation took so long, Lucinda thought it hadn't worked. I'm glad it did, Emily."

"You and me both! I couldn't imagine being dead... well, if I were dead, I probably wouldn't be doing too much imagining, anyway."

Andres smiled, which strung up another question in Emily's mind, "Hey Andres, do we sleep? Like honestly, what can we do and what can't we? I'm curious."

"Well, there isn't some type of handbook on this thing. We are fairly new to it all. It's pretty much a learning experience—we learn as we live through it. Even Lucinda, her knowledge is pretty limited on the whole vampire thing, but we are more than that. I'll tell you what I can, but some of it gets pretty gruesome. Are you ready for it?"

"Hell yeah, hit me. Maybe not literally," Emily smiled, realizing how corny her joke was, but Andres didn't seem to have noticed she'd made a joke.

"We are vampires, but that's actually up for debate. Our kind does not sleep. We get tired, restless even but do not have the human urge to sleep. After long periods without rest or sustenance, though, we become... crazed, which has been a detriment to others like us. Causing us to be pursued endlessly by the hunters, they don't think we can be trusted due to the 'crazed' nature we can resort to if unfed for long periods. If you ever encounter a hunter, kill them without hesitation because the moment you hesitate, you're dead. Be careful. Even though we are immortal, we can be killed. A shot to the head or decapitation will definitely do the trick. From a human, though, you do have the advantage. Your speed plays a great role in your self-preservation. What else, you have heightened senses; you can climb objects with little effort. Also, we can induce hallucinations or paralysis through our... saliva. This gift is how we can remain in this hotel without raising suspicion."

Andres looked away from Emily, embarrassed that he had done exactly that to Emily the first night they'd met. When Andres made the comment, a memory flashed in Emily's mind of the two of them in the basement together having a moment of intimacy. Then another memory of her being bitten by him.

"Andres? Did we...?"

Andres smiled at her, not wanting to respond, but he did so anyway, "No, we didn't. I did bite you, though; sorry about that. It's as I said earlier, the hallucinations sometimes can't be manipulated and instead create a moment of... bliss."

Emily pondered the memory of the two of them together, slightly wishing it had actually transpired. Emily liked something about Andres, and she could tell he liked her as well.

"Is there anything else I should know?"

"I almost forgot. As I told you before, we are thought to be vampires by some, but others have another name for us... Zombies. Due to the small difference that we consume human flesh. Traditional vampires do not. They live off of blood alone."

"What!?"

"Yeah, it's pretty gruesome, but it's what we do. We never truly get the sustenance we need from blood alone, that is a temporary easily accessible means of satiation. On only blood, we cannot survive as a species. The reason for tiredness and restlessness is due to a lack of flesh. You'll be fine on your diet of blood for now. However, it is imperative within the week, you have at least one."

"I get it you don't have to continue with that. I should have believed you when you'd told me it would be gruesome."

"There are actual blood-sucking vampires like Dracula, don't quote me, but I don't think they turn into bats. There is a long history between our two species. Although we are similar, we are not the same, which has been the basis for many wars between the two races. Vampires are born and zombies are created. Vampires do possess the ability to turn, but it isn't as simple as the Hollywood movies. To be turned and not born, you have to descend from a vampire bloodline. Otherwise, the vampire venom is more likely to kill you. Normally a Witch is directly involved in the turning of a zombie. The transition happens when the body is already dead. The human flesh thing is but a small price to pay. Unlike Vampires, we can walk in the sunlight, and stakes don't quite do the job. One other perk we inherited is we can communicate telepathically. None of the three of us can do it ourselves, but we know it's a possibility. I wish we were able to though, it would serve quite useful in the field. Now that you are pretty much informed, would you like me to show you how to rest?"

"I guess so. If necessary."

Andres Led Emily out of the ballroom and into a smaller room where Luis and Andrea were lying down quietly. Seeming not to be disturbed by them entering the room.

Andres instructed Emily to lay down on the bed.

"But Andres, we haven't even had a first date."

He smiled at her as she laid down as instructed.

"Now, place your arms across each other on your chest. This will allow your energy to remain in you during your rest. Otherwise, you can pass on your energies, emotions, memories to whoever your arm connects with."

Emily did as instructed, and Andres continued to explain the process to her, "In your young stage, you have no control over resting, and it will come suddenly, abruptly. It's almost exactly like meditation except more... interactive. In this state, you will be somewhat trapped in your mind yet still conscious of the outside world, if that makes sense. When in a state of rest, you can completely access any memories you have of your current life and your previous life. I think it will be something you find yourself enjoying."

Emily stopped talking as she listened to Andres. She slipped into something like a coma. She could hear him talking but was unresponsive. Emily felt Andres slip into the bed beside her. Lying down and quickly falling into a similar state. The memory that replayed in her mind in the ballroom resurfaced. It was of her and Andres, the night in the basement hallway. It replayed in Emily's mind she seemingly had no control over what memories she viewed.

Emily snapped out of her trance with a hard punch in the shoulder. She sat up reflexively, looking around, spotting Luis and Andres, who looked at her with intrigue.

"You and Andres seem to be quite... friendly with each other," said Andrea with a smirk as she nudged Emily with her shoulder.

Emily assumed it was none other than Andrea who punched her awake.

"What are you talking about?" asked Emily.

They had all been abruptly awoken to a memory they had all been forced to experience. Andres looked at Emily, seemingly more embarrassed than the rest of his companions.

"Emily, I... we... your human hallucination of us together, we all saw it... repeatedly."

"What!?" Emily uttered in disbelief, cupping her face in her hands.

"Oh, it was only a hallucination? Rats! For some reason, it isn't as interesting anymore," said Andrea as she flopped down back onto the bed.

Luis got up feeling empathetic and laid a hand on Emily's shoulder, "It's okay, don't be too embarrassed. As a result, we made a very important discovery."

Emily looked up at Luis, and a thought came to her mind, *An important discovery?* Everyone stared at Emily with much interest.

"Indeed, Emily, you are a telepath. None of us can project our memories onto others without physical contact. When you master this ability, there is no telling what the possibilities could be. The fact that we all heard your thought just now proves it," Luis sounded genuinely excited.

"Ok, but between the four of us, can we keep this between ourselves? I don't trust Lucinda. I know it's a lot to ask, considering what she's done for all of us."

Andrea and Luis stared away in silent protest, but they ultimately agreed to her request. Andres agreed without hesitation, "Your secret is safe with us."

There was a sudden knock on the door. Andres got up and looked out the peephole prior to opening it. There stood Lucinda with what looked to be a stack of cards and passports. She handed the documents to each individual and patted Andrea on the head before giving her what looked to be a birth certificate.

"Que es esto?" asked Andrea. She did not understand why she did not receive an ID like the others.

"Esta es su forma de identificacion. I don't want any suspicion to arise at the airport if you present the fake ID. You look your age, Andrea, maybe even younger, and to avoid any complications in your mission, you will pose as your age as well 13."

Andrea pouted as she stared up at Lucinda, who stood over her as she sat on the bed. Emily inspected the fake ID everything was incorrect, her last name, place of birth, and her weight. *What? 130? I don't weigh a pound over 125...* Thought Emily as she looked the Id over. Andres, Andrea, and Luis laughed briefly at Emily's astonishment towards her new identity. Lucinda looked at the three of them with an eyebrow raised before returning to the task at hand. Emily's last name had been changed to Santos, implicating a Latin lineage.

"You are all posing as siblings. This should be easy for you all since you already operate as such. Andrea and Luis, you have a different assignment from Emily and Andres; hence you will be boarding a different plane. Is there anything that needs to be repeated?" When there was no response, Lucinda continued, "Andres, Emily, here are your tickets, flight leaves in two hours. I suggest you make haste. Andrea and Luis, come with me so I can brief you on your assignment."

Andrea and Luis followed Lucinda out. Emily and Andres followed after them briefly before separating.

"I've... never been outside of Mexico before," said Andres, his voice laced with concern.

"Don't worry. You'll be fine. I think you'll blend in fairly well."

Andres hadn't uttered a single word since leaving the hotel. They entered the plane and took their seats next to each other.

"I-I've never been in a plane," said Andres, which alerted Emily as to why he hadn't been speaking.

"That's ironic. A vampire that's afraid of an airplane? I'm sure you've faced grizzlier foes."

"Sure, but none that took place thousands of feet in the air."

"Fasten your seatbelts. We are preparing for takeoff," said the pilot on the loudspeaker as Emily suddenly felt a tight grip on her hand.

"Andres, we'll be alright. Take my word for it. I've been on plenty of planes without incident. What's the worst that could happen, anyway? Can't we regenerate at will or something?"

Andres didn't answer as the plane began to enter the air. Emily had been wondering what her parents must be thinking. She hadn't called them since she'd been on vacation. It had been an entire week since she was supposed to return. More importantly, she found herself wondering about Amelia. It seemed like time was on fast forward as they pulled into the Crimson Springs airport. They had arrived quicker than Emily was prepared for.

"See, I told you nothing to worry about. Come on, let's go catch a cab," Emily led Andres to the cab pickup line in which they stood patiently.

"Where too?"

"741 Spring Drive."

The cab driver looked in his rearview mirror staring back at Emily and Andres. Their eye color intrigued him.

"Relatives, I take it? Brother and sister?"

"Yes, actually."

"I can tell. You two have beautiful eyes. I can't say I've ever encountered anyone with icy grey eyes."

"It runs in the family. We have two other siblings with the same trait. Mom had grey eyes, and fathers were blue. The luck of the draw turned out to be in favor of the grey."

Andres nudged Emily gently as if insinuating she was saying too much. Emily felt as though she was saying just enough to level any suspicions.

"Well, here we are. That will be $49.50."

Emily swiped her card in the card reader on the back of the cab seat. The driver pulled off, leaving Andres and Emily standing outside of her house. It seemed different from what she remembered, more detailed.

"Andres, I need you to remain hidden. I have to go in alone. I can't just show up at odd hours of the night after being missing for a week with new eye color and a strange boy. You understand, right?"

He stared at her blankly before hesitantly responding, "Fine; I'll be on the roof if you... need me. Be careful, okay?"

Emily smiled at him and made her way for the entry door. She heard the scuffles of Andres climbing up the side of the house. It was 9 p.m. her parents should be sound asleep. They worked long hours during the day and were always asleep no later than 8:30 p.m. Emily had to see them. She couldn't just let them go on thinking she was dead.

Emily made her way into the house. It was completely quiet, and everything seemed in order. She went upstairs to her parent's bedroom, opening the door slowly, taking care not to wake them. They were lying fast asleep and looked so peaceful she didn't want to disturb them. She didn't know when she'd get another chance to see them after tonight. Lucinda made the rules now, and Emily knew her life was no longer her own. Deep down, she knew that a part of her died that night in Mexico.

Emily could feel her blood warming. She didn't know why this was happening. The same sensation she had felt before she had her first blood meal came over her again. The air felt thick, and the searing pain in her throat made it impossible to swallow. Emily found herself easing closer to the bed, almost as if she was no longer in control of her legs.

Mrs. Wright woke up suddenly, asleep dazed and confused. There was an intruder in the house, and she did not look like an ordinary burglar. She was young, and her eyes were glowing an eerie yellow hue.

Mrs. Wright was terrified as she opened her mouth to scream. A mere gasp escaped her lips as Emily jumped atop her, her fangs elongated and pierced into her neck. She drank the blood ravenously, making sure not to spill a single drop. Amid the attack, her father woke up from his sleep. Silently, he reached for the pistol in the end table. Emily sensed his presence, turning her head slowly toward him. Mr. Wright aimed the gun directly in Emily's face as his hand quivered in terror. This was Emily's home, and she knew that the gun was merely a starter pistol. The action was enough to bring Emily out of her trance.

"Dad?" Said Emily as she regained consciousness from her frenzy.

"W-who are you? W-what are you?" He stared in horror as the intruder feasted on his wife. "G-get O-out of here o-or I'll shoot."

"Daddy, you... you don't remember me?" Emily couldn't believe it; in this twisted reality her parents did not know who she was.

Emily's mind went blank as her eyes glowed yellow once more, and she attacked her father. Emily ripped his throat out with her bare hands. His hand hung off the bed, still gripping the starter pistol. It dropped to the floor as his life slipped away. In Emily's state of being, it was as if she wasn't acting on her own. Something had come over her, a hunger that she needed to satisfy.

Emily lifted her mother's arm and began to devour it, ripping out large chunks of flesh so clean that only bone remained. Once the flesh was stripped away Emily made light work of the rest of the body. Taking her only minutes to devour her mother completely. Emily then turned toward her father and began to consume him as well.

Andres could smell the blood from atop the roof. A feeling of regret came over him once he understood what Emily had done or was doing. He didn't interfere. This was her first kill, and at this point, she could not stop until it was finished. Emily had become crazed, and until the hunger was satisfied, there was nothing anyone could do.

Amelia stopped in front of the house on 741 Spring Drive. She looked behind her as she sensed the presence of something.

"It was probably nothing," said Amelia to herself as she made her way toward the home.

Something was compelling her to enter as her feet carried her up the steps and to the grand entry doors. Reaching for the bell, she noticed the door was ajar, so she proceeded to enter. As she walked up the stairs, she began to recall a memory of being in the house as a child. Playing dress-up with a small girl of the same age. In the vision, the girl's face was blurred, and she could only see an outline of the girl. It was very vague and didn't make any sense to her as she turned the corner into the master bedroom of the house.

It appeared she knew exactly where she was going as she reached the door to the master bedroom. Amelia noticed the door happened to be ajar. The air was thick with a strong metallic smell. She couldn't quite place what it was.

Amelia pushed the door open slowly in the darkness, and there, crouching over a lifeless body, was a silhouette of someone she felt like she'd known. The individual looked to be ingesting the body it was hovering over, which sent a chill down Amelia's spine. Whoever it was had been so occupied with devouring the corpse it had not noticed someone had entered. Suddenly it came to her, Amelia's memories came rushing into her all at once as she began to recollect who the silhouette belonged to.

"Emily?" Amelia called out reluctantly, causing the individual to look up in a frenzy.

Emily acknowledged her name but couldn't control herself as she lunged straight toward Amelia from the bed with great force. The creature jumped straight on top of Amelia, knocking her off balance and sending Amelia backward with a thud. Slightly disoriented, Amelia attempted to get away, but her dress was restricting her.

The moonlight shone in on the face of what Amelia thought to be Emily. It looked like her, but different at the same time. This being took on Emily's appearance but was not her. The creature Amelia thought to be Emily opened its mouth wide with an evil grin as it began to sink its fangs deep into her neck. A blood-curdling scream escaped Amelia as she began to conjure an energy ball in her right hand.

The energy ball quickly fizzled out as Amelia's life force was drained by the person, she once considered to be her best friend.

www.ingramcontent.com/pod-product-compliance
Lightning Source LLC
Chambersburg PA
CBHW020616260626
47157CB00003B/1044